# Dedication

To my Nova Scotian friends who have shared their lives
with me.

# Concealed by the Tide
## A Tide Harbor Suspense

*Where love and murder lie just below the surface.*

Book 1

By Zara West

New York

Published by Tidal Waters Press

# Prologue

*Minas Basin, Nova Scotia*

The fisherman squinted through the sea-salt splattered window of the wheelhouse and into the black of the night. Up ahead, the blinking lights of the channel buoy rose and fell on the swells. Below, Seastroke Energy's innovative tidal turbine sat on the seafloor, a billion-dollar masterpiece of ingenuity, ready to churn out thousands of kilowatts of electricity.

He cut the engine. Not going to happen. Not when Seastroke's competitor was willing to pay him a fortune to halt the installation.

He signaled his crewmate. "It's time. Take the helm."

With the ease born of years hauling lobster traps on wet decks, he moved to the stern and gingerly drew the metal canister from its plastic wrapping. He stared down at the small beer barrel. The directions he'd found on the internet had better be right.

"You know what you're doing?" His companion looked over his shoulder, his face eerie-white against the dark.

"Yah, sure." He picked up the depth charge. "As soon as the water soaks into the powder, it's going to make a terrific bang."

"Big enough to destroy the turbine?"

"Doesn't have to."

His buddy pushed up the brim of his baseball cap. "Yah, crazy? We've been paid to blow it."

"He's going to get exactly what he paid for. You heard me tell him homemade devices aren't foolproof. But he wanted to do it on the cheap. Wanted to keep his hands sweet-smelling. If we blow it to smithereens on the first try, Mr. Money Bags will only pay us once."

Grasping the depth charge in his rubber-gloved hands, he hefted it to the gunwale. "This way, he either pays us for a second go go-round, or if the explosion is loud enough, it'll rattle those puffed-up shirts down at Seastroke Energy's headquarters in Boston. Make them anxious to pay us a little protection money."

"You talking blackmail?"

"Exactly." He glanced back at his companion. "In fact, if we're lucky, both will pay."

He reached back and tossed the barrel into the sea.

*Splash.*

Water kicked up over the gunwales.

"Gun it, mate."

The driver throttled up, and the boat took off, heading back to the harbor.

Minutes later, a column of water shot up in the air with a *whoosh*. Spray rained down on the deck. Shockwaves from the underwater explosion ripped beneath the hull and drove the boat forward.

The bomber grasped the cabin housing as the boat dipped and bobbed and smiled at his companion. "Done." He took a swig from his flask and swallowed. "Now we wait and see what turns up."

# Chapter 1

## Summer

*I*diots. Summer Avery took a last glance at the *New York Times* article about the amateur bomb attack on Seastroke Energy's undersea energy generator then stuffed the news clipping into her backpack. Bombing the turbine was a surefire way to turn people against the local fishermen fighting the turbines. Nobody liked terrorists.

The Tide Harbor folks needed to win over the press and the authorities, not antagonize them. Without someone to organize them and get positive publicity, the bombers would end up in jail, and in six months, Seastroke's tidal energy monstrosity would be spinning away, killing fish.

They needed help. They needed her—EcoGreen Action's star activist, community-liaison, and former high-power marketer.

She fingered her mother's locket. This was her chance to show her dying father that you could fight the big corporations and bring them down.

She leaned back in her seat. At least she'd been able to catch the last ferry of the season going to Yarmouth, Nova Scotia. But after eight hours of straight-through driving from New York City to Bar Harbor, she was exhausted.

She clutched the arm of her seat as the ship tipped to one side then the other. The three-hour boat ride would be a welcome break, even if wind and rain pelted the windows and the odd roll of the high-speed catamaran car ferry was stirring up the contents of her stomach.

Her mind required a distraction, and she had just the thing.

She pulled out the technical article on Minas Basin marine life and settled in to bone up on maritime ecology.

Just as she reached the end, a child screeched. The sound drilled through her and raised the hairs on the back of her neck. If there was something that set her on edge, it was a child in distress. It brought back too many memories better forgotten.

Summer slapped her hands over her ears and peered around the seatback. Inside the passageway to the midsection, a man with the build of a linebacker grappled with a small girl who barely reached his waist. The child's face was white with terror, her eyes bulging, and her high-pitched shrieks ear-shattering. He encircled her in his arms and pulled her against him.

The little one yelled louder.

Summer tossed the research study onto the empty seat next to her and glanced around. It was the end of the season, and the few passengers in the ferry's lounge were doing what everyone did—looking anywhere but at the parent-child drama. Well, she wasn't everyone. The bewildered man looked like he needed help.

She stood. Beneath her feet, the ferry rolled and twisted. She faltered and latched on to the armrest to keep from falling. Her stomach, unfortunately, kept right on going. Stupid seasickness. Why did it have to be rough the first time she was on a boat?

She swallowed back the nausea, cursed the eco-bomber for choosing cold, foggy Nova Scotia for his antics instead of some oil rig in the balmy Gulf of Mexico, and wobbled on her favorite high-heeled boots toward the screaming girl.

Three feet away, she stopped. "Your child seems to be in distress. Can I help?"

The man's head jerked up, and his dark brown, almost black eyes met hers. He held the girl in an armlock against him, wincing under a barrage of kicks to his shins. "Stay back, lady. Don't—"

Summer softened her voice. "I've had a lot of experience with children." Well, she had, even if it was a long time ago.

The girl screamed again as the man struggled to control her. He really needed assistance.

She formed her lips into her best I'm-confident smile. "Please let me help. Have you tried singing to her?" She moved forward.

At that moment, a pair of gabbling senior citizens, coffee cups balanced in their hands, wobbled down the aisle. The ferry rolled, and the old couple swayed, jostling the man and child. The man lost his hold. The girl broke free and, with a high-pitched yell, ran straight at her.

Summer crouched and extended her arms. "Come, sweetheart. I'll keep you safe."

The girl smashed into her, bringing with her the smell of cookies, milk, and rain-wet clothing. She gathered the small body tightly to her, the way she had when her brothers were little and frightened.

"Got you, darling."

"Nooooo—" The child struggled against her, knocking her off balance.

Summer crashed to the floor. Sharp little nails scratched her face. Teeth dug into her wrist. Hard rubber boots thumped her in the belly.

Throwing her arms over her face, Summer wiggled away from her mini-attacker. *Thunk.* Her head hit the metal base of one of the seats. Pain struck. Her head spun. Her stomach did another somersault.

"Lissie!" The man's voice, rich with the sea-salt flavor of the Maritimes, cut through the dizziness and headache.

Before she could figure out what had happened, the child was lifted off her and several people were helping her to her feet, handing her napkins to staunch the bleeding from the scratches on her cheek and neck. Someone said something about taking her to the first-aid station.

Summer sat up and rubbed the lump on her head. Growing up on a farm, she'd had worse.

She waved the do-gooders away. "Thank you, but I'll be fine."

An elderly man frowned. "Kid bit you. Could get infected."

She glanced at the teeth marks on her wrist. "Barely broke the skin. Just needs antiseptic. I have some in my daypack." She grasped the armrest to steady herself and rose to her feet. The ferry swayed, stilled a moment, then dropped away. Her aching head rolled. Bile crept up her throat.

She flopped onto the nearest seat, pressed her hands against her temples, and concentrated on breathing in and out. Mouth tightly closed, she swallowed the gathering saliva, willing the contents of her stomach to stay down. No way was she going to heave in front of all these people.

"You all right, miss?" There was that sea-salt voice again.

Summer glanced up. Focused on the child, she hadn't paid attention to the man. Now she did. Mercy, but he was a looker.

Deeply-tanned skin stretched tight over high cheekbones and spoke of distant African ancestors. A strong nose hinted at a Native-American heritage. Long black hair curled down his back in an unruly ponytail. A rough-edged man who spent time outdoors, for sure. Most likely a lobsterman, seeing as she was heading to the lobster capital of the world. A very attractive one—too rugged and masculine to be a chick-flick heartthrob, but he wouldn't look amiss in a military thriller or *Game of Thrones* episode, playing the hard-ass hero.

But right now, she didn't need a hero. She needed her stomach to settle before she upchucked on him and embarrassed herself even more.

She nodded and hoped he'd get the hint and leave.

He didn't. Mr. Heroic leaned his hip against the seatback, as if settling in for a long chat. "You sure? I could fetch ice for that bump on your head."

He was so close she could smell his scent—clean and fresh, like a pine forest. Heat swirled through her, and for a moment, she forgot about her roiling stomach. He looked like the type of man who could sweep a woman off her feet and drive away all reason with a kiss from his full, wide lips.

She glanced away. She had no business thinking such thoughts. Not with only ten days to get the locals protesting loud enough that Seastroke Energy scrapped their plans to repair the damaged cables running to the tidal turbine.

Besides, Mr. Lobsterman might be an eye-catcher, but he didn't know much about handling little children.

Summer swallowed down the acid creeping up her throat and peered up at the man. "What's wrong with the child? She acted terrified."

He rubbed the back of his neck. "My daughter, Lissie ... she's ... she's having a hard time. First time on a ferry. I'm sorry she attacked you. Is there anything—"

"No." She shook her head then wished she hadn't. She forced herself to ignore the gurgling warning in her stomach. "I'm perfectly fine."

A muscle twitched along his jaw. "I'm sure you are, Miss Fancy Toes."

Summer twisted around and glared at him. She might be dressed like she had just strolled down Madison Avenue, but she was no city slicker. She'd grown up grubbing in the fields, cultivating and picking the organic apples, pears, and berries her family sold at the local farmer's market. That was ... until her father lost the lawsuit against the drilling company that had poisoned their well, and they'd had to abandon the farm.

The ship rolled to one side, did a little shuffle, then rolled the other way. She slapped a hand over her queasy stomach. "Oh ..." She swallowed and swallowed, but there was only so much of what her ex-fiancé called her "maniacal willpower" could do.

Vomit rose up and burst forth. Most landed in the seasickness bag that miraculously appeared in front of her. She heaved and spit. Heaved some more. Spit some more. Retched until her throat and nose burned and nothing of her granola bar breakfast remained in her stomach.

With his free hand, her would-be hero smoothed back her hair. "Better?"

Avoiding his eyes, she yanked the stinking bag from him and set it on the floor. "Sorry. Something I ate."

"Or didn't." He handed her a pocket-sized package of wipes.

Refusing to think about what kind of man carried baby wipes, she took one out, blotted her mouth, and blew her nose.

He reached into his coat pocket and slipped out a plastic bag of sugary-looking bits. He waved it in front of her. "Best thing for *mal de mer*. Crystalized ginger." He took out a sharp-looking folding knife with a rosewood handle, cut off a small piece, and popped it in his mouth. "Tastes good, too."

"I don't have seasickness."

One side of his lips curled up. "That's what they all say. Try a piece, anyway. Made it myself. My momma's recipe."

Summer turned away. She did not want this too-handsome-for-her-own-good man to be kind to her or to know he cooked. He was everything she had once wanted in a man.

Heavens. Her face heated. How embarrassing. He'd seen her throw up.

The hand holding the baggie in front of her face didn't move. "Honest, it will settle your tummy. Here—take the whole bag."

"*Fine.*" She curled her fingers around it. "You cook?"

"Been known to whip up a soufflé or two." He winked at her. "Eating is one of life's greatest pleasures, you know."

The ship shuddered and rolled. She slapped a hand over her mouth and bent over. "Don't want to think about food."

"It's not that rough. I suggest you move to the center seats midship and face forward or go out on the stern and get some fresh air. I never ride in the lounge."

Summer squinted at him. "Really? So, why are you in here?"

He pushed a stray lock of hair off his forehead. "I was looking for a quiet place for Lissie."

She spun around. Totally distracted by the man, she'd forgotten the child. "Where is your daughter?"

"She's in the seat right behind you. The drug finally kicked in and knocked her out."

Summer peered over the seatback. The little girl lay draped across the cushions, swaddled in a faded and tattered handmade quilt, only the tip of her chin and a mass of dark brown curls visible.

She turned back. "You drugged her? That seems extreme."

"Not my first choice, but we have to get to Nova Scotia, and I can't have her attacking strangers along the way." He brushed his finger over the scratch on her cheek. "Sorry she hurt you—"

"It's nothing." She drew back, unwanted tingles running down her spine.

He reached into his shirt pocket and pulled out a small notebook and stubby pencil. He jotted down a phone number. "If you need medical attention, call. I'll pay."

"I can afford it." *Barely*. All her savings from the marketing job had gone to pay for her brothers' college tuitions and her father's medical bills, and there wasn't much money in eco-activism. It was something you did to help save the world by exposing nasty corporations who destroyed innocent people's lives, like her father's, not pad your bank account.

He held the paper out to her. "Please. Take it. The emergency rooms here charge Americans a hefty fee for their services."

Could the man be any nicer?

Summer pinched the paper from his fingers and tucked it in the pocket of her jacket. Time to get away from the tempting lobsterman.

She pushed up from the seat and wiggled past him, heading for where she'd been sitting. Why did he have to be the total opposite of her ex-fiancé—handsome, kind, and apparently a good cook and father?

She didn't need an entanglement now, not with the Tide Harbor anti-turbine activists waiting for her. Besides, he had a daughter. He was probably married. Thank heavens, once they were off the ferry, she'd never see him again.

Summer moved down the aisle. Now, where had she left her pack? It held all the essentials for her job—camera, laptop, and notes. Without it, she'd be up the proverbial creek, or in this case—tidal bay. She peered into each row, wobbling on the high-heeled boots that threatened to tip her over every time the deck swayed under her.

She glanced down at her feet. She loved these boots. The soft, white-leather designer boots had been a steal at half-price at Nordstrom's back when she had trod the halls of the biggest ad agency in Manhattan.

The ferry shifted, and she grasped a seatback. But Mr. Lobster Guy was right—they weren't made for rocky boats. First thing she'd do when she arrived in Tide Harbor was buy some sensible footwear. But she wasn't going to be buying anything without the credit card in her pack.

She lurched from one side to the other as she treaded the aisle again. Nothing. What the heck? Had someone stolen it? She surveyed the lounge.

"Here." Lobster Guy held up her red leather daypack. "Looking for this?"

Was she never going to get away from the man?

She stomped back to him and seized the strap from his hand, trying not to inhale his tantalizing scent. The ferry rolled, and another wave of nausea swept over her. She managed to mumble out her thanks and turn away. The last thing she wanted was to vomit in front of him—again.

"We have the same taste in reading, you know," he called after her.

Summer glanced back. He was waving the research paper at her and smiling.

Now she knew. His smile *was* devastating. No man should be that put-together.

Ignoring the heat flooding her body, she headed back down the aisle and ripped it from his grasp. "Thanks."

"I'm Gil Moses, if you're interested?"

"And here I thought you were Captain Nemo." She gave him the best smile she could manage with an upset stomach then turned on her heel and stumbled her way up the aisle.

Slipping into a forward-facing seat, she glanced at her watch. Thank heavens. Only thirty more minutes, and they'd reach port in Yarmouth.

The ferry tilted. Her stomach rolled. She remembered the bag of ginger candy in her hand and examined the pinkish-tan bits. It couldn't hurt to try one—sometimes folk remedies worked. She took out a piece and placed it on her tongue. Spicy sweetness trickled down her throat. It was delicious. She ate another piece. Captain Nemo *could* cook.

Summer peered back toward the rear lounge. She'd never been strongly attracted to a man before, and she wasn't going to start now. She was here to gain that directorship and win back her father's respect.

She jerked back around and faced forward. The last thing she needed was to fall for a lobsterman with an out-of-control child. So what if he could make candied ginger? So what if he had a charmer's smile? She wanted nothing more to do with men, especially one who was surely married. And that was that.

This attraction to Mr. Lobsterman was a passing quirk. In half an hour, they'd be docking, and she would head off to Tide Harbor and never see Mr. Gil Moses again.

Wait a minute. His name was Gil Moses? They had similar tastes?

Summer snatched up the research article and flipped to the bibliography. She ran her finger down the page until she found it. *Moses, G. "Fluctuating fish populations and tidal turbines in the Minas Basin."*

Too Tempting Lobster Guy was no lobsterman. He was a marine biologist with a research interest in the Minas Basin.

She fisted the paper in her hand. No way. She couldn't be that unlucky.

She stuffed the article into her pack. Besides, even if he were the same G. Moses, an up-and-up scientist wouldn't be pro-turbine. Only a fool or company shill would defend the installation of the fish-destroying abomination she was on a mission to stop.

# Chapter 2

## Gil

Gil peered down at his daughter. Lissie looked like an angel when she slept. He wanted to run his fingers through her curls—so much like his long-gone twin sister's—give her a hug, and kiss her like a normal dad. Show her how much he loved her. But he couldn't.

The minute he touched her, she would go berserk, and the poor people on the ferry didn't need to hear her scream again or come under one of her unpredictable attacks. He shook his head. Wait until Miss Hug-a-Child got a good look in the mirror and saw the scratches marring her gorgeous face. She'd send a bill, for sure. Gil straightened up. Maybe he'd face a lawsuit.

He picked up the frayed edge of the quilt covering Lissie then trailed his finger down his late mother's tiny hemstitches. With his mom dead, his tormented little girl was all he had left. Come a lawsuit, they'd take Lissie away from him, and that would play right into his ex-wife's hands. Prove her right. He smoothed down the faded cloth. He couldn't let that happen.

Gil pulled the paperwork out of his duffle and thumbed through it. He'd finally gotten a diagnosis for Lissie—severe autism with sensory integration issues. He turned to the back of the psychiatrist's report. There was even a proposed treatment plan. Not that his ex-wife had cared. She'd wanted rid of the baby from the moment she'd come into their lives.

Well, she was rid of them *both* now. The divorce and sock-in-the-stomach papers giving him conditional custody had arrived the same day as the doctor's report. Dolores had destroyed his career, his family, and his trust in women. He glanced again at his beautiful daughter. But she wasn't going to destroy Lissie.

Gil stashed the papers away and leaned back in the seat. Getting a divorce had felt like a failure. Turning over their home and their bank account had felt like a betrayal. But turning over Lissie so Dolores could stash her away in an institution and let her rot? That called for immediate action, even if that meant he'd have to figure out how to become a spy and care for her at the same time.

The call to move to the car deck filtered through the loudspeakers. The few people still in the lounge pressed down the aisle toward the exit. He watched them file past: the elderly couple who'd helped the city girl, the noisy young people returning from a trip to Montreal, a grumpy-looking businessman, newspaper tucked under his arm. Those people knew who they were and where they were going. Unlike him.

Gil slung the duffle over his shoulder. Oh, he knew where he was going. He just didn't know who he was anymore.

His stomach clenched. How did a person go from being a suburban dad with a lovely wife and a brick Colonial in Newton to a man with nothing but a small, miserable child he'd wrenched from the only life she'd known and a job he was totally unsuited for?

Well, it was too late to change what he'd done. As his mama would say, he'd weighed anchor and set himself adrift.

Through the windows, he caught glimpses of the pier and buildings. Everything wrapped in thick gray fog. Nova Scotia, the place he had sworn to never return to was waiting to suck him back in.

Beneath his feet, the floor vibrated as the thrusters eased the ferry into its berth. He waited until the last minute, metal clanging as the doors to the car deck opened. Then he bent over Lissie and tucked a curl behind her ear. Somehow, he'd find a way to help her. He had to. There was no going back.

The ferry bumped against the wharf. The voices of the other passengers faded. He could put it off no longer. Time to disembark.

He wrapped the quilt securely around his daughter and swooped her off the seat. Snugged against him, the small body stiffened instantly. Holding his breath, he squeezed tighter. According to the psychiatrist, Lissie's outbursts were the result of fear, not willful attempts to get attention or to show outright hatred like Dolores had insisted. Secure swaddling would make her feel safe.

Gil checked that her feet and head were covered. Then, with both arms encompassing her, he rushed through the passageway and down the stairs to the car deck.

In the hatchway, he stopped and searched among the waiting vehicles for his ancient Volvo. Blast! In his hurry to get Lissie down and out, he'd gone down the wrong side of the boat like some landlubber. The battered black car that had been his mother's was all the way on the other side.

He pressed his lips together to keep from cursing. They'd wedged a pickup pulling a speedboat on a trailer in front of him, too. He wouldn't be able to drive right off. Well, nothing for it. He'd do what he always did—the best he could. As Dolores liked to remind him, it was never enough.

Gil clasped Lissie against him and set out toward the Old Lifeboat, as his momma had nicknamed the car that had ferried them to safety in the States so long ago.

Lissie, stiff in his arms, made a high-pitched keening as he squeezed between the tightly packed vehicles, but so far so good—she wasn't screaming ... yet.

Cold September air whooshed in from the open hatch, carrying with it all the familiar scents of the docks—fish guts, diesel, tar, and rotting seaweed.

Against his shoulder, Lissie flinched. The keening increased in pitch, but she still didn't scream. He might make it yet.

Then he saw her. Tottering in those sexy, high-heeled boots, Miss Too-Helpful bent over and searched for something in the back seat of a blue Hyundai with New York plates, and he couldn't help looking.

She straightened up, a map in her hand, and swiped her glorious maple-brown hair from her brow. With her pert little nose and pouty lips, the woman was one gorgeous package. Her head rose, and eyes the color of sea-glass looked straight into his.

Gil tipped his chin in her direction, and she gave him a nose-in-the-air jerk of the head in response.

Righty-o. Pushing the woman from his thoughts, Gil turned sideways, working his way between the closely parked cars and taking care to keep Lissie from bumping into anything. Forget Miss New York. He had a whole passel of problems to deal with. He didn't need to add a brassy American into the mix.

He was one row from the Volvo when the driver of the car beside him blasted his horn.

That did it. Lissie sucked in a breath of air and, with amazing power for a small child, screamed. The sound stabbed his ears and echoed through the hull.

Gil glanced around. Heads were turning in their direction. He had to put her in the car before someone else tried to help him with his daughter.

*Keys.* With one hand, he fished them out of his jeans pocket and unlocked the car. He yanked open the rear door, hefted the kicking, screeching bundle into her car seat and snapped the protective bar into place.

Her screams stopped as she sucked in another breath and screeched even louder. She kicked wildly at the seatback and pounded the padded bar that restrained her. This would go on for hours until she sank into a stuporous sleep.

Lissie hated being in cars. Hated the car seat.

Gil shut the door, maneuvered his way around to the other side, and got in the driver's side. The nearly three hundred miles to Tide Harbor were going to be a trial.

Across the way, a crew member directing traffic gave him a sympathetic look and came over to help guide the pickup and boat trailer in front of him off the ferry. Lissie's shrieks rose a decibel as the trailer's wheels rattled over the metal plates of the decking.

Gil rubbed his ears. The treatment plan suggested he buy child-sized, sound-deadening ear protectors, similar to those mechanics wore, for Lissie. At this moment, he wished he had a pair for himself. He mentally put two pairs of soundproofing earphones at the top of his shopping list and followed the motor boat down the ramp and toward Customs.

He drew out his and Lissie's Canadian passports and glanced at the clock in the instrument panel. With luck, and a hard-of-hearing customs agent, he'd be on the road in minutes. If all went smoothly, in five hours, he'd be able to settle Lissie into a somewhat comforting environment with all her familiar things around her and maybe she'd calm down long enough for him to get an hour or two of sleep.

Gil tapped his fingers on the steering wheel as the female customs officer started taking luggage out of the car in front of him. He was pretty sure the agent wouldn't give him trouble, but you never knew. Women were often unpredictable.

He glanced over at Miss New York as she pulled up next to him in the adjoining customs line. She pointed to the scratch on her cheek and gave him a wink. Yeah, unpredictable.

But oh so sweet.

# Chapter 3

## Summer

Summer rubbed her cheek then slapped the steering wheel. Why had she taken that last glimpse of Mr. Gil Moses? His smile had haunted her for the entire three-hour drive to Tide Harbor.

Well, she was here now. Time to think about her plans for stopping the activation of the turbine and preventing any more from ever being installed. But first, she needed to get settled in and get some sleep.

She glanced up and down the street. Place looked dead. The few storefronts were closed up tight. Traffic signs barely visible through the misty fog. She pulled over to the curb and stopped the car. Complete silence blanketed her.

What had she been thinking coming here? She would have loved to work on EcoGreen Action's black-footed ferret project or be heading to Florida to help organize the protests against keeping dolphins in captivity. But no. Other EcoGreen Action staff led those projects. She needed to do something on her own. Be bold. Make a splash. Stop an international mega corporation in its tracks, and earn the respect of her superiors at EcoGreen.

Most importantly, she had to land the directorship position so she could do some good and make up for her betrayal to her father. That was why she was spending ten days of unpaid leave in a foggy fishing village that closed up tight at midnight. So, for now, Tide Harbor it was. Even if the main street looked to be about two-blocks long.

Summer peered through the droplets of mist coating the windshield. There was a hairdresser, a hardware store, some kind of brick edifice, a shuttered eatery, and a church. She squinted into the gloom. No, make that two churches. And, of course, the ubiquitous fast-food place on the far corner, as cold and dark as every other business in town. No chance of a hot cup of coffee to warm her insides.

With the car engine off, a chill damp crept over her. She tugged her too-thin, designer sweater more tightly around her. She might be a long way from her once-upon-a-time family farm, but if she wasn't freezing, she'd swear she was back in her hometown. And if the locals were anything like the folk she had grown up with, it was going to take a lot of effort to get them stirred up enough to make a huge corporation like Seastroke Energy pull its cutting-edge tidal project out of the Minas Basin. And she had less than ten days to make it happen.

She rested her forehead on the steering wheel. Maybe the turbine bomber had the right idea—blow the thing to smithereens.

*Plink.*

Summer jerked upright. A shadowy shape hovered outside the passenger-side window.

*Plink.*

What the heck? Some man was tapping on the glass with what looked to be a beer bottle.

She turned on the engine. No way was she going to deal with the town drunk at this hour of the night. She shifted into drive, put her foot on the pedal, ready to speed up, then let up. The idiot had stumbled in front of her hood and stood there, waving his arms.

Summer rolled down the window and stuck her head out. "Move, please."

The man lifted his face. She shrunk back.

Caught in the light from her headlights, the man looked crazy enough to attack her. His bald head glistened with wetness. One side of his mouth twisted down. His nose had been broken so many times it lay flat to his face. But it was his eyes that set her heart pounding.

Beneath thick, bushy eyebrows, one dark eye gave her a piercing stare, sharp as a knife, while the other, filmed with the whitish glaze of a cataract, sent icy sweat down her back.

This was not someone she wanted anything to do with.

She put the car into reverse and slowly backed up.

The man shook his beer bottle. "That's right, lady. You go back where you came from. Don't want no strangers here." He took a gulp from the bottle and swung it again. "The sea, she be angry. Very angry."

Ten feet back, Summer put the car in forward again and eased out into the other lane. If she could get past the drunk, somewhere several miles ahead was the turn-off to the cottage she'd rented. She couldn't wait to be curled up nice and tight and warm in a cozy bed, far from this ghostly madman.

She pressed gently on the gas pedal, keeping her eye on the old geezer. She might want to skedaddle, but the last thing she ought to do was hit a local. It would be hard to build a grassroots movement after injuring one of Tide Harbor's own.

She was almost past when, at the last minute, the crazy bastard lurched toward her with a shout. Clamping her hands more tightly on the wheel, she swerved farther to the left and floored the gas.

In the rearview mirror, she watched him throw back his arm and toss the bottle.

*Crash.* The bottle smacked into the rear-passenger side, filling the interior with the heady smell of beer. Trying not to think of the damage to the car, she whipped her eyes forward and zoomed down the street.

Summer didn't look back. Every small town had its weirdos. But that man was more than bizarre. He was downright scary.

****

Twenty minutes later, it wasn't beer-guzzling drunks that frightened her; it was the fact that she was totally lost. Her GPS had given up long ago on trying to find the road to the cottage, and despite paying extra for international service, her cell phone couldn't latch on to a signal. It was back to the Dark Ages.

Summer picked up the Google Maps printout she'd thankfully brought with her and studied it in the light from the glove compartment.

She peered at the two sandy tracks illuminated by her headlights then glanced back at the map. Somewhere ahead, there was supposed to be a vacation cottage. But which way?

She tipped the printout to get a better view in the dim glow. If she was reading it correctly, the more traveled left trail ended at the top of a cliff, and the overgrown right one went to the rental. That seemed backward somehow.

She traced the lines on the map and came up with the same answer. Okay, so the right it was.

Gripping the steering wheel, she slowly inched her way down the narrow track, wincing every time the wheels dipped into a water-logged puddle or churned over a rock. Heaven help her if a tire went flat out here in the middle of nowhere.

Ten harrowing minutes later, the cabin appeared out of the fog. It was nothing like she had expected. The realtor had sung its praises over the phone. Sea view, all the amenities, cozy and private.

She got out of the car and slammed the door. She glanced back down the narrow track she'd just traveled. Well, it was private all right. But if it had a sea view, you'd have to hack your way through a thicket to get to it.

And as far as being cozy? The outside hadn't been painted in years. Moss, a bilious green in the car lights, crept up the peeling siding and covered the rough, cedar-shake roof. Dead weeds huddled around the doorstep. One windowpane was cracked, while another sported what could only be a bullet hole. A pile of beer and whiskey bottles sat to one side. Either there were a lot of heavy drinkers in Tide Harbor, or the town drunk spent all his time here.

Oh, she so didn't want to think about that.

Summer rubbed her cold hands together. Would he be coming here, after her? She didn't think so. The man had been pretty blotto—hopefully, too drunk to find his way five miles down that excuse for a road.

She let out a breath. No way could she go back to Tide Harbor. Not only was she dead tired and the road daunting, but the bed and breakfast there cost way more than EcoGreen Action's living allotment for activists in the field. She'd checked. This rental had been dirt cheap. She toed the gravel and cursed the agent. Now she knew why.

The chill air, heavy with the scent of pine and sea, wrapped around her and seeped under her collar. She had no choice. She'd freeze to death standing here.

Opening the trunk, Summer hefted out her suitcase, scooped up her backpack and, ignoring the prickles running up and down her skin, headed to the door. She was going to have to stay here no matter what. The agent had better be right about the key being under the brick by the door.

# Chapter 4

## Gil

*T*hud.

Gil flipped onto his stomach and scrunched the pillow over his head.

*Thud.*

He groaned. Who was knocking on the door this early in the morning? For that matter, who knew he was here? They'd arrived in the middle of the night at the house he had rented in Tide Harbor.

He opened one eye halfway and glared at the old-fashioned clock radio on the nightstand. 5:00 a.m.

*Thud.*

Whoever it was wasn't going away, and if the banging kept up, Lissie would soon be screaming.

Gil threw back the comforter, yanked on his jeans and a tee-shirt, and stumbled his way through the unfamiliar house. He opened the front door a crack. "Yes?"

A round-faced woman with shockingly blue eyes peered up at him. In her faded dress, orange fisherman's slicker, and grubby yellow slippers with daisies on the toes, she looked like an escapee from a fishwives' homeless shelter.

"Morning, Mr. Moses. Brought you some breakfast fixins, I have." She nodded down at the wrinkled shopping bag slung over her arm. "You getting in so late and all with that little girl of yours, thought you could do with some eats."

Gil looked up and down the road. No car. No other houses. Where had the woman come from? "That's very kind." He took the bag from her. "And you are ...?"

"Oh my." She smiled, revealing large, yellowed teeth. "Why Mrs. Eagles, of course, from down the way a bit. Everybody knows me. Heard Mrs. Campbell rented out Windswept Cottage to you and your little one for the winter. Figured you'd need some settling-in help. I'm a fine housekeeper. Do the cleaning for Mrs. Campbell. I'm a widow woman on a pension. Can always use a little extra work."

He rubbed his face. It was going to be hard enough to maintain his cover while trying to ferret out the turbine bomber for Seastroke. The last thing he needed was a local busybody underfoot. He sniffed. Especially one who smelled like week-old fish. And Lissie didn't adjust well to strangers. "That's fine and well, but—"

"Nannaaaa." Lissie's cry echoed through the small house. "Nannaaaa."

The sound sent shivers through him. Despite the fact that Dolores had been getting Lissie up and off to daycare in the mornings, his daughter still cried for her dead grandmother, the woman who'd loved and cared for her since infancy. In a moment, she'd be screaming.

Gil turned, dumped the grocery bag on the coffee table, and rushed to the bedroom.

Eyes shut tight, Lissie jumped up and down in the portable playpen he'd set up for her when they had arrived. At four, she was too big for it, but it was her favorite place to sleep, curled up in a ball, thumb in her mouth.

"Nannaaaa." Her forearms flapped up and down in the awkward little dance she did that disgusted Dolores so much.

He bent over and lifted her out. "Daddy's here, sweetheart. Daddy's here."

"Nooooo." Lissie struggled, batting him in the face with her small fists, kicking him with her bare feet. "Nannaaaa."

Gil fought against the pain of her rejection and readjusted his hold. She wasn't angry at him. She wasn't used to him taking care of her. She missed her grandma. He missed his mother, too.

He set her down, and she threw herself facedown on the floor. Her arms and legs thrashed up and down, and from deep in her throat came the slow, steady growl that signaled the start of a major fit that could go on for hours.

"Oh, the dear child."

Gil whirled around. His would-be housekeeper had followed him in and stood in the doorway. "Misses her mommy, she does, Mr. Moses." The old woman toddled over and, ignoring the wild kicks and thrashes, settled down on the floor beside Lissie. She slipped her hand under her pajama top and rested it on her back. "Hush, my little sugar buns. Auntie Victoria is here."

He held his breath and took a step forward. Lissie hated to be touched skin to skin, and in a second, Mrs. Eagles was going to learn that fact. But instead of going berserk, Lizzie's frantic movements slowed. Her cries became a low, lonesome-sounding moan. And rhythmically tilting her head from side to side, Mrs. Eagles moaned along with her.

Gil stared at the pair. The old woman rocked and hummed. Lissie's thumb slipped into her mouth. The keening died away. And at last, his daughter's eyes opened, and she looked around. Her eyes found his. "Dada."

Gil gave himself a shake. Did the woman have some kind of magic touch? He peered over at her. "What? How did you ...?"

Mrs. Eagles pushed herself up from the floor with a grunt. "It's the warmth and pressure that does it."

"But she hates to be touched."

"No, she doesn't. She needs it." Mrs. Eagles cupped one of Lissie's feet in her hand. "Don't you, sugar bun." She frowned at him. "Every human being needs to be touched. What kind of scientist are you not to know that? Learned it in school, I did. About those poor baby monkeys who preferred the soft, cuddly, fake mommas to the cold metal ones that fed them."

"But the doctor said—"

Mrs. Eagles waved her hand as she led them into the bright green and yellow kitchen, slipped out of the fishy slicker, and washed her hands at the sink. "Gotta use yah own two-cents. Now, let's get some good food into the two of you. Then I'll start freshening things up around here. Place has been closed up a month. Reeks of the damp. Show you the lay of the land, too."

She nodded at the huge picture window in the eating alcove. "You need to watch the tides out there. The view's grand, and the yard is well-fenced. Last tenant had a dog. But with a little one, you have to be a bit in tune with the ocean, if you know what I mean."

Gil settled Lissie on a kitchen chair and glanced out at the water. The Bay of Fundy stretched before him, glistening in the early morning sun. After years away, and despite all the tragedies, he was surprised he still felt the pull of the sea. He wanted to be out there, breathing in the salt air, listening to the slosh of water in the bilge and the *put-put* of the engine.

He turned away. "I'm Nova Scotian. Grew up on a lobster boat. I know the sea."

Mrs. Eagles pulled a blueberry muffin out of the grocery bag and set it in front of Lissie. She handed him another. "Not on the Fundy side, I'd lay bets."

He took a bite. Tiny wild blueberries burst with flavor. The moist cake melted in his mouth. He hadn't had a home-baked muffin this good in ages, not since his momma died. He swallowed.

"South shore. Sailed out of Seal Cove."

"Did you now?"

"My pa was a lobsterman."

"Aye. So was my husband, rest his poor soul." The woman plugged in the coffee maker, added coffee and water, and then leaned back against the counter as the coffee beaker filled. "So I'm hired, eh?"

Gil choked on his muffin. He'd been hustled. Blazes, he didn't need an old woman underfoot all the time. He'd have enough to do taking care of Lissie and finding the crazy bombers. Still, it wouldn't hurt to have a little help once in a while.

"You've been very kind and seem quite competent. Perhaps you could babysit occasionally?"

The woman frowned. "Nope. Full-time, live-in." She took a mug from the cabinet and poured a cup of coffee. "How you plan to do your work? Go out on the boat? Who's going to care for this little girl of yours?" She handed him the mug. "Sugar? Milk?"

"Black." Gil took the mug and sipped. The woman made a fine brew, too. "I planned to send her to a local preschool." He fished around in his pocket and found the scrap of paper. "Miss Flowers' Playhouse."

"And did you tell Betty exactly what she was getting?"

"I haven't talked to Miss Flowers yet."

Mrs. Eagles shook her head. "She's a good woman, Betty. But high-strung, if you know what I mean."

"Nana." Lissie slapped the table. "More, Nana."

Mrs. Eagles put another muffin in front of her. "That's a girl. You eat up."

"Bit, bit, bit, bit, bit." Lissie crooked her neck over the muffin and picked it apart as she had the first, setting the mushy blueberries in a row on the tabletop. She pinched a berry between her thumb and index finger and popped it in her mouth. She picked up the next and did the same.

Gil let out a huff of air. "My mother, her nana, made muffins like these. She passed away three months ago."

"Did she now?" The woman tilted her round face toward him, a bit of tongue showing between her lips. "A sign, I should think."

Gil set down the mug. "How about five days a week?"

She held out another muffin. "Full-time. I do all cooking, cleaning, and childcare."

Gil chomped into the muffin and savored the sweet goodness. The old lady could cook. Still, what with the alimony, money was going to be tight. He had the rent to pay, and he would need to maintain a boat. "How much?"

"Room and board. That's all, Mr. Moses. Room and board. Got my pension for the every-days. Not that an old lady like me needs much."

Gil rolled his shoulders. "Fine. Room and board. Weekend off."

Mrs. Eagles opened her mouth to protest.

Gil held up his hand. "That's nonnegotiable. You can sit on the deck and watch the tide roll in or whatever. I'll write up a contract for a month, and we'll see how it goes."

"Don't worry, Mr. Moses. Best decision you ever made. You'll not regret it. I promise." She wiped her palms on her dress. "You want me in the bedroom next to Lissie's?"

Gil threw up his hands. "Sure, it's not like there's a lot of choice in a three-bedroom bungalow."

"Right enough. I'll be able to hear her through the wall if she needs something." Mrs. Eagles trotted around the kitchen table. "I'll go fetch my things and make myself at home."

"You need a lift?"

"Oh no. Got my things right outside."

Gil glared at the woman. "*Outside*?"

"By the door. Mrs. Campbell said you were a good man, Mr. Moses. That's good enough for me."

Gil trailed her through the living room, kicking himself for not asking for references. For all he knew, he could be taking in a homeless person—or a thief.

He eyed his new employee as she pushed open the door. Not that she looked like a criminal. With her swollen ankles, work-reddened hands, and hunched-over back, she looked precisely like what she claimed to be—a pensioner housekeeper.

Nevertheless, he knew his lawyer brother would be shaking his head and saying in that snotty tone of his, "Always too trusting for your own good, Gil. You can't tell who someone is by merely looking at them. Devils can have the faces of angels."

Gil's shoulders sagged. Aaron *had* been right about Dolores.

He stepped out the door. One glance at the large suitcase and two cardboard boxes on the front deck, and his stomach did a little warning dance. Where had she come from? Why was she lugging around all these belongings? Something was definitely not on the up-and-up about Mrs. Eagles.

Gil studied the woman again. Wiry gray hair, wrinkled bags under her eyes. She had to be in her late sixties or early seventies. He looked her up and down. How much damage could an old lady do?

Later, he'd check with Mrs. Campbell. Tide Harbor was a small town. Surely, Mrs. Eagles was what she appeared to be, and if not, he'd send her packing.

"Here we go, Mr. Moses. Only these few things."

She grabbed the two boxes, and he hefted the suitcase. It weighed a ton. He glanced at the elderly lady scuffing along in her slippers in front of him.

"Feels like you have a whole house in here."

"Nothing crazy. No guns or such. Just my treasures, lovey."

Gil gritted his teeth and twisted his way down the short, narrow hall and into the bedroom next to Lissie's and opposite his. He dropped the suitcase on the floor. It landed with an ominous *clunk*. "Better not be."

There was a loud *thump*.

"Lissie." Gil dashed into the hallway and across the way into the kitchen. The room was empty, her chair knocked over, the screen door ajar.

Panic swelled in his chest. What kind of father was he? He'd left her alone.

He charged outside. "Lissie?"

Scraggly pines and brush surrounded the patchy brown and green lawn on two sides. Straight ahead, the yard opened up a steep cliff overlooking a semi-circular cove. Five-foot high fencing ran around the yard. Could she have climbed the fence and fallen?

He rushed to the fence and sucked in a breath. No small body lay smashed on the tiny rock-strewn beach twenty feet below.

He looked along the cliff edge. Someone had chiseled a narrow footpath down to the shore. Had she climbed the fence and gone down to path?

"Mr. Moses."

Gil swung around.

Mrs. Eagles waved. "It's all right. Your daughter's here. In the kitchen."

He sprinted back inside, his heart racing.

His new housekeeper put a finger to her lips and pointed to the cabinet under the sink. "She's found herself a little hidey-hole."

Gil bent down and peered into the darkness. There she was, his beautiful daughter, curled up in a mess of cleaning solutions, spray bottles, and scrub cloths, sucking her thumb.

He reached in and gently tugged on her arm. "Come to Daddy, sweetheart. Come."

Lissie slunk farther back.

He stuck his head into the cabinet and tried to wrap his arms around her. She stiffened and let out a piercing screech.

Gil jerked his head out and squeezed his eyes closed. She was nearly five years old. School age. She should be in kindergarten, learning to tie her shoes and recite the alphabet. Instead, she hid in kitchen cabinets. She cringed from his touch. Screamed at the slightest thing. Was his ex-wife right? Did she belong in an institution?

He scanned the bare kitchen with the dated green Formica countertop, the cheap appliances, the battered table that had served countless summer tourists. At least in an institution, she'd be in a clean, modern facility and watched over constantly.

He rubbed his temples. Stealing Lissie away might have been the biggest mistake in his life.

The woman patted his arm. "She's safe enough for the while."

Gil threw her hand off. "But it's filthy under there. Full of chemicals."

"Nothing dangerous, Mr. Moses. I don't believe in those high-powered cleaners. Only organics for me. Mrs. Campbell agrees. Can't have her guests having allergic reactions." His newly acquired housekeeper nudged him. "Your daughter's scared. New place. New sounds. New smells. Let her be for a while." She looked him up and down. "You go shower and dress. I'll keep my eye on her. Promise. I'll sit right here at the table and write up a grocery list. Then you can go shopping." She tilted her head and gave him a half wink so like his mother's his breath caught in his throat. "A big, loving daddy like you can't live on blueberry muffins alone, you know."

Gil closed his eyes and fought the urge to hug the old woman. He was going to have enough trouble tracking down the bombers. It would be a relief to know Lissie was well cared-for.

Maybe hiring Mrs. Eagles would be the right thing, after all. Then he remembered the suitcase and boxes, and his resolve wavered.

Or maybe not.

# Chapter 5

## Summer

Summer pushed her cart down the aisle of the supermarket, flipping cans of soup and boxes of granola bars into the basket.

She tossed in a bag of chips and a jar of salsa. The cabin was buggier than a New York City garbage truck, but it had an electric heater to compete with the damp and, as she discovered this morning, a stunning view of the bay from the minuscule deck at the back.

Not much in the way of appliances, though. A hot plate and a tiny refrigerator didn't allow for gourmet meals. Not that she was much of a cook, anyway. A duck with a spoon tied to its back could cook better than she did, according to her brothers. But then, she hadn't had a mother to teach her.

She turned into the cereal aisle and crashed into an old lady pushing a shopping cart heaped high with food. She caught the woman by the arm and waited for her to regain her balance. "So sorry. Are you all right?"

"No trouble, dearie. Nothing broken." The old woman moved her wagon out of the way. "New to Tide Harbor?"

Summer nodded and started down the aisle. The woman trailed after her.

"Thought so. Interesting accent you got. You must be Old Man Keddy's new tenant. Awful place, that one. Miles from nowhere. Favorite spot for the locals to go boozing. He couldn't rent it at all this summer. Must think you a godsend." She peered into the cart. "A seagull couldn't survive on that junk."

Summer maneuvered her cart around a display. Just what she needed—a stick-her-nose-in-everything village gossip. She pointed back down the aisle. "You've left your cart back there."

The woman raised one eyebrow and shook her hand in the air. "Nobody in Tide Harbor would take Victoria Eagles' cart, dearie. Besides, my employer will be back in a sec. Went to find the molasses. Going to bake lassy bread for him and his little one like I used to make for Mr. Eagles. 'Best darn bread in the Minas Basin,' my man always said. Slathered it with butter every time."

Summer gripped the handle of the cart and gave the woman a curt nod. Next, the old chatter-mouth would be telling her what Mr. Eagles ate for breakfast. She knew the type. She'd grown up in a small town full of gabby ladies like this one.

Summer stopped to grab a box of cornflakes. "That's nice. Got to run." She sped up and whirled around the corner, right into a tall, familiar man holding an even more familiar child.

A jar crashed to the floor. The overly sweet smell of blackstrap molasses wafted around her. The child's mouth opened, revealing two missing lower teeth, and for one precious moment, everyone froze.

Then the most ghastly screech she'd ever heard filled the store. "*Mommmmmmmmmmy!*"

It went on and on and on.

Summer clapped her hands over her ears and glared at the man. "You!"

Gil Moses pressed the little girl's face to his chest, muffling the sound a bit. He glanced at her. "Yes, me." He spun on his heel and strode out of the supermarket, taking his screaming offspring with him.

Mrs. Eagles waddled up behind her. "Poor little thing. The slightest thing sets her off. I told Mr. Moses to let me stay at home with her while he did the shopping, but he wouldn't hear of it."

"What's this Mr. Moses doing here, in Tide Harbor?

"Well, I am not quite sure, dearie. Something to do with the fishes, I suppose. That's about the only thing we have."

A dark-haired, broad-shouldered man, standing in line at the cash register glanced over. The back of his leather jacket featured a ferocious-looking bear-like animal with cat ears and claws. He called across, "Heard he's here to work on Seastroke Energy's tidal-energy project, Aunt Victoria. Gonna convince us it's a good idea."

Summer squeezed the handle of her cart tighter, her pulse resounding in her ears. He *was* Gil Moses, world-renowned fishery expert. But what was he doing here, working for Seastroke? Surely, he knew the effect turbines had on fish populations.

She pushed her cart to the side, grabbed her purse and, avoiding the sticky puddle on the floor, rushed out the door and into the parking lot. This was her chance to find out what exactly Dr. Moses was doing here.

She was in luck. Gil Moses was still there, struggling to get the girl buckled into her car seat. For a second, she hesitated. The man was harried enough, but she had to talk to him. Find out whose side he was on.

She crossed her fingers. Hopefully, he'd be on her side, and they could work together. And if he was here to cover up the ecological damage, she had to ferret out his weak spots before he discovered why she was here.

The child shrieked again. And heaven help her, she had to do something to help him handle that little girl.

"Mr. Moses." She moved closer to his car, trying to stay out of the sight of the red-faced child.

He jerked up, hitting his head on the top of the door opening. "Not now."

"I need to talk to you."

He rubbed his head. "Not now, I said."

From inside the car, came the huffing sound of a child on the verge of another screaming fit.

"My name is Summer Avery and—"

He stood up fully, the faded quilt dangling from his hand, and glared at her. "Miss Avery. Please—" Something more than simple recognition flashed across his face. "Ah, Miss Fancy Boots from the ferry." He finished wrapping the quilt around his daughter then stepped toward her and touched the scratches on her cheek. "I am so sorry about what happened."

The touch was tentative and gentle yet it stirred up heat in all the wrong places. For a moment, Summer froze then jerked back. She really shouldn't be attracted to this man— this most likely *married* man, who could be her most difficult opponent.

He dropped his hand. "Your cheek is healing? And the bite? No infection?"

From the car came another ear-shattering screech. He turned and tucked the quilt tighter over the child.

Summer peered over his shoulder. Forget the turbine, she wanted to do something to help that poor child. The girl was too old to be having tantrums, and she didn't seem to respond to her father at all. Odd, the girl behaved almost as if he were a stranger she feared.

She studied the awkward way he handled her. For all she knew, he could have kidnapped the girl. The child certainly seemed petrified of him.

"About your daughter—"

"Here's your groceries, ma'am." The leather-jacketed man from the register line came up behind her.

She spun around and stared at the two plastic bags being held out to her. The man gave her a dazzling grin.

"Mine?" She took the bags and peered inside. Junk food. It was her stuff, all right. "But how? I didn't pay."

He patted his back pocket. "All taken care of."

"My stars. You *paid* for me? I can't let you do that." She shifted both bags to her left arm and went to pull her wallet out of her backpack.

He offered his hand. "Cully Teed, at your service. Consider it a welcome to Tide Harbor."

She took his hand in hers, noting the callouses on the palm and the dirt under the fingernails. A working man— she studied his face—a very fine looking one. He had wide-set brown eyes with crinkle lines at the corners from too much sun or too much smiling, an expressive mouth, a powerful jaw, and even white teeth.

Perhaps, this was a man she could befriend. He was plenty attractive, and he didn't come with the baggage Gil Moses did.

Summer broadened her smile and squeezed a little more firmly. She'd need local allies, like him. "Most pleased to meet you, Mr. Teed. I can't thank you enough for the kind gesture. I certainly chose the right place to vacation."

"Anything for a beautiful lady." He smiled broadly. "Please, call me Cully."

"And I'm Gil Moses."

Summer jumped. Heavens, the man could move quietly. She hadn't even heard him come up behind them.

Moses held out his hand.

Cully glared at it, the sunshiny look gone from his face. "Heard Seastroke Energy sent you. Tide Harbor don't take kindly to strangers telling us what to do."

Summer glanced from one man to the other. They were of a size, both over six foot and powerfully built. And they had taken an instant dislike—their eyes held that beady-eyed stare her father's roosters wore when facing off in the henyard. For a moment, she feared they'd come to fisticuffs.

Moses took a step back. "Don't know what you heard, but I'm here to study the lobster populations at the site before they complete the installation."

"Yep. Mrs. Campbell likes to know who she has staying at her place. My buddy Gary—that's her nephew—he's pretty handy on a computer. Looked you up. You're on Seastroke's payroll."

"There you are." Mrs. Eagles trotted across the parking lot. She glanced at the two men. "You go in and pay for the groceries, Mr. Moses. I'll watch Lissie for you." She leaned in the car door, took a hard candy out of her pocket, unwrapped it, and popped it in the child's mouth.

The screaming stopped. A look of surprise spread over Lissie's face. A furrow creased her forehead. Her eyebrows rose in concentration. Her tongue worked the candy around her mouth, licking and smacking.

Gil spun around. "We don't feed her candy. No sugar. Nothing artificially colored." He ran a hand through his hair. "I'll fill you in on her diet when we get home. Just don't go giving her any more sweets, Mrs. Eagles." He dipped his head and headed back into the supermarket.

Cully turned to Summer. "Up to no good, that one. Stay away is my advice. Lots of folks here don't want any that turbine-y thing out in our bay. Wish the government would simply let us do our fishing and leave us to take care of our own neck of the basin. What's some company from the States know about the Minas Basin?"

Mrs. Eagles poked her head up. "Don't you be chasing off my new employer now, Cully."

"He's here to cause trouble, Aunt Vickie. Milk him for what's he worth and get out of there."

"Got my reasons for staying." She glanced at Summer. "He's a good man."

Cully grunted. "*Bah.* He's giving you a place to live for the moment. But Masie will eventually forgive you and let you back into the apartment."

"Masie can dig her own cesspit and stick her head in it. This little girl needs me." She slipped into the back seat next to Lissie.

Cully peered in the car window. Lissie was rocking and moaning. "What's wrong with her?"

"Who's to know? Remember the Hazelton boy who got drowned in the caves. He was something like her—all sensitive to sounds and movement. Not like you, you big lug." She slapped him away. "Your skull's as hard as Old Crow Rock. Your mamma used to tip you head-first out of bed in the morning, and you'd go right on sleeping."

Summer laughed. "So, you have a hard head, Mr. Teed?"

"So they say." Cully tapped the side of his skull with his fist. "Good thing, too. Survived three seasons with the Bearcats as a defenseman without a single concussion."

Mrs. Eagles leaned farther out the window and shook a finger at Summer. "You watch out for this guy, Miss. He's our local hockey hero. The Bearcats won the trophy the year he played. Wins the sea kayak race over to Cognecto every summer, too. Thinks he's the biggest fish in town."

Summer eyed the man. He seemed like a nice enough guy. Besides, all she had to do was find one local willing to step up and bring people together. Cully Teed sounded pretty anti-turbine.

She tipped up her chin and smiled. "I like my fish big."

Cully took the hint and moved closer. "Say, I was planning to take my boat out for a spin. Want to join me?"

Summer widened her smile. Even better. Getting in with the locals was step one in the organizer's playbook.

"Sure. Sounds perfect."

# Chapter 6

## Gil

An hour later, Gil parked his car at the Tidal Turbine Research Center in Parrsboro and got out. He sucked in a breath of the sea air. Stuck in his university office at MIT, he'd forgotten how invigorating fresh air could be. He took another deep breath, filled his lungs, then exhaled. All the tightness and worry lifted from his chest. Somehow, everything was going to work out.

Mrs. Eagles was a charm. Lissie was calmer than she'd ever been back in Boston. And he was finally doing what he loved after years of pontificating in the classroom with minimal time for research so Dolores could have the suburban life she demanded.

He glanced out at the deep, cobalt-blue water rippling like watered silk across the Basin. The only thing that would make the day more perfect was getting his hands on a boat.

He crossed the parking lot and pushed open the door. Hopefully, the research center would lend him theirs.

Two hours and a heap of paperwork later, he was standing on the dock, staring at the decrepit hulk he'd been assigned by the overly efficient gentleman in charge of turbine research. From one end to the other, the boat showed signs of wear and neglect. He doubted it was all that seaworthy. The bilge pump would be working overtime for sure.

It had been grand once—a smaller version of the Cape Island boat his father had owned. With the high sweeping bow and low stern for ease in taking on and letting off the lobster traps, it was perfect for a one- or two-person operation. But the battered decking and peeling white paint told of a hard life.

At near high tide, the boat rode several feet below the pier. Gil swung down and stepped onto the deck. The open-back wheelhouse wouldn't provide much cover from the elements, but the equipment was up-to-date with GPS, radar, and satellite radio, and there was a small cuddy with built-in benches which could serve as beds in an emergency, but which were currently covered in old papers, greasy rubber gloves, and a mess of ropes and lines.

He opened the deck hatch and peered down at the engine. Unlike the rest of the boat, it appeared to be well-tended. According to Mr. Efficiency, the research center only used the boat to check on the site status.

Gil ran his hand over the console and smiled. With a good engine under her and with a little tender loving care, the boat could be brought up to snuff. It would never be a looker or fast, and its name *Hell'za Poppin'* would drive him crazy, but none of that mattered. It was a boat, and for now, it was his.

He glanced out at the harbor that gave the town its name. It had been years since he'd been on the water captaining a boat. He couldn't wait to get out there.

He patted the steering wheel. "Let's start by cleaning you up, old lady. Then I'll see about giving us a jaunt. Work the kinks out for both of us." He bent over to finish hooking up the GPS wires.

"Good morning," a voice with a familiar twang called down.

He looked up and winced.

Summer Avery stood on the wharf, dressed in the same too-tight sweater and slinky jeans she'd worn at the market. What was with this woman? She kept popping up everywhere. Not that he minded. She sure was an eyeful. Golden-brown hair. Perfect curves. He'd have to be a dead man not to be attracted.

But she was not for him. Everything from the expensive gold chain around her neck to the kinky-heeled white boots that didn't belong anywhere near a working fishing wharf cried, "Pamper me." After Dolores, he had no appetite for high-maintenance women, especially know-it-all ones.

He patted *Hell'za Poppin's* railing. "Don't mean you, ole girl." He'd take an ancient boat any day over some woman who wanted to tell him how to handle his daughter.

A man came up behind Summer, his features hidden beneath the shadow of his ball cap. "Looky here. Our Mr. Moses has got himself a boat ... of sorts. Fixin' to take her out, eh?"

Gil squinted up. *Ah.* It was the rube from the grocery store. What was his name? That's right—Cully Teed. He should have given the guy the taking down he deserved for his rudeness, but his mother, and a lot of messy bar brawls in his youth, had taught him violence did not change people's attitudes. Always take the high road, Momma cautioned, and keep your head above the mud.

He made sure his voice was university professor polite. "Yes, that's the plan." He shielded his eyes with his hand. "That you, Miss Avery? You here to buy fish for dinner."

A slight frown marred her forehead. "No." She shifted the pack on her back. "Mr. Teed is going to take me for a ride on his new lobster boat."

Gil gave a wave. "Sounds delightful. Enjoy your trip." There, Momma would be proud. He'd kept it pleasant.

He turned away and picked up a rag. Now, if he kept his mouth shut, the pair would leave, and he would have a peaceful morning cleaning the boat and taking it for a spin. Summer Avery and what she did was none of his business.

Instead, his gut churned. He hated to see any woman being played by that bonehead. The guy was a lecher. His intentions were written all over his face. Miss Fancy Boots deserved better. Any woman deserved better.

He peered up at Summer. "You did tell Mr. Teed about your seasickness issue, didn't you?"

Miss New York's smile faded.

Cully's chin went up. "You a gull feeder, city girl?"

She glared at Gil from the corner of her eye. "I get a bit nauseous, if that's what you mean. But I'm sure I'll be fine."

"That's what they all say." Cully shook his head. "Sorry to disappoint, but you'll have to stay here. I can't have you whooping up all over the boat. Ain't even paid for yet. And I plan to put it through its paces, not mosey around the inlet here. Not today. Everybody on shore's going to be looking for me in the new boat."

"But I—"

Cully wrapped an arm over her shoulders and gave her a squeeze. "Now, come on. Don't want your tummy upset, do we? But when I get back, how about I treat you to a coffee and donuts at Bake and Bite? And later, we can scoot over to the White Rock for their fish and clam fry. It's half-price on Mondays."

Miss Avery stuffed her hands into her jean pockets and glanced around. "Sure, whatever."

Cully adjusted his ball cap. "If you truly want to go out on my boat, you should go down to the drug store in Parrsboro and get some seasickness meds or one of those wrist-bandy things the tourists swear by. Then I'll take you out." He gave a wave and strode down the dock.

Gil winced at the broken look on Miss New York's face, and his stomach sank. He'd done that. He cursed under his breath. Why did his good deeds always go wrong? It wasn't like him to be mean to a lady. Somewhere in heaven, his momma was scowling down at him right now.

Still, Lissie had attacked her. He owed her for not raising a stink about it. And if she was a delight to look at, that was merely a side benefit.

"Sorry I lost you your boat ride."

She shrugged. "I've been touring the town, seeing the sights. Lady in the gift store said I shouldn't miss the harbor. Is it true the tide goes so far out all these boats will be sitting in the mud?"

"Yah, sure. Tides here are near fourteen meters. That would be fifty feet Stateside. But you'll have to come back to see it. Tide's rising right now. Low tide will be close to midnight."

"Oh. Expect I'll be sleeping then." Miss Avery stuffed her hands into her jean pockets. "This your boat?"

"Borrowed." He wiped down the combing. "Not much to look at, but she'll do. Not going out to the open sea. Just doing some tests."

"What kind?"

He scrubbed harder. "A survey of the lobster population. Get a baseline before they start up the turbine." That much was true.

"You working for the tidal energy company?"

He pressed his lips together. He doubted a tourist from New York City had anything to do with the Minas Basin bombing, but his Seastroke contact had drilled into him the importance of maintaining his cover at all costs. No one could know he was working for them or that his job was to catch the bomber.

"I'm funded by a grant from the provincial government." Not exactly a lie—he did have a grant.

The smile that blossomed on Summer Avery's face made his gut twist. Now she thought him one of the good guys.

She shifted her pack. "So, you taking the boat out?"

"That's the plan. Need to see how she runs."

"Could I come? I bet the view is amazing from out there."

He stopped polishing. How could he turn her down after nixing her excursion with Teed. "Sure. I'll take you out, Miss Avery, if your heart's set on it." He pointed over his shoulder. "A little vomit won't mess up *Poppin'* here."

She peered over the edge of the wharf, one hand on the strap of her knapsack. "The boat's awfully small and beat up. Is it safe?"

"Definitely seaworthy. Besides, we'll not go far. A spin around the harbor. The water's calm."

Summer took a long glance back toward the parking lot.

Gil waited. Miss Fancy Boots would come up with some excuse or another. High-maintenance women didn't joy ride on old fishing boats.

She moved closer to the edge. "How do I get down there?"

*Darn it.* There went his peaceful morning. He should have kept his mouth closed. Still, the woman had guts. He admired that. Dolores wouldn't have come within twenty feet of this boat.

Gil tossed down the rag. "Okay, turn around and grasp that post. Now reach down with your foot and find a crosspiece."

Summer wrapped both hands around the piling and reached out with her heeled boot, giving him a perfect view of her perfectly rounded bottom. He bit his lip.

"That's the way. Just like climbing down a ladder."

Summer's foot flailed. "There's nothing there."

Gil pressed his tongue against his teeth and grasped her by the hips. "I've got you, Miss Avery. Let go." He held her against his body. He could feel every curve. Smell her floral scent. A wave of desire shot through him, and he quickly swung her into the boat. He turned away and busied himself checking out the fuel gauge, converting liters to gallons and back again. Anything to get his thoughts back under his command.

He glanced over at the annoying woman. This was so not a good idea. The next hour in close quarters with Miss New York was going to test his self-control for sure. And patience.

She was holding on to the gunwale, her mouth set in a rigid line, her knuckles white. She was petrified, and they hadn't cast off yet.

Every time the boat sloshed against the wharf, she lost her balance and tipped precariously to one side or the other. In a minute, she'd be in the drink.

He strode across the deck and caught her by the arm. He peered down at her feet. "Those boots don't belong within a thousand miles of a boat."

She held out one foot then the other. "Not an admirer of my footwear, Mr. Moses?"

"You might want to take them off. You'd be a lot more stable."

"Barefoot on this worn-out boat? No way. Might get a splinter." She firmed her footing. "They're my boots. I'll manage."

Gil bit the inside of his cheek. The woman was impossible. But he'd asked for it.

He frowned at the calf-high, leather footwear and shrugged. "Suit yourself. Come up to the helm." He handed her a life jacket. "Put that on. Then I'll show you where we're heading." He drew her forward into the wheelhouse and helped her finish doing up the straps.

She set her pack at her feet and glanced around. "Where are the seats?"

"It's a working boat. Don't have any. There's a bench in the cuddy, but it's a mess. You can hold on to the grab bar over there." Gil looked at her. "No boats where you're from?"

*Hell'za Poppin'* jostled against the pier. She wrapped her fingers around the bar. "No, just farms."

"Farms? I though you a city girl."

"Don't you know you can't read a woman by her stylish fashion? My parents had a small farm in Northern Pennsylvania. I grew up living and breathing mud and manure."

He moved to the helm. "Probably no worse than breathing fish guts. My daddy was a lobsterman born and bred. But we fished for haddock and cod, too."

Gil started up the engine, listened for any odd knocking, and relaxed when it ran like a well-oiled machine. The boat might look beat, but as long as its innards worked, that was all that mattered.

He glanced behind at his unplanned passenger. Even though she had a good grip on the handhold, he could see her jaw trembling. He needed her to settle.

He spoke in his most soothing voice. "Relax, Miss Avery. I'll take it slow. The water's smooth as glass today." He hoisted himself up to the wharf, undid the lines, then climbed back down. "You can stand up here. Next to me. Might let you steer the boat."

Miss Avery raised an eyebrow. "Drive this thing?"

"Sure. You can drive a car. You can steer a boat. Here— come take the wheel."

She shook her head and pressed her hand to her mouth. Gil chewed his lip. *Uh-oh.* Bad sign.

"You don't happen to have any of the candied ginger I gave you?"

She swallowed. "I ate it all." She peeked up at him. "It was delicious."

"Too bad. It really helps."

"How do you know?"

"Been seasick."

She wrinkled her nose. "Fishermen don't get seasick."

"Sure they do. Got plenty of buddies who upchuck their way out of the harbor on every trip. Besides, if the sea's rough enough, anyone will turn queasy. And if you're already hungover, a rocking boat don't help."

"Sounds like the voice of experience."

"Done a few dumb things in my life." He gripped the wheel. And marrying Dolores had been the dumbest.

Summer gave him a small, closed-mouth smile. "So have I. So, are we going?"

"Yah, sure." He put the engine in gear then worked his way out of the dock, heading toward the mouth of the harbor, taking it slow. The boat rocked as it hit the cross current of the incoming tide, and then they were out in the Basin, motoring across water as calm as a lake.

He inhaled deeply. What more could a man want? It was one of those glorious autumn days. Blue sky. Sunlight glinting on the sea. The hills a blaze of color. No wind to speak of.

And a gorgeous woman by his side.

# Chapter 7

## Summer

Summer brushed her hair out of her eyes and studied the man at the helm. She couldn't believe her luck. This was the perfect opportunity to find out more about Gil Moses. He had no idea who she was. He thought her a nosy tourist, and she needed to keep it that way. How hard could that be?

She waved her hand at the coastline. "I've never been this far north. The scenery is breathtaking. So lush. So unspoiled."

She didn't have to pretend about the landscape. Tide Harbor truly was one of the most beautiful places she'd ever seen. It belonged on a postcard or a travelogue. She shifted her daypack. A tourist would be taking pictures. She needed her camera.

Holding on to the handhold with one hand, she picked up her pack and struggled to open it. The strap tangled in her wind-tossed hair. She yanked. "Ouch."

Her reluctant captain turned to look at her. "Now what are you doing?"

"I'm trying to get my camera out."

He glanced at her boots. "Camera? You can't stand up straight, and you want to take photos?"

"Yeah, this is most likely my first and last fishing boat ride. I want to record it for posterity." She pushed her hair out of her face again. "I need a hair tie, too."

He flicked a dial on the instrument panel and came over. "Here. Let me help."

She grabbed the handle bar. "*Wait.* Who's driving the boat?"

He had the nerve to laugh. "I engaged the governor. It will keep the boat going straight ahead while I untangle you."

She looked all around. "But what about other boats?"

He held his hands up. "This no superhighway. The only other boat out here is your friend Mr. Teed's." He pointed to a white speck speeding through the water. "And he is way over on the other side of the harbor, showing off. Now let's get you free."

He put his fingers under the near strap, loosened the hair twisted around it and freed the pack. But at the same moment, the boat dipped, she wobbled on her tottering heels, and their bodies smashed together. He clasped his arms around her and steadied her.

The embrace sent warmth surging through her body. She felt cared for, for the first time since her mother died, and she liked it too much.

She jerked away. What was she thinking? No way should she be seeking comfort from a man who could easily be a major roadblock in her career. Not now. Not here. Not ever.

She pushed him away. "I'm fine now. You can go back to steering the boat."

Captain Nemo clung a moment longer then stood her back on her feet. He turned back to the helm and squinted through the windshield.

It wasn't fair. The accidental hug had sent tingles through her, while he looked like he had done nothing more than uncoil some fishline.

She yanked a hair tie from the outside pocket of the pack and twisted it around her unruly hair. Then she slung her camera around her neck and peered through the lens. Something yellow bobbed up ahead.

She tapped him on the shoulder. "Look. Over there. What's that?"

"That's the buoy marking where the turbine is installed. Should be in operation soon. They've fixed the damaged cable." He slowed the boat and checked the GPS. "I'll be collecting samples in this area once my equipment arrives, both before and after the turbine starts producing electrical power. I think they plan to get it turning next Tuesday."

*Tuesday?* That meant she only had six days to get the locals to take action.

Summer snapped a picture of the shoreline, hoping to capture a landmark so she could find the turbine site again—from land next time.

Holding tight to the railing and willing her stomach to settle, she peered down at the water where the fish-killing contraption was set to go. "What's the turbine like?"

"Seastroke Energy's design looks like a wind turbine with short blades affixed to a heavy triangular base. We should be right over the site in about two minutes."

"Over it?"

"The turbine sits on the bottom. It's why there's such concern here locally. The Minas Basin is one of the world's largest lobster spawning beds, and the fishermen believe the turbines will drive the females away or destroy the fry."

Summer lowered the camera and moved up next to him. "There's nothing to take a photo of." Her mouth turned up at the corner. "Well, that's a major disappointment. I was hoping to get a picture of one tearing a whale to pieces."

"Nope. Never happens. The propeller isn't going to trap large mammals, like whales or dolphins. Haven't you visited the Tidal Research Center in Parrsboro and seen the models there?"

"Not yet. Only my first day here. Cully's invitation to ride in his boat was a spur of the moment thing. But I do plan to visit the center as soon as possible." She snapped a photo of the buoy.

"I'd be happy to give you a tour."

Summer shook her head. She didn't need to spend more time with a too-enticing marine biologist.

The boat rocked more strongly. He looked at her with those unreadable dark eyes. "Wind's come up. It's getting rougher. Shall I take you back?"

Her feet shifted under her as a wave splashed over the side. Based on the way her stomach gurgled, this was going to be her only time to photograph the area for the anti-turbine promo she was planning.

She swallowed the bile gathering in the back of her throat. "Let me get another photo or two. Then yes, you can take me back."

She snapped a series of photos of the town nestled on the hillside and the cliffs rising from the sea then clicked a picture or two of him.

He put up a hand and ducked away. "Hey. I'm not the scenery."

She grinned. "Could have fooled me. You fit right in, Captain Nemo."

"Do I? I thought Nemo was a pirate." He gave her a wink, swung the boat around, and kicked up the speed.

"He did good deeds, too." She hesitated. She so hoped Gil Moses was one of the good guys, but she had to be sure. Time to stop circumventing the real question.

"So, what exactly are you doing here in Tide Harbor? You're an expert in your field. You have a professorship at

MIT. You've led major scientific expeditions. Surely, rocking around on this little boat is a comedown."

"Looked me up, did you?" He gazed out the windshield. "I had to get out of the city. Find a quiet place to raise my daughter. I'm from Nova Scotia. A small fishing village like Tide Harbor seemed ideal. So, I wrote a grant and took a leave of absence."

She touched the healing scratch on her cheek. "What's wrong with your daughter?"

He rubbed his forehead. "Lissie ... she's autistic. You know what that is?"

"Autistic? Oh dear, I am so sorry. I thought—" She reached out and put her hand on the sleeve of his yellow nylon windbreaker. "Please forgive me for the things I said."

He shrugged. "I'm used to it. Most people don't understand. Lissie's behavior is so ... bizarre."

"I shouldn't have interfered on the ferry. It's one of my worst faults. I can't stand to see animals or children in distress."

He softened his voice. "Nothing wrong with that. The world would be a better place if people took action when they saw injustice."

She gave his arm a pat and wedged her camera back in her bag. "I've never met a child with autism. Don't know much about it. There's that woman with a weird name—uh, Temple Grandin. Listened to her Ted Talk. It was fascinating to hear how differently she sees the world."

Gil glanced at her. "Grandin *is* amazing. But there are all types of autism. Lissie isn't like Grandin. She's nonverbal. Her senses are supersensitive. Everything sets her off—sounds, smells, movement, noises, touch."

He let out a slow breath. "But she's never scratched and bitten a stranger before. She's more likely to bite and tear at herself. I was trying to wrap the quilt around her. The doctor we saw suggested cocooning her in a blanket to calm her when she screams. I don't know why she attacked you except she was totally bewildered by all the noise and movement on the ferry. We rarely took her out in public places."

"Seeing how distressing it was for her, that was probably wise." She slung the pack back on her shoulder. "You said 'we;' you married?"

"Divorced."

Summer nodded. "So, you're on your own with her. She's lucky to have a father like you."

He cleared his throat. "That woman you saw me with at the store—Mrs. Eagles—she showed up at my door. Seemed to instinctively know how to handle her." He turned the wheel, and the boat made a graceful circle around the buoy. "I wouldn't be out on the boat with you otherwise. But it's time to get back. You have a date to get ready for."

"A date?"

He wagged his eyebrows. "With Cully Teed for a half-price fish fry."

Summer gave herself a little shake. Gil Moses had so beguiled her she'd totally forgotten she was on a mission, and it was Cully Teed she should be cultivating, not Captain Nemo.

# Chapter 8

## Gil

Thankfully, by the time they reached the harbor and docked, the tide was cresting and the side of the boat floated even with the pier. Gil let out a thank-heavens breath. The last thing he wanted to do was touch her again. A fashionista tourist was not for him. He had a child waiting and a household to get organized.

Gil leaped onto the dock and made fast the bowline. "I hope you enjoyed your trip, Miss Avery."

She laughed. "Enough with the Miss Avery. Call me Summer, please."

"As you wish—Summer." He tipped his chin at her. "Your stomach, okay?"

She rubbed her belly. "It is. How did that happen?"

"I think you forgot about being nervous. Seasickness is mostly in the head."

She tugged her backpack higher on her shoulder. "I was so embarrassed on the ferry."

He grinned. "Hey, you're not the first girl whose hair I held while she upchucked."

Summer tossed back her head. "Is that your patented method to attract a woman—catch her at her most embarrassing moment and remind her of it?"

"Did it work?"

"No. But maybe"—she gave him a wink—"this won't be my last boat ride after all."

He offered his hand, and the feisty woman, despite her footwear, managed to get on the pier without landing on her bum. He watched her work her way toward the car park, gingerly wending her way between tar-covered rope coils, spilled oil, and stinking fish crates and couldn't resist one last dig. He called after her, "Hey, Summer, if you're going to hang around boats, I suggest you get some new footwear."

She turned and wrinkled her nose at him.

At least the woman was a good sport.

He waved and moved to tighten down the stern line, far more relaxed than when the woman had boarded his boat— he glanced at his watch—a little over half an hour ago.

He looked at his watch again. *Oops*. He was going to be late taking Lissie to visit the preschool.

****

By the time Gil was in sight of Windswept Cottage, he was feeling more and more uneasy. How long could he keep his cover story going? Summer seemed to accept his explanation of why he was here, but she was merely a tourist passing through. His pseudo-marine sampling was sure to rile up the locals. Lobstermen, like Cully Teed, were highly territorial. They'd see him trapping lobsters out of season and harvesting the eggs and spawn for counts as poaching on their future livelihood.

He gripped the steering wheel tighter. What if the folks here discovered the lobster study was fake, that his true purpose was to lead the authorities to the bomber? Messing with the marine life was bad enough. Chasing down and getting a local man in trouble with the law could be worth his life.

He turned into the driveway and shut off the engine. He'd been a fool to take this job. He was no private investigator. He should have advised Seastroke to hire a professional detective. But the idea of ferrying Lissie far away from Dolores had trumped his commonsense.

Gil got out of the car and headed up the steps to the front door. He stopped and rubbed his temple. He was a competent marine biologist, but his only qualification for catching the turbine terrorist was he was Nova Scotian—he knew the locale, and he knew boats.

"Dadadadada." Lissie stood in the doorway, her head rolling from side to side to side, her arms flapping, and her body shaking.

Gil's heart pinched. She looked like a mad marionette.

"Lissie." He stepped inside and put out a hand. "Stop—"

A smiling Mrs. Eagles came up behind her. "That's my happy little princess."

Gil's hand dropped. "*Happy*?"

"Of course," Mrs. Eagles said. "That's her happy dance." She peered at the child. "Right, Lissie?"

Lissie flailed her hands harder and jumped up and down.

Tears gathered in his eyes. All these years, Dolores and he had yelled and stopped her when Lissie did her "dumb duck routine," as Dolores called it. And this old woman, in a few hours, had seen what they had not. Lissie not only was communicating that she was happy, but she could respond to what people said. He thought of all the times he'd scolded her for acting weird. No wonder she didn't want him touching her.

The housekeeper turned and headed toward the kitchen. Lissie bounced along behind her. "Wait till you see what Lissie's made," she said over her shoulder. "She's been staring out the window all morning, waiting for you to come home."

*Lissie* made something? Gil shucked his jacket and hurried after them.

"Look." Mrs. Eagle spread out her hands.

On the kitchen table, hundreds of raisins were lined up in a huge circle.

"Worked for over an hour on it, she did." She nodded to Lissie. "Tell your daddy what you made."

Lissie opened her mouth in a big O.

"That's right—a circle, like your mouth."

Gil moved around the table. The circle was too perfect for a four-year-old to have made. "You helped her with this?"

"Oh no, she did it while I was making the beds and sweeping. Came in and found it."

He scratched his head. Lissie had always played with her food. Lining up green beans. Stacking up carrot slices. It drove his ex-wife crazy.

He remembered one day coming into the kitchen and finding Lissie lying on her belly, screaming, as a cursing Dolores swept up a long line of Cheerios that extended an arrow straight from the cupboard to the kitchen door.

He studied the circle again. It was amazing. Lissie was not stupid. She was not an idiot. She could think and communicate. She knew what a circle was. No matter what happened with the job, he'd made the right decision to bring her here and to hire Mrs. Eagles.

He bent down and gazed into his daughter's eyes. "You made a circle, Lissie. A perfect circle. I am very proud of you."

Lissie rocked backward and forward and flapped her hands.

He stood up and nodded his head at Mrs. Eagles. "You humble me. In one day, you have taught me more about my own daughter than I have learned living with her for four years."

Mrs. Eagles patted his arm. "It's okay. Sometimes the idea of what we think we see gets in the way of what we really see."

Gil glanced back at the table. "Too bad we'll have to destroy it so we'll be able to eat dinner."

Mrs. Eagles pointed her chin at Lissie. "I don't think that would be a great idea. Let's let Lissie decide when she wants to remove her circle."

"Where will we eat?"

"I'll make up lap trays, or we can spread a blanket on the floor and have a picnic. Would you like that, Lissie?"

Lissie's head rocked from side to side.

Mrs. Eagles untied her apron. "That's all settled then. Now, off to Betty's." She pointed to the door. "Remember, Lissie, we are going to go visit my friend, Miss Betty, today. She has all kinds of interesting things for you to see. And you get to ride in Daddy's car." She hung her apron on the hook, slipped into her fishy slicker, bundled Lissie in her snow jacket, and shepherded her outside.

Gil stared after them. No screaming. No battle to get Lissie's limp arms into the sleeves. It was like he'd fallen down a crazy rabbit hole and ended up in Wonderland.

He took a step toward the door then stopped. He whipped out his cell and snapped several photos of the raisin circle. Then he tucked the phone back in his pocket and headed out, his brain whirling. If Lissie could make perfect circles, what else could she do?

Two faces peered up at him as he stepped outside.

Mrs. Eagles gave him a frown. "Hurry. Car door's locked, and it's freezing out here." A gust of wind buffeted them, scattering the fallen leaves in the yard.

"Sorry. Took some photos of Lissie's circle." Gil hurried over and unlocked the doors.

Mrs. Eagles slipped into the back seat with a huff.

He turned to Lissie. "Into the car seat you go." He picked her up. Her body went rigid. Her fists whacked him in the face.

"What are you doing?" Mrs. Eagles asked.

*Oof.* A foot kicked him in the stomach.

"She has to be in the seat so I can drive safely. If she has a fit while I'm driving—"

"Fit smit. Let her get in by herself." The old woman patted the seat. "Talk *to* her, not at her."

Gil lowered Lissie to the ground, humiliated. His housekeeper was right again. He'd been treating Lissie like a recalcitrant cat he was trying to force into a pet carrier. Still, it took all his willpower to let go and step back. For all he knew, she'd take off running and be impossible to catch, like she had many times before.

"Do you want to sit with Mrs. Eagles?"

She didn't run. Instead, Lissie turned and jumped up and down in front of the back door. Gil pulled it open, and she climbed into the seat.

He leaned in. "I'm going to have to buckle her up."

"Sure. Everybody buckles up. I wear a seat belt, you wear a seat belt, and Lissie wears one. Right, sugar buns?"

Gil handed the buckle across to his housekeeper, and she snapped it in.

"Good girl." She popped something into Lissie's mouth. Lissie smacked her lips.

Gil jerked up, bumping his head on the car ceiling. "I said no candy."

Mrs. Eagles opened her palm. "Not candy. Raisins." She gave him a straight-mouth look. "That healthy enough for you?"

Gil huffed. "Sorry. Raisins are fine. But you shouldn't be rewarding her with sweets."

The old woman sat up straighter. "Well, the way I see it, I've spent two days with this lovely child, and she hasn't screamed or had a 'fit,' as you call it. I think she deserves a reward, and she likes raisins. Now get in and drive us up to Miss Betty's. I will stay there with her for the next two hours. Me and sugar buns will have a grand time playing with all the toys while you go do all that important work with those turbine-y things."

# Chapter 9

## Summer

Summer pulled up in front of her rented cabin. In the daylight, her fears from the first night seemed way overblown, just like her worries about Gil Moses. After a ride on his boat, she didn't think he was going to get in her way. It wasn't enough that the man, with his pirate black hair and eyes, was handsome as all get out. He had a sense of humor and an air of competency that made her want to trust him. That, combined with his innate kindness, was something she'd never found in a man before.

And he truly cared about his daughter.

She pushed open the car door. That poor little girl. She had no idea what she would do if she were Lissie's parent.

If she weren't here to stop the turbine installation, she could see herself shacking up with Captain Nemo.

A shiver ran down her spine. Now that was a dangerous thought.

She rolled her shoulders. Better she keep focused on her work. She'd start by jotting down everything Gil had told her about the turbine. Next, she'd find a free wi-fi spot, get online, and search out news articles about the local protests as well as double-check Gil's grant and Cully Teed's assertion that he worked for Seastroke.

Gil had sounded like he was telling the truth, but he also knew the cable had been fixed, which was news to her. And she had read everything published about the bombing of the turbine.

She climbed out of her car and grabbed her backpack. But right now, it was time to forget about the sexy marine biologist and set her sights on twisting Mr. Cully Teed around her finger. A local hero with his ties to the inshore fishing industry was her best chance of getting an effective protest movement started.

*****

Two hours later, Summer woke with a start. Where had the time gone? She'd sat out on the little deck at the back of the cabin to record her notes and plan out her strategy for tonight and had been lulled to sleep by the sound of the surf below the cliff.

Summer tossed her notebook down and checked her watch. The last thing she needed was to be late meeting Cully. But neither did she want to make a bad impression.

She rushed inside and peered into the tiny bathroom mirror and slathered on foundation to cover her freckles. She did her eyes then dabbed on her trademark coral lipstick.

A low V-neck blouse in filmy jade green, flowing pants in the same fabric, and a pair of strappy heels completed her outfit. She was probably overdressed for whatever the local bar scene was, but she'd learned long ago that what one wore was part of marketing what you were selling. And right now, she was selling herself as a big city powerhouse who could focus the world's eyes on little Tide Harbor.

Besides, the travel-worn jeans she'd been wearing the last two days had a distinctly fishy smell. She added finding a laundromat to her list of must dos.

But she'd deal with that tomorrow. Tonight, she'd kick back, have a little fun, and hopefully discover what the local folks thought about tidal energy taking over their bay.

She took one lingering look in the mirror then tossed her compact in her purse and headed to the door. Time to forget Gil Moses and charm Cully Teed.

****

The White Rock Tavern was filled with the overpowering aroma of fried fish. Bare wood tables and black captain's chairs hosted a crowd of young folks. A miniature stage at the far end was lit with neon blue and violet lights. Holding a mic, a skinny kid belted out a rap song to the laughing encouragement of his peers.

Cully rose and met her at the door, placing his hand on the small of her back. "This way."

She arched away from the pressure of his palm. Best to make plain from the start that she was not going to exchange her favors for his cooperation.

Cully gave her a sucked-in-cheek stare that sent a tingle of warning through her, but he dropped his hand and showed her a broad, toothsome smile. "I know. I know. We only met. I'll keep my hands off." He winked. "For now." He strode forward into the noisy bar area, leaving her to follow.

*Heaven's bells.* Guess she'd offended his male ego. If she hoped to get his help, she would have to smooth things over. But that didn't mean she'd fall into his arms, either. The snub at the wharf still rankled.

Throwing her shoulders back, she followed Cully down the aisle to the long center table.

"Hey, guys, look what I reeled in."

Four people, each in various states of inebriation, turned to gaze at her.

Cully nodded in their direction. "Meet the Tide Harbor Friday Nighters." He pointed to the table occupants and went around clockwise. "Gary Campbell, my co-pilot. Ingrid Thibault, she's the town's hairdresser. Knows everyone's

63

secrets. Betty runs the local preschool. And that over there on the end is Owen Young, my oldest and craziest friend. Used to fish with my da."

So, that was his name. Summer stared at the man. This was the character who'd put a dent in her car on her way into town. How dare he sit there, calmly guzzling more alcohol. She opened her mouth to give him an earful.

Cully took Summer's hand in his and gave it a possessive squeeze. "This is Summer Avery, everyone. Despite her name, a late season vacationer. She's renting the Keddy cabin out on Fly Head."

"Yikes." The woman, whom Cully had introduced as Ingrid, clapped her hands together. "How'd you end up in that rat trap?"

Now was not the time to get in a spat with an old drunk, so Summer tucked her anger away for another time and sent the overly bleached-blond an I'm-friendly smile. "Some guy at the real estate office in Parrsboro sent me there."

"Some idiot, you should say." Ingrid curled in her lower lip. "Must have been Keddy's sister-in-law's kid, Jonathan. Doesn't have a pinch of brains."

The narrow-chinned man with thinning brown hair Cully had called Gary elbowed Ingrid in the ribs. "Didn't you date him once?"

Ingrid held up one finger. "Once."

Gary took a sip of beer. "Ingrid's dated everybody hereabouts. *Once.*"

Ingrid tipped up her chin. "Everyone except you."

Gary wagged his finger at her. "That's because you are going to marry me."

"Never."

"Be nice, everyone." Cully pulled out the chair next to the old guy and guided Summer into it. "Miss Avery will think us a nasty lot."

Ingrid snorted. "We are a *nasty lot.* Comes from hanging out with the likes of you."

Cully wiggled his eyebrows. "Imitation is the highest form of praise."

Ingrid tossed back her beer then slowly licked the foam off her top lip. "You would know, darling." She smacked her lips, making kissing sounds.

Cully glanced around. "Anyone order the eats yet?"

"Waited for you, boss." His words slurred. "Your turn to buy."

Summer snuck a peek at the old seaman, and a shiver skittled through her. Up close, the weathered old bird looked even more sinister than when he'd appeared out of the fog the night before last. Between the weird, off-kilter, filmy white eye and his rotten teeth, he gave her the creeps. She shifted her chair over and picked up a menu.

Cully settled into the seat on her other side and tugged the menu out of her hands. "Don't need that. I'll order for you."

She opened her mouth and closed it. Cully Teed was not winning any points with her. If she didn't have to play nice with the locals, she'd had told Mr. I-Know-Best what she thought of men who presumed they could tell her what to do. Instead, she folded her hands in her lap. "Sure. You know what's good here."

He signaled the waitress over. "Patti, we'll have the clams, fries, and beers all around."

"So, where you from?" Ingrid asked Summer.

She turned in relief. Perhaps Ingrid could become an ally, and she wouldn't have to deal with Cully. "A small town in rural Northern Pennsylvania. Not much different from here." She waved her hand in a circle. "Trees, brush, beer drinkers, and more beer drinkers."

Gary rested his elbows on the table and leaned in so close she could smell the alcohol on his breath. "That where you got that weird accent?" His voice was raspy and raw, as if he had burned it.

Summer shook her head and strove to keep her tone light. "Me? An accent? No, no, no. You're the ones with the weird accent."

One side of Cully's mouth winked up. "Do we now? Well, we'll have to fix that, won't we?"

"Really?" Summer laughed. "You're going to *fix* my accent?"

"Yep." Cully laughed. "Ingrid, time to teach our guest some local lingo."

"Come on, Gary. Time for the show." Ingrid stood and pushed in her chair.

Summer turned in her seat. "A show?"

Ingrid and Gary headed for the blue-lit alcove.

The blonde-haired woman fiddled with the dials and picked up the mic. "Next up ... Stan's 'Fisherman's Wharf.'" She threw her arm over Gary's shoulders, and together, they belted out the words in perfect harmony.

Summer glanced back at Cully. "Wow. They can sing. But how will their singing sad folksongs about old fishing schooners and tides of tourists get rid of my accent?"

Cully leaned back in his chair. "Just wait. I figure you drink enough beer and listen to Stan Rodgers for the next several hours, and it won't be us having the weird accent."

The waitress put a beer in front of her and placed two napkin-lined baskets, heaping full of fried clams and fries, in the center of the table. She wiped her hands on her apron. "You take care, miss. The local brew is strong." She squinted at Cully. "And you watch out, lover boy. The way I hear it, there's a mighty pissed Mountie waiting to catch you drinkin' and drivin'."

"The lady's riled because I didn't ask her out on a second date."

Summer helped herself to a French fry. So, Cully Teed was a ladies' man. As if she hadn't guessed. She made a mental note to stay sober and took a sip of the reddish liquid in her glass. *Ugh.* It was horrid. She forced the bitter brew down and studied her new friend as he leaned across her and said something to wild-eyed Owen about a boat.

She had a feeling that despite his easy-going countenance, Cully Teed was a lot like the beer—warm and frothy with an acrid aftertaste. Still, she couldn't help needling him.

She peered over the top of her glass at Cully. "Lover boy?"

Cully placed his hand atop hers. "Means nothing. Patti's one of my cousins. Always teasing."

"Is everyone related around here?"

"Just about," Owen said, his words slurring. With an unsteady hand, he set his glass down. But he missed the tabletop, and the half-empty glass tumbled to the floor. Beer splashed everywhere, spotting the thin fabric of Summer's blouse and pants.

The old man jumped up with much more energy than his worn appearance suggested, knocking over his chair. "Sorry, miss." He grabbed a handful of napkins and swabbed at her.

Summer drew back. "Stop. You're making it worse."

The old man's mouth curled into a tight little knot. "No, you are, stranger. Told you, don't want you here. Go home before something else happens ... to you."

Cully seized him by the collar and hauled him uptight. "You're soused, old fool. You go home. Sleep it off. And not in my new boat. Don't let me find your stinkin' carcass anywhere near it."

Owen nodded and, with a sniff in Summer's direction, lumbered away.

Cully patted her hand. "Sorry. Old man must have had a few before we arrived."

Summer dabbed at the spots and swallowed down the bile gathered in her throat. The guy was an old drunk spouting nonsense. Nobody else seemed to find his ranting at her threatening.

She gave Cully a smile. "No harm done. The outfit's washable. By the way, where is the local laundromat?"

"Take your stuff to Gary's aunt. She does the washing for the summer people who rent her cottages. Guess you kind of qualify. Keddy isn't going to offer. Him being up at the old people's home in Advocate."

"I don't want to put anyone out. Surely, there's a laundromat?"

"Not here. Got to drive into Parrsboro for big city conveniences. But don't worry, Aunt Nan won't be washing it herself—she's got a hired girl. And besides, it not like you're the only one. She's doing that Moses guy's, too."

Here was her chance to find out what the locals thought. "Cully, you said something about this Gil Moses working for Seastroke Energy; how's everyone around here feel about putting that tidal turbine in your bay?"

Cully gave her a narrowed-eye glare. "That depends."

Summer took a fried clam from the basket and bit into it. "Depends on what?"

"Why you're asking."

She chewed the sweet, crusty clam and weighed her response. "Just curious."

Cully put his hands on the table and pushed back in his chair. "About tidal turbines? A girl from New York City? Hardly anyone knows about the blasted things. Ain't a major tourist attraction. But now we got two strangers poking around. Seems a mite suspicious to me."

Summer forced the clam down her throat. Time to get down to business. First on the agenda: win their confidence. "Well, I'm against the turbines myself, and yesterday, in the parking lot, it sounded like you weren't happy about them either."

Gary and Ingrid slid back into their seats. Ingrid gave her a nod. "Cully Buddy is always riled up about something. Has a temper on him." The hairdresser squirted ketchup over the plate of fries and picked one up. "What is he hot under the collar about now?"

"Tidal turbines."

Ingrid twisted her lips to the right. "Well, that's not what I expected. Usually, it's women. Now tidal energy"—she wagged her fry at Cully—"that's a dead issue. Nothing's going to stop Seastroke from putting that turbine in now it's fixed."

Gary nodded his head in agreement. "They're coming, for sure. I looked Mr. Moses up on the internet. He's been hired by Seastroke Energy to do a survey of the basin and determine the environmental effect of their new design on lobsters. Expects to be here at least six months. Left his university position to do it."

Cully snorted. "Left his fancy job? That's suspicious in itself. Bet they are paying him a fortune to produce the results the corporate big wigs want. Stupid government. Have the gall to let companies like Seastroke come here and mess around. Bring in outside *experts*. But no time to listen to us—the fishermen who actually understand the fish." He socked the table with his fist. "Some politico muck-a-muck crawls in bed with the corporations, and us little guys get the short end of the towline."

Summer took a small sip of the beer. "So, what's so bad about the turbines?"

Cully leaned in so close his cheap aftershave prickled her nose. "It would take me days to give you the lowdown."

Gary finished off his beer. "Why don't you take her down to the research center where they have models of the monstrosities, Cully? Show her the dratted thing. Anyone with half a brain would know that huge paddles spinning away on the sea floor are gonna upset the fishies."

Mr. Bearcat quaffed his beer then wiped his hand across his mouth. "Tell you what, Summer girl. I'll meet you for breakfast at Bake and Bite then drive you over to the center. Tell you all you need to know about the blasted turbines."

Summer couldn't believe her luck. She'd be able to pump Cully Teed and find out exactly why the fishermen hated the idea. She'd learned the hard way that a protest movement was best built on the local community's complaints. No one appreciated a stranger coming in and telling them what to do.

"But it will be quick. I'm planning another spin across the harbor. Work out the kinks in the new boat."

"You have a new boat?" Summer asked.

Everyone laughed. Ingrid took another fry. "Sure does."

Betty glanced over at Cully. "It's here?"

Cully gave a little roll of his shoulder. "Just delivered from David MacDonald's."

Ingrid took another fry. "Yeah, I saw you racing around the harbor this morning. New boat's spiffy looking."

"Should do. It cost a fortune."

Gary leaned back in his chair. "It's got two sleeping compartments, a kitchen and a head. Wouldn't mind sailing to Bermuda on it."

Cully laughed. "Not going anywhere now we have the lovely Miss Avery to keep us company."

Summer amped up her smile. She'd gotten what she wanted. Now she needed to keep him hooked. "So, what kind of fish do you catch?"

"All kinds." He reached across and chucked her under the chin. "But mainly, I'm a lobsterman."

She swallowed back her increasing distaste for Teed's domineering behavior and infused enthusiasm in her voice. "So, I'll get to see you catch a lobster?"

"Not in season yet." He tipped his head and winked. "But once you get those seasickness pills and come out on the boat with me, there's lots of other things I can show you."

"That's great." Summer struggled to keep that neon smile beaming. There was no question what Cully Teed wanted, but there was only so far she would go to protect the environment. She'd have to keep her can of pepper spray near at hand. And stay off his boat, for sure.

# Chapter 10

## Gil

Gil pulled into the marine supply parking lot and got out of his car. He straightened his shoulders and tamped down his apprehension. Time to get started working undercover.

He pushed open the glass door to Labranche's Marine and looked around. Despite the battleship gray walls and floor, the store was a cacophony of color. Coils of rope in neon colors lined one wall. A rack of yellow, red, and black fisherman boots lined the other. The rest of the place was jampacked with chains, empty gas cans, fishing gear, and in the far back, florescent-orange weatherproof coveralls covered in reflective tape.

He headed to the back. He'd start with the protective suit. One thing was for sure, he was going to be spending a lot of time out on *Hell'za Poppin'* and the fall chill was settling in faster than he'd expected.

It didn't take long to have a stack of equipment on the battered wood counter.

The clerk eyed the pile. "Planning to be fishing these parts? You need a license, you know."

"Have one." Gil took out his credit card. "I'm here to carry out research on lobster populations. You know any old-timers I can talk to about the way the currents flow in the harbor and where the most lobsters are caught?"

The clerk wrinkled his brow. "Most are pretty tight-lipped about their lobstering grounds, but you could try my uncle, Owen Young. He's usually drunk, but once upon time, he was one of the best lobsterman in Tide Harbor. Always brought in a full catch." He glanced at the clock. "This time of day, he's probably down at the wharf, nursing a bottle. He looks rough, but he's a gentle soul. Tell him Ethan sent you."

*****

Car loaded, Gil headed for the dock. Owen Young was easy to find. The disheveled fisherman was leaning against a piling, chugging from a rum bottle and staring at Cully Teed's new boat.

Gil walked up and stood beside him. "Sure is a looker."

Young snorted. "Lines are poor. Not goin' to last like the old ones nor ride as well in the water." He ran his gaze over him. "So, you're the other stranger 'round here."

Gil held out his hand. "Gil Moses. Ethan over at Labranche's said you might talk to me about the harbor here—the currents and such."

Young ignored the offered hand and wrinkled his nose as if sensing a bad smell. "You the guy got *Hell'za Poppin'* polished up?"

"Working on it. Got some new equipment for her. Help me unload, and I'll take you for a spin and a drink afterward. Got a six pack of beer in the car."

Young grunted as he pushed up to his feet. "Twenty dollars an hour."

"Yah, sure. Come along." Gil led the way back to his car, shaking his head. Boy, would his brothers tease him if they ever caught wind that he was paying a drunk to spend time with him. But he had to start somewhere, and maybe a tongue-loosened drunk would help him track down the bomber more quickly than the more wary fishermen.

He put the six-pack of beer on the floor beside Young and started up the engine. The sooner he caught this crazy bomber, the sooner he could return to the work he loved—carrying out scientific research.

*****

By the time they were out on the water, the blue sky had faded to gray, and Owen Young had proven to be different than he'd appeared at first. Standing at the stern, he stood straighter and more steadily than he had on land.

Gil called back, "You miss going out fishing, Mr. Young?"

"Yeah." The man turned to face him. "I'm the best there is at lobstering, but nobody will take me out on their boat. Bad luck, they say. But they make their own bad luck. Messing with the sea. Stirring things up. Is that what you're planning to do? You one of those turbine guys? You're using their boat."

"Not exactly. I'm here to study the effect of the turbine on the lobster population. I will set out traps, monitor what I catch, and release the spawn back into the sea at the same location."

Young came up behind him. He peered out the windshield. "You heading for the turbine site?"

"I heard that it's a good place to catch lobster."

"The whole harbor is a good place to catch lobster, and other things."

"Ethan said you knew all the best places."

"My nephew hasn't the foggiest notion 'bout lobstering. Never been on a boat. But you have."

"I've done my share of pulling traps. My father was a fisherman down the south shore."

"Doesn't mean you know what is going on here."

Gil gazed at the cragged face. "What do you mean?"

"Some people 'round here won't like you stirring things up. Very possessive, they are, about the waters they fish."

"My previous research showed that the sampling technique I've developed doesn't harm the lobsters."

"Not worried about the lobsters, boy. Worried about *you*." He shook his finger at him. "It's too dangerous here." He peered down into the water. "Bad things are hiding in these depths. Lots of secrets. You should leave now. Take that city girl with you."

The yellow buoy loomed ahead. Gil slowed the boat. "What bad things?"

Young spat over the side. "You ain't dumb. Work it out."

Gil pressed his lips together. The man did a good job acting the doddering drunk, but he was beginning to sense a wary intelligence behind that decrepit appearance. The man knew something, for sure. If only he'd stop talking in riddles. He'd have to ask him outright.

He broke apart the six-pack and held out a can. "So, you think there will be another bombing? Is that what you are trying to tell me?"

Young waved the can away. "Bet your father taught you better. No drinking on a boat, boy."

He set the can down. Nothing about Owen Young made sense. Not his behavior and not his crazy talk.

He tried again. "Why are you telling me to leave? Do you know who the bomber is? Will he strike again?"

"Wrong questions." Young gave him a hard-eyed glare. "Don't be a fool, Mr. Scientist. Leave before you get hurt. The sea isn't kind, you know. And you are too darn trusting. Look, you took me out on your boat, knowing nothing about me. Get yourself killed if you keep it up."

Gil's heartbeat accelerated. Was that a threat?

He scanned the horizon. Not a boat in sight. Not even that cocky Cully's. If Owen Young wanted to kill him, all he had to do was knock him out and cast him over the side.

But he hadn't. The man was no murderer. But he could be the bomber.

He stared at the man. "Be straight with me. Are we talking about the idiot who dropped the depth charge? I can help stop him."

"Can you now?" Young looked at him sideways. "How? You're a stranger in town. A target. Everyone's watching you. But no one's watching me. Stopping him is my job."

On a certain level, Young was right. He did have an advantage, but he was also a drunk. "I have resources. I have money. I have a boat. I can call in the authorities."

"Don't want anything from you, stranger, except a ride back to port."

Gil circled the boat around. "Will you at least let me know when you know who it is?"

"*Humph.* Maybe."

Gil sucked in a breath. Maybe was better than no.

"Okay. Do what you have to. But stay safe. And come to me if you're in danger."

Owen snorted and faced toward the stern. "Danger? We are all in danger. The sea she be crazy."

Gil focused on the sun glinting off the water. The man was impossible. He'd have to keep his eye on him somehow and continue his own investigation.

This whole expedition had been a waste as far as getting any information. But at least, he'd eliminated one suspect: Owen Young.

# Chapter 11

## Summer

This was the night that would make all the difference.

Summer parked in front of the Cape Cod bungalow that housed Betty Flower's preschool and flicked off the headlights. She whistled. The small parking lot was full. Cully had done it—gotten the anti-turbine folks off their couches and turned out for the initial organizational meeting.

She gave herself a hard shake. She was ready.

After a brief tour of the Tidal Research Center with Cully, she'd spent the morning in Parrsboro, shopping for more appropriate footwear and ordinary clothes so she would fit in better. And for the last three hours, she'd sat in the library, using their free wi-fi and going over everything in the EcoGreen organizing materials. Now it was time for her show.

Getting them excited and willing to make their voices heard wouldn't be a problem, but a successful protest campaign hinged on creating a tight, cohesive group with a focused mission.

Sounded easy. It wasn't.

Too many times activist groups splintered because of strong personalities unwilling to compromise or who had their own agendas—people like Cully Teed. She bit her lip. Dealing with people like him was what EcoGreen paid her to do, and how she handled him would make or break her chances for winning the Atlanta job.

She retrieved her backpack and headed to the house.

"There you are." Ingrid swung open the door. "We've all been waiting for you."

"Sorry. Thought you said seven?"

Ingrid flipped her hand. "It was seven half an hour ago."

"What?"

Betty swished past, carrying a tray of home-baked cookies. "She's pulling your leg. Get in here and meet everyone."

Summer closed the door behind her and gazed around. The connected living-dining room of Betty's small Cape Cod had been turned into a children's playroom. The long, narrow space sported bright yellow walls, primary-colored toys neatly arranged on shelves, and the overpowering aroma of paint, glue, and milk. But instead of children, the room was full of grownups.

Summer surveyed the people who'd shown up. Gray-haired seniors and flannel-shirted fishermen sat on folding chairs lining the room. They were the type of people environmental groups relied on for doing the basic organizing. They had the time and local knowledge.

Two high-school-aged girls were sprawled out, cross-legged, on the alphabet-themed carpet, giggling at a tall, reedy man talking on his cell. Young people could be annoying at times, but they were the ones with the energy and passion to make waves. She was glad they were here.

And there was Cully. Mr. Bearcat stood in the doorway between the playroom and the kitchen, holding a steaming mug of coffee and wearing a did-I-do-good-or-what? tooth-baring grin. There was no question that he expected a reward for his efforts.

Betty crossed in front of him and set down the plate of cookies on a low table. She nodded toward the corner of the room. "We saved the reading rocker for you, Summer."

Summer pasted on her best I-am-here-to-help smile and worked her way over to the rocker, greeting the locals and shaking hands as she passed.

Cully came up behind her and held the back steady as she sat down. He leaned in so close she could smell his aftershave—some spicy blend that was probably called Hot Passion—and whispered in her ear, "I'm disappointed. I expected some leg. Told the guys you were a looker to get them here. How about you borrow something sexy from Betty?"

She didn't have time for his nonsense. "You wish. Find a seat, Cully, and let me do this my way."

Summer turned to face the group, drawing out her handouts and EcoGreen Action brochures from her pack. First, she had to allay the natural fears that she was going to boss everyone around.

She raised her voice and addressed the group. "Welcome. I'm Summer Avery. I want you to know I am not here to tell you what to do. Rather, I'm here to bring the resources of EcoGreen to your assistance. We are a non-profit organization who can provide anti-turbine research, contact the press, link you with other groups, and spread word on social media. I have a background in marketing, and

I know how to get important people's attention." She glanced around the circle. Good. People were nodding and smiling at her.

She continued, "So, let's go around and learn who you are and why you are against the tidal energy project. Then we will come up with ways to make a noise loud enough that Seastroke sits up and takes notice."

****

By the time everyone had shared their views and eaten all of Betty's cookies, Summer knew she had a winning movement bubbling up in front of her. Ingrid and Betty were natural leaders. The high school girls and the young man they had been ogling, who'd turned out to be the local pastor, were energetic. The fishermen were passionate about the sea, and the old people were ready to donate their free time. Already, they were brainstorming possible events to raise public awareness and bring in more supporters.

She glanced across the room. Cully had moved to the opposite end and stood leaning against the wall, tossing a child's red ball from one hand to the other. So far, he'd not said a word, and she hoped he would stay quiet a few minutes longer. All she had left to do was wrap everything up.

She looked over at the easel pad Betty had supplied. "Things couldn't be going better, everyone. Time is short, but your enthusiasm is huge. I will make sure the press hears all about you and your cause." She fingered her notes and smiled. She couldn't wait to call her boss and tell him the world would soon be hearing from Tide Harbor because Summer Avery was a kick-ass organizer.

She clapped her hands to get everyone's attention. "What with the petitioning and soliciting support from the council members and local businesses, topped off with the Save the Sea Day event on Saturday, Tide Harbor should soon have a large enough group to stop Seastroke Energy powering up the turbine. I'll set up the website and social media accounts right away." She took a deep breath. "So, if we are all decided, I say let's get to work." She stood up.

"Hold on." Cully tossed the ball across the room and pushed off the wall. "All that stuff is fine, and you folks go right ahead and have fun, but we have a Seastroke guy right here in Tide Harbor, working for the company. It seems to me we should be taking our complaints directly to him."

Summer's cookie-stuffed stomach did a nose dive. This was what she had been afraid of.

The fisherman next to her shook his fist. "Cully's right. We've been too welcoming to the bastard."

The older woman across the way nodded in agreement.

Cully strode into the middle of the room and stood with his hands on his hips. "I volunteer to organize the fishermen around here. Let's make Gilbert Moses squirm like a worm on a hook." He glared at Summer, his resentment at her brush off plain. "Put that on your list, too, city girl."

She sucked in a breath. "Mr. Moses is not here to promote the turbine installation. He's a marine biologist doing a research study. He even might discover something that helps our cause. I don't think—"

"That might be the sweet talk he gives to you"—Cully raised one eyebrow—"but you can't trust a company shill. He could be here to bribe officials, interfere with our protests, do a coverup. Who knows?"

"We should vote …" Summer glanced around the room. Everyone's head was nodding in agreement with Cully. If she called for a vote, she'd lose them.

Cully gave her half-shrug and threw the door open. "Come on, guys. Let's go over to the Tav and talk about how to catch a Boston big fish."

Summer gathered her papers and hurried to catch up to them.

"Wait." Ingrid grabbed her by the arm. "You're not going to convince those guys to change their minds, especially after they get some drinks in them. Meet me at the Tav for lunch tomorrow, and we'll come up with a counter plan."

Summer patted Ingrid on the back. "I'd love to."

That would give her an opportunity to talk privately and see if Ingrid would agree to be one of the leaders of the anti-turbine group. From what she'd seen, Ingrid was the only local who had the guts to stand up to Cully.

*****

By next morning, Summer was feeling more positive. She had formed a protest group in record time, and while she didn't think Gil deserved the fishermen's animosity, he'd put himself in this position. He'd just have to deal with it.

The Tav was humming with the luncheon crowd. Ingrid waved to her from a table near the karaoke stage.

Summer hurried over. "Sorry I'm late. I was calling in favors from people I know. I got three confirmations from newspapers that they will send reporters to Save the Sea Day on Saturday."

Ingrid laughed.

"What's so funny?"

"*You.* What is that you're wearing?"

Summer looked down at her newly purchased sweater. "Hideous, isn't it?"

"Neon green is definitely not a fashion statement, especially with red sneakers."

"Drove over to Parrsboro to do laundry and found a thrift store. There wasn't much choice." Summer avoided glancing down at her eye-watering green sweater and her getting-more-worn-by-the-day jeans.

If her co-workers in New York could see their nose-in-the-air fashion plate, they'd laugh harder than Ingrid.

Summer sighed. She'd worked hard to get rid of her rural roots when she had been in marketing. But boy, she had to admit her thrift finds were far more comfortable, and warmer, than what filled her suitcase.

Ingrid tipped her head sideways. "There's a cool boutique in downtown Amherst that might be more your style."

"I haven't time to bother. Got what I needed. Found a flannel nightgown and a comforter. At least I won't have icicles dripping from my nose at night anymore."

"You ain't seen cold yet, girl. November's coming."

"I won't be here in November. EcoGreen will be sending me somewhere else." Nice, warm Atlanta, if things went right.

"That's a shame. You're such fun to tease."

Patti set down platters of burgers and fries. "Enjoy, ladies."

Ingrid pushed one toward her. "I hope you don't mind that I ordered for you. I only have a half-hour before my next customer arrives." She bit the end off a fry.

Summer took a bite of the burger and savored the juicy flavor and satisfying fullness in her stomach.

"Now, tell me about those fishermen Cully led off. How do we get them to focus on our planned actions and not some marine biologist who's not bothering anyone?"

"Oh, he's a bother, all right." Ingrid cupped a hand to the side of her mouth. "So, are you really against the turbine?" she whispered.

"Of course. I wouldn't be here otherwise."

"So, prove it. You'd be doing a lot of people 'round here a favor if you got that Gil Moses right in your pocket, so to speak. Then you tell little old me everything he says and does."

Summer whispered back, "You want me to spy on him?"

Ingrid tilted her head and smiled. "Bull's-eye. I'd gladly do it. He's definitely bed-worthy. But my guy radar says he wants you, babe. Couldn't tear his eyes away, according to Cully."

Summer bit her lip. Getting close to Gil Moses was the last thing she should do. And spying on him? Sometimes getting personal could be an effective tactic, but Gil Moses wasn't one of the bigwigs at Seastroke. He was here to study lobsters, not lobby for the turbines.

She glanced at Ingrid, who was giving her a crooked eyebrow pout. She could understand how the locals might zero in on Gil. Way up here on the shores of Nova Scotia, he was the closest they could get to the company threatening their livelihood.

They needed to focus on local government and businessmen, not Gil Moses.

Wait a sec. Had Ingrid said Gil Moses was hot for her? The thought sent a wave of heat through her. Gil might be off limits, but it didn't mean she couldn't flirt a little bit. Let the guy see what he was going to be missing when she left.

Ingrid tipped her chin toward the door. "Wish he'd taken me out on his boat. Maybe then he'd be looking at me, not you."

Summer jerked around. Two dark eyes met hers. Speak of the tempting pirate. Here he was, Captain Nemo himself, in all his sexy glory.

# Chapter 12

## Gil

He really shouldn't be spending more time with the woman, but he had to find out if what he'd heard was true.

Gil cleared his throat. "How are you doing today, Miss Avery?"

Summer set her burger down and peered up at him with those sea-green eyes of hers. She looked so innocent. "Just fine. I thought you'd be out in the boat."

"I was. I did a spin around the harbor earlier."

"That explains the fish smell." She wrinkled her nose. "You need something?"

"We need to talk."

Ingrid's purple-polished fingernails tapped the table. "Hey, you guys. Introduce me, Summer."

"Oh, sorry. This is Gil Moses, the marine biologist." Summer dipped a fry in ketchup. "Talk about what?"

"Exactly what you are doing here. I've heard *you* work for some crazy environmental group—Green Dirt or something."

"EcoGreen Action. Looked me up, huh?"

"No, your good friend, Cully, informed me while we were standing in line at Bake and Bite. When were you going to share that with me?"

"Didn't seem relevant. I'm not here to stop you from studying the lobsters. Research is a good thing. We just want to prevent turbines from being put into operation in the Basin until a lot more studies of lobsters, like yours, are done."

"Enough with the lobsters and stuff." Ingrid fluttered her fake eyelids and patted the seat next to her. "Come. Join us."

Gil glanced around the busy tavern then back at them. "If you don't mind?"

"Mind?" Ingrid ran her hand down his arm and rested it on the back of his hand. "Why, I'm the official Tide Harbor welcome committee. Now, you sit yourself right down and let me take care of you."

Gil tipped his head toward Summer and slid in next to Ingrid. "I was planning to grab a quick bite before picking Lissie up from Miss Betty's. Only have about twenty minutes."

Ingrid shoved her plate of fries toward him. "Have some of mine while they cook up your order. You like fish?"

"Sure."

"Then you'll love the special." She called to the waitress, "A beer-battered haddock platter, Patti." She wrapped her fingers around his arm. "Now, tell me what you think of lovely Tide Harbor."

Gil glanced at Summer. "It's one of the most beautiful spots on Earth."

Ingrid's lips pouted. "Too bad you're here in nasty, rainy October, instead of summertime when Tide Harbor is all blue skies and sandy beaches. Poor you." She picked up a fry and held it to his mouth. "Eat. At least you can enjoy some of the best fries on the peninsula." She made a kissing sound. "Come on, lover boy, take a bite."

Gil pinched the fry from her fingers and popped it in his mouth. He chewed slowly, staring all the while at Summer. "Good, but it needs some Boston hot sauce."

The waitress pushed a platter in front of Gil and nodded at Ingrid. "Caught a live one, did you?"

Ingrid wrapped an arm over Gil's shoulders. "Sure did." She snugged closer. "Now, Mr. Moses, what are you here to do? You gonna to study the fishies or are you working on the turbine itself?"

Gil speared a piece of golden-brown, fried haddock. "Lobsters are my area of expertise."

"Are they now?" Ingrid leaned against him. "I love lobstermen."

Summer glared at him. "Got to be going."

He swallowed his fry. "Hold on. We need a minute to talk."

He half rose. Ingrid shoved him down. "Wait. You finish your platter, darling. Summer and I are going to give you a treat." She stood up, clasped Summer by the arm, and dragged her toward the karaoke stage.

Gil leaned back and enjoyed the tug-of-war. It seemed Summer didn't want him getting friendly with the local woman, not that he was interested. The question was: was she jealous or protecting her cover?

Up on the stage, the two women were going back and forth with Summer declaring she couldn't sing and Ingrid insisting she could. Ingrid looked at him then whispered in Summer's ear. Whatever she said made the difference.

Suddenly, Summer whipped off her baggy sweater, revealing a skimpy black camisole and a lot of skin. She sent him a full-face smile then wrapped her arm around Ingrid's waist and belted out the lyrics to the Beatles' "All You Need is Love."

Gil sat up straighter. With her wild curls, Summer Avery looked like she was trying out for the part of Orphan Annie in a school play. She'd get it, too, except she had a voice that would drive even the tone-dead to wear earmuffs. But she sure could move. And her skintight, black sleeveless top revealed enough cleavage to keep any red-blooded man's attention.

He finished his fish and set down his fork. What he wouldn't give to touch that golden pink skin, even knowing she'd not been honest with him.

"Like what you see?" The waitress nodded at the stage as she added up the check.

Time to stop gawking.

Gil pulled out his wallet and winked at the server. "The curlyhead can't sing. But don't tell her I said that." He glanced at his watch. He'd have to leave now to get to the preschool in time. Mrs. Eagles was a wonder, but after spending two hours supervising Lissie at the school, it wasn't fair to make her wait on him. "Put the ladies' on my card, and thank them for the concert."

Bill paid, he rose to his feet and headed to the door.

"Wait, Gil." Summer waved to him from the stage. "I need to ask you something." She stumbled off the low stage and ran toward him. Her foot caught on a chair leg. She fell forward.

He hurried to her and caught hold.

"Thanks."

She shifted against him, and his fingers touched the bare skin of her midriff. Her skin was as soft as he imagined, but also amazingly chilled considering how hot he was. He inhaled the clean scent of her freshly washed hair, a honeysuckle fragrance that reminded him of his childhood home in summer.

He felt her shiver and pulled her closer. "You're freezing. Get your Kermit-the-Frog sweater on right now."

Summer pursed her lips. "Kermit the Frog?"

"My daughter's hero. She loves the Muppets." He took the ugly thing from Ingrid and helped her into it.

He glanced at his watch. "I really have to fly out of here. What did you want?"

"Your invitation to visit the Tidal Turbine Research Center—I'd like to take you up on it."

Gil bit the inside of his lip. He really shouldn't spend more time with Summer Avery. But they did need to talk. "Well, sure."

"My hero." Summer leaned in and kissed him on the cheek. Her breasts brushed against his chest.

His blood pounded. If he hadn't been standing in the middle of a restaurant, he'd have his hands all over her, pressing her against him, plundering that luscious mouth.

Summer smiled at him. "How about tomorrow?"

*Tomorrow?* He forced himself to think. "No. My equipment is arriving in the a.m. I'll have to inventory it and outfit the boat. Get going on my research. Saturday, I will be taking the boat out and setting up my traps. How about Sunday?"

Disappointment flashed across Summer's face. She stepped back. "Okay. See you then, I guess. Ten at the center?"

Gil nodded. "Sure. Got to run."

****

Outside, Gil climbed into his car and leaned back on the seat. What had he done? He really shouldn't spend time with

Summer Avery. She was a professional agitator come to rile up the locals, and she hadn't been honest enough to tell him.

Then there was Cully. The guy had given him an earful at Bake and Bite and made it clear Summer Avery was off limits.

Still, the research center was mostly a tourist site, anyway. He'd have to watch what he said and—he opened the window and sucked in a breath of air to get the scent of her out of his nose—despite his inexplicable attraction to her, keep his hands to himself.

His cell phone rang. Drat, he was late picking up Lissie.

He glanced at the screen. Private number. He hesitated then thumbed it on.

"Gil, what were you thinking?"

The fish and fries in his stomach turned over.

"Dolores." He squeezed the phone, tempted to hang up. His ex-wife was the last person on Earth he wanted to talk to at the moment. But he would not be a coward. Not now when Lissie was opening up. "I did what was best for Lissie."

"Some *best*. Taking off half-cocked like you always do. Dragging her to that backwoods place you come from. The agreement was you got custody, but only if she got the most up-to-date treatment and care. What kind of care can you give her there? And"—Gil pressed his hand against his aching forehead. He knew what was coming next—"what about my visitation rights? I can't fly up to the sandpit you're living in every other weekend, now can I?"

He drummed the dashboard. "I didn't think you cared."

"Of course I care." Her voice went Boston prim. "I've retained a lawyer, and I will take you to court and sue for full custody unless you bring Lissie back to Boston by the end of the month, abide by the visitation schedule we arranged, and prove you are providing proper care." Her tone lowered in pitch. "Though, maybe by now you're ready to do the rational thing and put her in that fine residence I found for her. Is she driving you crazy yet? Are your shins covered in bruises like mine were?"

"Dolores, please—"

She made that New England nasal *humph* that always made him cringe. "You'll be getting the paperwork from my lawyer shortly, so don't be stupid. Bring the little snit back, Gilbert. *Bring. Her. Back.*" The phone went dead.

Gil started the engine, turned out of the parking lot, and headed to Miss Betty's, his mind a mess, his stomach a ball of soured fish. Go back? Go back and undo all Mrs. Eagles' magic? Go back and be harangued into locking Lissie up like she'd done something wrong?

Never.

How had he ever fallen in love with Dolores? But he knew how. Before Lissie, Dolores had been a completely different person. Gentle. Thoughtful. Loving. Someone with whom he could share his deepest hopes and dreams. He'd loved that woman from the instant he saw her.

He'd been crewing on a Liberty Fleet tall ship. She'd been a passenger. A literature major at Radcliff. Thin, elegant. Long, black hair falling over her shoulders.

He'd watched her from the rigging, moving like a swan among the group of giggling co-eds and beer-blasted Harvard boys, never thinking she'd notice a member of the crew or fall in love with a lobsterman's son from Nova Scotia. They'd had a good marriage, traveling the world, going to concerts, hosting parties for their friends.

Then Lissie had come into their lives, and Dolores couldn't handle her. And no matter what he did, no matter how much he loved them, he couldn't fix the problem.

He turned down the side road, pulled up in front of the preschool, stopped the engine, and waited for the trembling shaking him to the core to ebb.

The Beatles were wrong. Love was not enough.

# Chapter 13

## Summer

Summer took out her laptop and set it up on the only non-sticky spot on the table. Having to use her phone as a hotspot at the cabin was sucking her minuscule expense account dry. But trying to concentrate in the hustle and bustle of Bake and Bite was driving her crazy. She'd never seen a fast-food place so busy every hour of the day.

Enough daydreaming. She took a sip of her hazelnut latte then opened her notes from the previous night's anti-turbine organizational meeting. She had two days to pull off the informational fair they'd planned. Save the Sea Day they'd voted to call.

"So, how's my EcoGreen Action lady doing this grand day?"

Summer twisted around and came face-to-face with Cully Teed.

He slipped into the chair beside her and set a bag heaped with donuts in front of them. "Great meeting, wasn't it?"

She looked up. "Amazing how many people showed up at such short notice. And I can't believe all the people who volunteered to go door-to-door with petitions. Wouldn't happen in New York City."

He grabbed a sugar-coated donut and stuffed it into his mouth. He chewed noisily and shoved in the rest. "That's one thing about small towns—we know how to pull together. Helps we're all related." Cully extracted another donut. "So, did I do good or what?" He held up the sugary concoction in a celebratory salute and took a big bite.

Summer tapped her fingers on the tabletop. She had a thousand pressing things to do to get the fair off the ground tomorrow. The last thing she needed right now was a guy whose ego required schmoozing, no matter how helpful he was. In fact, the whole Save the Sea Day wouldn't be happening without Cully's help. He'd had signs made and hung, helped to build displays and floats, and had set up boat tours of the harbor to impress the visitors and the press who had already started to arrive.

She pushed her computer back. "The meeting went great. The publicity is coming along marvelously." She flicked her hand at the screen. "But I have tons more coordinating work to do if we want to be ready by tomorrow."

"Really?" He turned her laptop to face him. "You're not checking out the enemy?"

"*Enemy*?"

He tugged on one of her curls. "Mad for Turbines Moses."

She pulled away from him. "Dr. Moses is not pro-turbine."

Cully took another bite. "So you say. Those Seastroke people are pretty sneaky, though. They've sent undercover people here before to bamboozle us. He is taking their money."

"Come on. Going after Gil Moses is a waste of time. It's changing the company's mind that's going to stop the tidal energy project, and we're making progress. The petition drive over in Wolfville and environs brought in hundreds of new signatures. I was getting ready to send copies to Seastroke Energy's board of directors." She firmed her voice. "Besides, Dr. Moses is doing research that might actually support our cause and change the government's approach to green energy. Every little bit helps. So, please concentrate on our protests and not your dislike of the man."

"Now, don't get all snappish. Thought we were wearing away that New York brashness." He pulled back, peered into her eyes for a moment, grabbed a donut, and stuffed half of it into his mouth. He chewed noisily, shoved in the rest, and swallowed.

"I am not being snappish, merely sensible." Summer wiped her mouth with her napkin and reclaimed her latte. She took a swallow.

"I am being sensible, city girl. That man has no intention of carrying out any research."

She set the cup down. "Sure, he does. His specialized research equipment should have arrived yesterday. Gil said something about unpacking it and outfitting the boat today."

"Did he now?" Cully snapped her laptop closed. "Then you can spend the day with me."

Just what she needed—another man bossing her around.

Summer scowled at him. "I was reading that."

"Read it later. Grab the donuts, and let's go." Cully jumped up and headed for the door.

Summer yelled at his back, "Slow down. I have to pack up my stuff."

Cully spun around and came back, his mouth turned down in a frown as false as a clown's. "Sorry. My mind is elsewhere at the moment. And the truck is running." He helped her up and waited while she tucked her laptop in her backpack. Then he snapped up the donut bag in one hand and, with the other, gripped her elbow, guiding her out the door and to the waiting truck—not Mr. Bearcat's fancy silver one, but a rusty thing with faded red paint and two kayaks in the back.

Inside the cab, Cully's buddy, Gary, sat in the driver's seat, his mouth a tight line, his hand tapping the dashboard.

"What took so long?"

"Found me a New York Apple."

Gary glanced over.

"Morning." Summer gave him her brightest smile. Gary was not much of a conversationalist, but at least he wasn't a drunken sot like Owen.

Gary sucked in his cheeks. "What'd you bring her for?"

Cully lifted her up onto the seat. "Be nice to the lady. She's my lucky charm."

"Yeah right." Gary spat out the driver's side window. "Whatever. Toss her stuff in the back and let's go."

Cully stowed her pack behind the seat then slid in next to her. He pulled out his cell and sent a text.

Summer glanced from one man to the other and tried to ignore the little voice warning her that she barely knew Cully and didn't know Gary at all. Could she trust them? But it was too late to escape.

The truck zoomed out the parking lot and turned left, throwing her against Cully's sturdy body. His arm came over her shoulders and steadied her.

She studied the man beside her. Why couldn't she be attracted to Cully Teed, instead of Gil? With his tangle of blond curls and his dimpled cheeks, the fisherman radiated an innocent charm and a can-do attitude. He was against the turbine, too.

Mr. Helpful grabbed the donut bag and bit into another donut. Well, maybe the way he gobbled donuts was a bit off-putting, and he did like to be in control. But as far as she could tell, there was no harm in him. He was attracted to her. That was all.

Yet, something seemed off in the way he acted around her. Almost like he was pretending to be Mr. Jovial Flirt when in truth he was more like the toothed-predator on the back of his jacket, waiting to take a big bite.

Oh well, she never could figure out how men thought. It was why she didn't have a guy waiting for in New York.

She sucked in a breath. "So, where are we going?"

"To see Gary's auntie. Then we'll give you a tour of the area." Cully patted her hand. "I owe you big time for what you are doing for the town. So, forget about tomorrow for a moment and enjoy the incredible view."

Just then, the trees opened up. Summer had a view of the ultramarine water of the bay through the windshield. It was hard to believe that, under that water, people wanted to put metal contraptions that would sit there, rusting away while it changed the currents and displaced marine life. Even Gil had been uncomfortable with the idea.

Several minutes later, the truck pulled into a narrow driveway and stopped next to a small white bungalow with a wraparound deck. Behind the house was another breathtaking view of the Minas Passage.

Summer leaned forward to see better. "Wow. Is this your aunt's place? You can see right across the basin here."

Gary nodded. "Yeah. This is the narrowest point of entrance to the Minas Basin. Highest tides in the world come through here."

Simultaneously, both men opened their doors and jumped out. Cully turned back and rubbed her knee. "We'll only be a minute, city girl. You wait here and rest." He plopped the bag of donuts in her lap. "Have a snack while you're at it."

The truck doors slammed, and the two men bounded up onto the deck, knocked, and were let inside.

Summer set down the donuts and glanced out at the view again. If her reading of the maps and the lay of the small island in the foreground was right, this house overlooked the tidal turbine site. Even though the turbine itself was not visible, this was definitely a photo opp. It showed the beauty of the place, and if she could set this view next to a picture of the actual turbine, that would go a long way to raising the wider public's ire. It would be perfect for the blog she'd created.

She wiggled her way over to the door, managed to open it, and let herself slide out. Now, where had Cully stowed her pack? She peered behind the seat. There.

She dug out her camera then, leaving her pack behind, slung the camera around her neck and made her way across the lawn to the back of the house.

Loud voices cut through the air. She spun around. Through the huge picture window at the back, Cully and a short, round woman gestured and yelled at each other. The woman turned, her face a mask of anger, and Summer recognized the busybody she'd met at the store—Mrs. Eagles.

Suddenly, a child's screech rose from somewhere inside. The woman said something, and Cully shook a fist at her.

Summer's stomach clenched. This was Gil's house, not Gary's aunt's. And Cully was terrifying his housekeeper. What was going on?

Photograph forgotten, she crept nearer to the back door until she could make out the words.

"Get out of here," Mrs. Eagle was saying, her voice trembling. "You're upsetting the child. And what will I tell Mr. Moses when he finds someone messed with his papers? Cully, you're going to lose me this job."

"You'll think of something. You always do. And you'll keep quiet about it." He lowered his voice. "A little birdie might tell the police what you did."

The old woman stepped back, her face washed pale. She extended her hand and pointed her finger at him. "Do what you will, Cully Teed, but know this one thing—don't you ever underestimate me."

"Oh, I don't. But be sure, I will turn you in if you even hint—"

At that moment, Lissie flashed through the kitchen, screaming at the top of her lungs, and burst out the screen door. She came to an abrupt halt when she saw Summer and shrieked, "Kerrrrrrrrrrrrmiiiiiiiiiii." The child leaped off the deck and headed straight at her.

The encounter on the ferry flew through her head. Not again.

Summer did her best to jerk to the side, but there was no way she could escape the oncoming demon.

*Smack.* The child crashed into her. She tottered but managed to stay standing and waited for the attack. But this time, there were no scratching fingers and kicking feet. Instead, two small arms wrapped around her waist and clung like a leech. Tears streaked down the child's face as she moaned over and over, "Kerrrmii. Kerrrmiii."

*Kermi?* Summer glanced down at her sweater. What had Gil said about the eye-blinding green? That's right. It was the color of Kermit the Frog. The child thought she was Kermit.

She cupped her hand above the little girl's curly head then remembered Gil had told her Lissie was sensitive to touch.

She dropped her hand and dredged up a song from her childhood. In her softest voice, she hummed the tune to "Rainbow Connection."

The child looked up at her with dark brown eyes flecked with gold that were too much like her father's and began to hum along in a childish monotone.

"What the heck are you doing there?"

Summer peered up.

Cully Teed stood on the back deck, glaring down at her, fists clenched at his sides. Big-smile, fun-loving Cully was gone. In his place was a large, dangerous-looking bear-of-a-man with a harsh mouth and squinting eyes.

Her blood ran cold. This was not a man to be on the wrong side of. But she'd done nothing wrong. Well, except eavesdrop a bit.

She indicated her camera. "I wanted to take a pic of the Basin."

Cully frowned. "From there?"

Summer glanced over her shoulder. *Oops.* She was too low and too far back to see the water. She thought fast. Right.

She pointed to the child. "Lissie caught me before I could find my way out there."

Cully's eyes narrowed even more. "Well, let her un-catch you and get yourself back to the truck. We're leaving."

Summer looked down at the child clasping her. "Lissie, I have to go now." She pulled back slightly. The girl held on tighter.

Summer tried again. This time, Lissie worked her fingers into the weave of the sweater and squealed. The more Summer tugged, the louder Lissie screeched.

Cully pressed his hands against his ears. "Shut the kid up, or I will."

"Wait. Don't move, Summer." Mrs. Eagles dashed down the steps. "Go back to humming. She likes that."

Summer stood still and hummed as loudly as she could.

Mrs. Eagles circled around them. "It's the sweater she's attracted to."

Summer nodded. "Yeah. Gil said she adored Kermit, and it's the color of the frog."

"Try slipping out of it."

"Take it off? But how? She's got her fingers twisted in it."

Mrs. Eagles came behind her and pinched the bottom of the sleeve. "Little by little. Lean against me so you don't lose your balance and work your arm out."

Gary came out on the deck. "What the heck is going on?"

Cully pointed with his chin. "Got herself tangled up with Moses' brat. Should lock kids like that away."

Gary scowled. "We don't have time for this, Cully. Had a call from boss man. Has another job for us. He's getting antsy."

"What next? Got to go, Summer. Be your friendly self and don't tell Moses I brought you here, okay?"

Summer's mouth fell open. She'd never be able to explain her presence to Gil. He already distrusted her. This would add fuel to the fire.

"Wait. Don't leave me." She struggled to get her arm out and lost her balance. She crashed into Mrs. Eagles, and together, they landed on the cold, wet grass.

Lissie let out a louder screech and crawled on top of her.

Cully laughed. "Good luck, city girl. See you tomorrow, if'n you can escape Little Miss Crazy and her joker of a father."

# Chapter 14

## Gil

Gil put down the box he was carrying and stared at the wreckage on his boat. Gauges and probes smashed. Wires and nets cut. The brand-new laptop computer missing. Someone had destroyed or stolen all the equipment he had transported to *Hell'za Poppin'* that morning.

He glanced around the dock. Boats slapped against the wharf. Flags waved in the stiff breeze. Seagulls soared overhead. And not one fisherman was visible. Not that the locals would turn in one of their own.

He took out his cell phone to call the police then slipped it back into his pocket. Calling in the Mounties would be useless at this point. Owen was right. No one was talking. The bomber was one of their own. The damage was done. The message received.

He jumped down into the boat and began sorting through the mess. The probes and depth gauges were a complete loss, but he could make smaller plankton nets from the big scampi trawl his unknown vandals had sliced up, and there were plenty of lobster traps around he could rig up to trap the larger size lobsters.

He'd have to use his own personal laptop for now until he could get the company to send another, and he could order more probes. But with a little ingenuity, he had enough to appear to be doing research, and if he lay low, the culprits might try again and give themselves away.

He stowed the salvageable items in the cuddy and padlocked the door closed. Next time, he'd be ready.

He picked up the carton—no sense losing the temperature equipment, too—hauled it back to his car, and put it in the trunk. He needed a way to trap them. In fact, if he were clever, he might get the bomber himself to tip his hand.

****

All the way home, Gil ran various plans through his head. He could leave equipment out at night and lie in wait to catch the vandals. He shook his head. No, he had to be home for Lissie. And besides, what would he do with some burly guys or teens if he caught them?

Once upon a time, nobody messed with him and his boat, but he was no longer that angry young man. Violence only led to more violence, and sometimes innocent people got trapped in the crossfire.

Like Ellen.

He banished the image of his sister's broken, bloody body from his mind and forced himself to concentrate on catching the Tide Harbor vandals. His sister was dead, and nothing he did would ever change that fact.

Gil rubbed the back of his neck. The best chance, and least confrontational way, to catch anyone on the boat would be to set up a streaming webcam like they had at the Turbine Research Center. But doing it without being seen by some nosey fisherman would be a challenge.

He turned into his driveway and brought the car to a stop. Yep, several deer trail cameras covering the dock area would work and not be too expensive. He'd just have to be sneaky about installing them. He was sure the fishermen would be watching him.

He let out a huff of air and peered out the car window. Scattered white clouds scuttled across the sky. A breeze rustled through the treetops. The water glittered in the Basin below. And Mrs. Eagles stood in the doorway, wearing a smile and waving. He was home and, for a short while, he could relax and forget about tracking down angry fishermen.

He got out of the car and slammed the door shut.

"You're late," Mrs. Eagles called as he took the carton out of the trunk. "Lissie's been waiting and waiting to go to Miss Betty's."

Gil waved back as he lugged the box up the steps to the deck. "Sorry. Get her coat on, and we can go as soon as I put this away."

Mrs. Eagles stepped back to let him pass by. "She has a new sweater to show you."

He spun his head in her direction. "A new what?"

"Sweater," Summer Avery said as she came out of the kitchen, her head a mess of wind-tangled curls, her petite body hidden in the too-big, gray wool sweater his mother had knitted for him.

The hair on the back of his neck rose. Miss Anti-Turbine was last person he expected to find in his home, and he didn't like it. Not when she looked absolutely adorable and desperately in need of a hug. It gave him all kinds of ideas he didn't want to have about the annoying woman.

In the last three days, not only had she riled up the locals so everyone he passed cold-shouldered him, but she was driving his bosses at Seastroke Energy crazy with her petitions. Not to mention that she was not available. Cully had staked his claim in more ways than one.

But none of that changed the fact that he wanted her.

He blinked, hoping the tempting apparition would disappear. But she didn't.

Lowering the box, he gave her his don't-mess-with-me look. "What are you doing here, Summer?"

Mrs. Eagles poked her head between them. "Gary Campbell dropped her off. Summer's waiting for her laundry."

He narrowed his eyes. "Her *laundry*? Is that why she's wearing my favorite sweater?"

"Oh no, your daughter claimed hers." Mrs. Eagles cupped a hand to her mouth and called, "Lissie, come show Daddy what you have."

Lissie duck-danced out of her bedroom, draped in Summer's unforgettable ratty green sweater that reached her feet. At the top of her lungs, she chanted, "Kermie! Kermie!"

"That's my girl. She thinks she's Kermit the Frog." Mrs. Eagles lowered her voice to a whisper. "Be kind."

He glared at the old woman. Of course he'd be kind.

He caught a glimpse of Summer's wary expression. She stood tense, her shoulders stiff, her hands clasped behind her back.

Here was the chance to show Summer Avery he wasn't the horrible father she thought he was.

Gil kneeled down on the living room rug and stretched out his arms. "Come. Let's do our Kermit dance."

For a moment, Lissie hesitated. Then, shrieking at the top of her lungs, she hopped up and down. It was an old game, one they had done since she had first fallen in love with the puppet.

Swallowing his pride, he hopped on all fours, croaking like a frog. Gil glanced over at Summer. Their eyes met. Even with her dressed like a waif, and him jumping up and down pretending to be a frog, heat and desire flashed through him. He gave himself a shake and croaked louder. She was not for him.

"Time to go, too, Miss Flowers, Kermit Lissie." Mrs. Eagles held out her coat.

Still hopping and shrieking, Lissie let the housekeeper bundle her up and lead her outside.

Gil rose to his feet and swept himself off. He nodded to Summer to proceed him out the door. "Thank you for sharing your sweater. I forgot to bring her stuffed Kermit in the rush to leave. That toy was one of the few things that soothed her." He stepped out the door and sucked in a breath of the chill air. "After I drop these two off at the preschool, I'll take you wherever you need to be."

# Chapter 15

## Summer

Minutes later, they were off, heading toward Betty's place on the hill above the village. With Mrs. Eagles and Lissie tucked into the back seat, Summer had no choice but to sit in the front, way too close to Gil Moses for comfort.

She adjusted her camera strap, leaned against the window and, ignoring the Kermie chant behind her, kept her attention on the landscape zipping past.

She glanced at her nemesis out of the corner of her eye. With his long hair tousled by the wind, and his jaw firmly set, Mr. Marine Biologist was too handsome for her own good, and she'd been wrong about him as a father.

As difficult as Lissie was to handle, he loved his daughter—loved her almost too much. It had taken all her willpower not to laugh when he had hopped and croaked around the room just to make Lissie smile.

She ran her finger along the edge of the windowsill. Her father hadn't had time to play with her. After their mother had died of the cancer her father believed was due to the water pollution caused by the company fracking the farm next to theirs, all his attention had focused on fighting the drilling company. There'd never been time for laughter or fun. Only endless papers and arguments, demonstrations and days in court.

Then she'd broken his heart by working on an ad campaign to improve the image of a drilling company, like the one he had fought and lost to. It hadn't mattered that the money she had earned paid for his sons to go to college or for his medical bills.

She glanced again at Gil. She'd been so wrong about this man. She couldn't imagine a father willing to play a frog for his autistic daughter as the villain in this turbine trouble. More and more, she was coming to believe he was here to do what he'd said he was doing—track lobster populations.

The car pulled up to the door of Miss Betty's pink-and-green ranch house.

Miss Betty, her gentle, heart-shaped face alight, her cheeks rosy from some exertion with her young charges, poked her head out the door and waved. "There you are. I was getting concerned. Come right in, Lissie."

Mrs. Eagles helped a Kermie-chanting Lissie from the car and scurried her inside. Miss Betty took a step to follow them then reversed herself and came over to the car door.

Gil rolled down his window and gave the preschool teacher that enticing smile he had once gifted on her. "Sorry we're late. Had some trouble on my boat."

"Oh dear. I hope it wasn't anything serious?"

Gil shrugged. "Not really. Just another mess to clean up."

Betty leaned further in, blinked her eyes at Summer, then turned back to Gil. "So, are we still on for tonight?"

Gil nodded. "Of course. I'll be here at five."

Betty gave him a quick peck on the cheek, leaving a red lipstick smudge behind. "You're a doll, Gilly." She flounced away, swaying her ample hips and generous bosom.

Summer bit her lip, angry that the slightly chubby preschool teacher already had her nails in Gil. She should let it go. Miss Betty was perfect for a caring marine biologist, but she couldn't. She leaned back against the door and draped her arm across the seatback. "*Gilly?*"

Gil started up the car and pulled out onto the road. He turned toward Tide Harbor. "Where to, Miss Avery?"

Summer straightened up. "Back to *Miss Avery*, are we?"

Gil gunned the engine and made a sharp turn down a narrow road that badly needed repaving. The car bumped and swerved as he avoided the worst of the potholes. At the end of the road, he stepped hard on the brakes and yanked the car over to the side, tires squealing, gravel kicking out against the underside of the car.

He turned and stared at her, his hands clamped on the steering wheel. "My equipment has been vandalized. I find you prancing around at my house. I know you're an eco-crazy nut out to diss the turbines without really understanding the research"—he shifted on the seat until he gazed fully into her eyes—"and all I want to do is kiss you."

She jerked it back. "You want to *kiss* me?"

"Is that such a shock? The enemy wants to kiss you?" He got out of the car, slammed the door behind him and, without a glance back, disappeared into the woods.

Summer stared at the pine trees. What was the matter with him? They were in the middle of nowhere. No traffic. No houses. She peered over her shoulder at the sandy trail. No road to speak of.

Touchy Turbine Man could be out there, nursing his imaginary rebuff for hours. He'd come back eventually, if only for his date with Miss Smiley-Face Flowers.

But no way was she going to sit here waiting for him. She wasn't a waiting kind of girl. She believed in action. Besides, she had a thousand last-minute details to take care of if Save the Sea Day was going to make the splash she'd promise the locals.

Summer pushed open the car door, and a gust of wind rushed in, sending chills up and down her spine. She tugged her coat closed, but it, and the borrowed sweater, were no match for the damp breeze whipping in from the bay. She wrapped her arms around her and bit her lip.

She could try hitching a ride. She gazed back down the trail. Good luck with that idea. She doubted there was much traffic on the dirt road they'd just rumbled down.

She put her hand on the doorframe and hauled herself out. Gil Moses was her only chance for getting back to town any time soon. Best if she went and calmed his ruffled man-feathers. Although what his problem was, she couldn't figure. He seemed to think she'd refuse him a kiss.

She touched her lips. Would she?

Maybe.

Maybe not.

But that was a moot point, anyway. Mr. I-Want-To-Kiss-You was nowhere to be seen.

Okay, so where had he stormed off to?

She pushed out of the car, shifted her camera towards her back, and worked her way toward the edge of the woods. As she went she cupped her hands and called his name, "Gil."

No answer. She called again, louder this time, "Gil."

The wind bustled through the pines, but no Gil Moses answered back.

She surveyed the woods. How far could he have gone? Surely, he'd hear her calling despite the wind. Well, she'd freeze to death standing here, and no way would she sit in a car, twiddling her thumbs because of some man's injured feelings.

She buttoned her coat up to her neck then, avoiding the wet spots as much as possible, she edged her way through the thicket of scrubby trees and pines.

In an open spot, she halted and called again. Only the roll of the surf and the cry of the seabirds answered. Her heart sped up. They must be up on the cliffs running along the shoreline. What if he'd fallen? Gotten hurt? She forced herself to move faster.

Up ahead, she caught sight of blue sky and a shimmer of water. She burst out of the trees and stopped dead. Below her lay a tumbling cliff face, littered with red and silver-gray rocks stretching down to a sandy beach. It had to be over a hundred feet down.

In the distance, a white lighthouse clung to a spit of land. Above, a pair of crows soared and squawked, angry at being disturbed.

She searched for the yellow buoy marking the turbine site. There it was. A bright yellow-fluorescent bead, unnatural against the blue-green water. It was a different angle, but the view was basically the same as from Gil's house.

Here was her chance to get the photo she'd intended to take before she had been distracted by Cully Teed's angry exchange with Mrs. Eagles.

She maneuvered the camera around to the front and framed the view. Not quite right. A treetop blocked the buoy. She shifted to the left. Big mistake.

Her foot slipped on the gravel, flew out from under her, and she fell flat on her back, knocking the air from her lungs and sliding a few feet forward.

She lay still for a moment, catching her breath and staring up at the blue, blue sky above her. For a minute, she considered staying there until the stupid man came and found her. But the ground was cold and damp, and if she didn't move, he was likely to find an ice cube in her place.

Summer sat up and froze, every muscle tight as a kite string. She was on a downward slope, her toes inches from the edge of the cliff. She looked right and left. There was nothing to grasp on to, only loose gravel and stones. Her only hope was a scraggly bush clinging to the cliff.

Slowly, she stretched toward it, swiping at it with her fingertips. The tiny motion was enough to set her sliding forward again. Frantically, she dug in her sneaker heel, but it didn't hold.

She let out a scream and clawed her hands into the stone and rock. Coarse sand lodged under her fingernails. Stones tumbled down around her head. Her ankle hit a rock. Pain shot up her leg.

She screamed again as her feet slid over the cliff face and hung out in space. Below, the ocean roared and the rocks waited. Her heart thundered in her ears. She was going to die.

"Summer! What the blazes?" Gil's feet crunched on the gravel. Then he was there, grabbing her by the arm, halting her slide over the edge.

He sunk to the ground, scooped her up, and cradled her against him, rocking her back and forth like a small child, whispering in her ear, "It's okay. You're safe now."

If he had yelled at her for being foolish, she could have been strong and blinked back the welling tears. She could have kept her cool and pushed him away. But no one had held her and comforted her in a long time. In this man's arms, she felt cherished for the first time since her mother had died. A sob escaped, and then another.

"Hush. It's okay to cry. You've had a scare."

It was like he had given permission. With a great aching wrench, the flood broke lose, all her hurts and losses and fears poured out in salty tears that trickled down her cheeks and lodged beneath her collar.

Gil clasped her more firmly against his hard, warm body, shielding her face from the wind. He rubbed her back and hummed a low tune.

Summer nestled closer, inhaled his scent, redolent with the sharp tang of the pines he'd walked through and wished she could stay in his arms forever. But all good things had to end, and she didn't deserve this man.

She'd done a good job keeping him out of her way since the boat ride. Why had she listened to Ingrid and set out to attract him with her outrageous behavior at the Tav yesterday? "He likes you. Get under his skin," Ingrid had urged. "Find out what he's really doing here."

Now, here she was, sitting in his lap, way too close.

Gil ran his fingers through her hair, working out the tangles. She was not worthy of such tenderness. If he ever found out she'd agreed to spy on him and knew Cully and his fishermen buddies had painted a target on him, and she hadn't told him, he'd hate her.

# Chapter 16

## Gil

Gil wrapped his arms around her and caught his breath. The image of her hanging over the edge had sent adrenaline surging through him. If he had been a minute later—he clasped her tighter—he'd have lost her.

Summer placed a hand against his chest and struggled to get free. "I-I—"

"Wait." He couldn't let her go. Not now. Not after what had happened. "I didn't mean to abandon you. It's just ... I was angry at myself. I lost control when I shouldn't have, knowing you and Cully are a thing."

"*A thing*? Heck no!"

"I'm glad." He lowered his lips to hers. "May I?"

She nodded, and he pulled her back into his arms. Every muscle in her body tensed against his. Someone had hurt this woman. He had to go slow.

His lips met hers, and he exalted. They were warm, tentative, gentle, and utterly delicious. And she was kissing him back.

Then she stiffened.

He drew back slightly and tempered the kiss. Her lips opened beneath his, and their mouths joined, fitting together perfectly. She tasted fresh and clean, like the air around them. He wanted to lick and suck and never stop.

Somewhere above, a gull cawed, clouds swirled, and the sea breeze wafted through the trees. For a moment, they were the only two people in the world. He was hers, and she was his.

He ran his hand along her cheek and wove his fingers into her hair. The last of the tension left her. She softened in his arms, and he risked kissing her harder, deeper. His tongue explored the softness of her mouth, the smoothness of her teeth, the press of her lips on his. It was more than a kiss. It was a melding.

Summer shifted in his lap and pressed closer. Heat suffused his body. He hugged her tighter. He needed her to know he wanted her. That he would protect and cherish her. That he would never hurt her.

She moaned and snugged against him. And he wished it weren't so cold. That they weren't sitting on the edge of a cliff. And that they had all the time in the world.

But they didn't.

He slowly ended the kiss and stared out at the sea. Why couldn't they have met in some other place at some other time? Why couldn't they have been on the same side? Then he could have trusted her. Told her what he was really doing in Tide Harbor.

A boat hove into view, heading toward the yellow beacon marking the turbine site. His muscles tensed.

"Gil?" Summer blinked and sat up. "What's wrong?"

"There's a boat." He pointed.

"A boat?"

"It's been circling the buoy for the last few minutes."

Summer spun her head around. "All the time you were kissing me like it was the end of tomorrow, and you were watching a *boat*?"

"Oh." He cupped her chin in his hand. "No, Summer. Oh goodness, no. That kiss was ... earthshattering. It's just ... I heard the engine and caught a glimpse."

"Heard the engine? I don't even see a boat. Darn you. Help me up."

Gil bent his head. "I'm sorry. That was insensitive of me."

Summer whacked him on the chest. "*Insensitive*? I call it pig guts insulting."

"Look." He helped her to her feet. "I've wanted to kiss you ever since that moment on the boat and ... well, we got carried away. Fear does that. I saw you going over the edge and thought I'd not catch you in time. It's the result of all the adrenaline flooding our bodies." He glanced back out at the water and narrowed his eyes.

Summer wrinkled her nose. "Oh, so we kissed to align your chemistry? Glad I could be of service." Her foot slipped on the gravel.

"Hold on." Gil caught her and cradled her in his arms. He rubbed his nose against hers. "Don't go playing prickly porcupine with me. You enjoyed that kiss as much as I did." He grabbed her hand.

Summer wriggled and pulled. "Let go."

"I need to show you something first. Make up for my ... inattention." He slung her into his arms and gathered her to his chest.

"Put me down. I'm too heavy to carry."

"No, you're not. I've caught fish that weighed more." He turned and worked his way down the rock face.

Summer clutched his windbreaker. "What the heck are you doing? I nearly fell down this cliff."

"I'm on the sea path."

"There's a path?"

"Yah, sure. Hold on."

He leapt from rock to rock, her hands entwined in the fabric of his jacket. He liked having her close, feeling the heat of her pressed against him and her heart pounding in rhythm with his. At the bottom, he lowered her onto a flat rock and reluctantly unpeeled her hands.

He glanced back up at the cliff she'd almost tumbled over. He'd come so close to losing her, and despite their disagreements. he couldn't bear to see such a bright, vibrant woman lost in a foolish accident.

She looked around. "How do you know where you are? I thought you weren't from Tide Harbor."

"I'm not. But I've been here before, as a kid. Came here many times with my brothers to sea kayak. And I know the lay of the land, the geology. It's part of my job."

He'd always love this particular section of the Minas Basin coastline. Reddish monoliths rose from the sea like frozen giants and towered over them. The ground was littered with rough gemstones.

"We used to row between the rocks at high tide, watching out for the boulders hidden beneath the water. It's low tide right now, or we wouldn't be standing here."

"How high up does the tide reach?"

"It varies." Gil pointed. "On a normal day, up to that darker band of rock."

"This whole beach goes under water?"

"Yep, but don't worry—high tide's not for hours."

She frowned at him. "Has anyone ever gotten caught?"

"It happens. A while back, they had to helicopter a pair of hikers out who got trapped down a ways in Cognecto Park."

"Ugh. I'm a terrible swimmer." Her fists clenched. "Can we go now?"

"In a minute. I see something." Gil kicked at the stones on the beach. Taking his penknife from his pocket, he bent down and pried a stone out of the gravelly sand. He handed it to her.

She turned it over and over. "It's got a purple cast to it. What is it?"

"A nugget of sea-worn amethyst. Not much to look at right now, but polished up a bit, it would make a beautiful pendant."

"I can't believe you picked a gemstone out of all these rocks. They all look the same to me." She rubbed the crystal between her fingers then held it out to him on her palm.

He closed her fingers over the stone. "Keep it. You can take it to the rock store in town and have them set it"—he looked away, chewing on his lip—"as a souvenir." Because that was what it was, right? She would rile up the locals. Then she would leave. Go back to New York and her high-powered environmentalist group, and he would be left here.

Summer stuffed the garnet in her jeans pocket. "Sure, a memento of the day I nearly killed myself."

She looked so fragile at that moment that he wanted to pull her back into his arms. But he could see the tension and suspicion returning. They were enemies, and it was better they stayed away from each other. Kissing her had been a mistake he couldn't repeat.

The distant sound of an engine prickled his ears. He turned and stared out at the bay. Could that boat still be out there?

Summer tugged on his arm. "What the heck is so fascinating about a stupid boat? Can you identify whose it is?"

"Can't tell. The sun's glaring off the water."

"Then let's go. I have things to do."

"Wait."

All of a sudden, a spray of water rose up in the air, like the waterspout of a gigantic whale.

"Oh." Summer slapped a hand over her mouth. "What was that?"

"The turbine bomber just dropped another depth charge."

"In broad daylight. I don't believe it."

"Neither do I. Whoever he is, he's one cocky bastard, and he's going to have to be stopped. That makes two tries." Gil turned to look at her. "He's not one of your anti-turbine groupies, is he?"

"Heavens no." She twisted her hands together. "No, of course not. EcoGreen only supports non-violent actions."

"Do they?" He gave her a long, piercing stare, but there were violent protestors out there. Owen Young had said as much. And there was a bomber on the loose. Owen Young said he was close to finding out, but it was taking too long. Until the bastard was captured, everyone was in danger.

He had to warn her. "I think you are mistaken."

"Are you accusing me of lying?"

"No, merely naïve. There *is* danger out there, you know." He looked back at the basin. The boat was gone. "People who drop bombs usually escalate when they don't get the notice they want. Dropping the bomb in daylight is concerning. What might the idiot do next? The locals can run the protest movement you've started. Why not leave now?"

"Because my work is not done. That turbine is still set to start spinning those fish-killing propellers—four days from now. Besides, there is no danger. My protestors are good people—local business owners, school children, and little old ladies. Even Betty, Lissie's preschool teacher, is against the turbines. I'm telling you now, I am not leaving until that monstrosity is pulled up out of the ocean."

The woman was impossible.

"Well, don't say I didn't warn you." He swung her up in his arms and headed up the path.

# Chapter 17

## Summer

By the time they reached the car, Summer was regretting everything—the kiss, the way she fit so perfectly in his arms, and that fact that she was hot, bothered, and so turned on she could hardly breathe.

But she couldn't say the same for the clench-jawed man whose arms wrapped so securely around her.

Without a word, he dropped her on the seat and circled to the driver's side. He started the engine.

"Where to?" His voice had lost all softness.

Summer let her head fall back. "I left my car in the Bake and Bite parking lot."

He grunted and set the car in the direction of town.

Summer fastened her seat belt and tucked her hands into her pockets to warm them.

He wanted her to leave Tide Harbor. Give up her protest. How dare he? Without her marketing skills and contacts, the press would lose interest, and the local group would fizzle.

Maybe Cully was right. Gil Moses *was* a company shill. But no matter who he was, he was the last man on Earth she should be kissing. He worked for Seastroke Energy. She worked for EcoGreen Action.

Her fingers brushed the amethyst in her coat pocket. She would not think of it as a memento of that kiss. Not at all. Instead, it would be a reminder that this was too beautiful place to install heavy industry. Because if this turbine was successful, more would come. Buildings would shoot up to house the electric cables and the repair equipment. Docks would be built for the repair service boats. Overhead high-tension wires would be strung through the pristine forests to transport the electric across the province. That was why she was here.

She glanced over at Gil. As much as she was attracted to him and as much as she liked his kisses, Captain Nemo had made it clear—he wanted her gone.

Fine by her.

With her leaving in five days, hopefully for Atlanta, and him saddled with a needy child she had no idea how to handle, a relationship with Gil Moses would be a tidal wave of a disaster, anyway.

Now, if only she could convince her stupid heart of that.

She risked a peek at him. Chin firm, jaw set, lips pinned tight, eyes focused on the road, he wasn't anything like she'd first thought. This was the kind of man women searched all their lives to find—gentle, self-effacing, a good father, and yet incredibly strong and masculine. And if that was how he kissed when he was distracted, imagine what he'd be like in bed fully focused on what he was doing.

Oh no. That was not what she wanted to think about.

She pressed her legs together, interlocked her fingers, and studied him out of the corner of her eye, noting the strain in his neck, the slight twitch along his jaw.

Ingrid was right, and the kiss had proven it. He was attracted to her. Yet he knew he shouldn't be.

A man like him deserved a Betty Flowers, all pretty-pink and sweet-tongued. Someone to scramble his eggs, take care of his daughter, and cuddle with him at night. Not someone who was going to bring down his employer, and surely—she pictured Cully Teed's twisted grin—cause him a barrelful of hurt.

Ingrid wanted her to worm her way into Gil Moses' confidence and share what she had learned with the anti-turbine group. But after that kiss, the idea of leading him on made her sick. She couldn't do it.

*That kiss.*

Guilt pressed down on her chest so heavily she could hardly breathe. Gil's kiss had not been a sudden kiss. Nor a possessive kiss. It was a thoughtful kiss. A cherishing kiss. One that had the makings of forever in it. And sweet heavens, she didn't deserve that kind of kiss and never would.

She pushed the amethyst deep into her pocket. Forget Gil and his kisses. Time to focus all her energy on her goal—stopping Seastroke's turbine project.

She folded her hands in her lap. She'd have to lie to Ingrid and her co-conspirators. Claim Turbine Guy was closed mouth about anything turbine-related.

She glanced again at Gil, who was silently staring ahead. Actually, that probably wasn't much of a fib.

A weathered-gray house rose into view on her side of the road, and Gil put on his signal and turned into the drive.

"Why are you stopping here?"

Gil frowned at her. "To pick up your laundry so I can have my sweater back." He jumped out of the car and headed for the house.

Her laundry?

Ugh. That's right. Mrs. Eagles had explained her presence at Gil's saying she was waiting for her laundry. This must be Nan Campbell's place, where they did the wash for the renters.

She gazed at Gil's retreating back. She should run and stop him. Tell him it wouldn't be done until tomorrow.

She pressed her hands to her cheeks. Tell him something. But it was too late, anyway. In a few minutes, Gil would be back, knowing her for a liar. Looking at her with even more distrust. She straightened up. Well, good. She could blame Cully and Gary's desertion for her inability to spy any further on Gil.

Still, he'd be one furious male when he learned she had no laundry waiting.

Summer leaned back and closed her eyes. Maybe he'd think her asleep.

The car door opened. Gil's distinctive scent filled the car. The seat creaked as he lowered his weight.

"Okay, Miss Avery, stop playing hibernating bear. Open those big green eyes and tell me exactly what you were doing at my house today."

Summer made an act of stretching and yawning. "What?"

"Cut it out. There's no laundry here, and you know it. Mrs. Campbell has never heard of you."

Summer fingered the raised cable stitches running down the sweater. She could weave a lie as well as anyone. It was an essential skill for a marketer designing ad campaigns for products she hated.

"Gary Campbell, her nephew, took me for a ride in his new truck. He stopped to visit Mrs. Eagles." She glanced over at him. "She's his aunt, too. And Lissie wanted my sweater and ... well, there was this Kermit thing, and Lissie wouldn't let go, and Gary didn't want to wait."

Gil stared out the windshield. "So, you're telling me Mrs. Eagles lied?"

Darn it. She didn't want to get the old woman in trouble. Mrs. Eagles had tried to protect her.

"No. It's what Gary told her to explain why I was with him. And I didn't ... uh, correct him."

Gil slumped slightly and bit his lip. "Okay. I'll accept that." He started the engine then spun around and glared at her. "But I don't want you near my house again. I don't trust you."

Her stomach tightened. He'd trust her even less if he found out Cully had been there, too.

Summer tilted her head and shrugged. "No. You just want to kiss me."

He pulled out into the road. "Trust me. That won't be happening again."

*****

Twenty minutes later, Summer watched Gil drive out of the Bake and Bite lot and speed back down the road, on his way to meet Betty Flowers.

Well, good riddance to him.

She opened her car door and slipped into the driver's seat. She should go home to her damp, moldy cabin, but the idea of being alone, thinking about that kiss with nothing to distract her, would drive her crazy. She glanced at the fast-food place. She could go back into Bake and Bite and continue the computer work Cully had interrupted.

*Wait.* No, she couldn't. Her laptop was riding around in the back of Gary's truck. Great. All her notes were on that computer, all the social media accounts, and she had no idea where Gary lived. She needed to find Cully now.

She swiped on her cell and hit his number. It rang then went to voicemail. She left a message and, for good measure, sent a text.

No response.

Figures the guy would be incommunicado just when she needed him.

She glanced at her cell phone. Four thirty. Would he be at the Tav this early? She could check. Get something to eat—she shook her head—or not. Her money and credit card were in her knapsack, too.

Her stomach grumbled in disappointment. It had been a long time since her coffee, and Cully had drunk half, at that. Right now, even those sugary donuts she'd turned down sounded good.

Summer started up the car and pulled up to the parking lot exit. Right or left? Oh, pig's feet, she'd go hang out at the Tav and see what was happening. The waitress might know where to find Mr. Bearcat. If she remembered correctly, she was related to him somehow.

# Chapter 18

## Gil

Before he was out of his car, Mrs. Eagles was yelling at him.

"Where have you been? You have a parent-teacher conference in twenty minutes."

"I remember." Gil hustled Mrs. Eagles and Lissie into the house.

Mrs. Eagles gave him a wink. "You might ask Miss Betty out to dinner after, as a thank you for being so patient with Lissie."

"That's okay with you?"

"Aye." She stepped back and let him through the door. "Lissie and me will bake muffins for tomorrow's breakfast then watch that movie she loves so much."

"*The Muppets*," Gil grunted. "Better you than me. I must have seen it a thousand times."

Mrs. Eagles laughed. "I don't mind. I'll work on my knitting."

He gave her a quick smile. "You're a lifesaver, and to think I tried to turn you away at the door."

The old woman beamed up at him. "No problem. That tide's left the harbor. But I do have a favor to ask."

"No trouble. I owe you. What do you need?"

"Well, that's the thing. It's something in my husband's old boat."

"Boat?"

Mrs. Eagles examined her fingernails. "Yes. The *Hell'za Poppin'*, the one the research center is lending you, was my husband's, you see, before they got it and ... well, I was wondering if you found anything of his there?"

Gil rubbed his chin. "I didn't see anything but old netting and lobster buoys in the cuddy."

"Well, if you do find something personal, would you let me know? I have so little to remember him by." The old woman's face held a weight of sorrow.

Gil patted her on the shoulder. "Of course. Any idea what he might have left?"

She shrugged her shoulders inward. The small movement made her look smaller and older. "They never found his wood-handled knife. The one I gave him for his birthday. Had his initials carved in it—a W and an E. Could have fallen between the planks, I'm thinking."

"I'll take a gander for it tomorrow."

The old woman smiled. "I knew you would help. You've got hero written all over you. Now, off you go. Spruce yourself up and treat Betty to a nice dinner. She's a sweet girl. Really loves her little ones. She's been great with Lissie, too."

A glance at the clock told him it was time to get moving. Gil took a moment to comb his hair back and gather it into a hair tie. Dolores had hated that he refused to cut it. "What up-and-coming future dean has long hair," she'd railed at him. But he'd refused—a small act of defiance in the face of her constant demands.

Besides, he hadn't been interested in becoming a dean. He wanted to do research again. Real research that would make a difference in people's lives.

He passed back into the living room and noticed the electric-green sweater Lissie had been wearing tossed on the sofa. He picked it up and held to his nose, savoring the intoxicating bouquet of honeysuckle. Then he threw the eyesore down.

It sure was ugly. He wished she had been wearing it this afternoon on the cliff.

Seeing Summer Avery wearing the sweater his mom had knitted made his gut wrench. Combined with wind-tangled hair and broken-in jeans, she'd looked less like a thick-skinned, unapproachable bombshell and more like a lost little girl.

He could resist the bombshell. He touched his lips. He hadn't been able to resist the big-eyed pixie with the sad eyes.

Gil headed out to pick up Betty.

Kissing Summer had been a mistake. She was everything he didn't want or need. And once she learned more about him, she'd regret that kiss, too. From now on, he'd stay far away from Summer Avery.

He'd take Mrs. Eagles' advice and invite the preschool teacher to dinner after the parent-teacher conference. She was gentle, motherly, and doing a great job with Lissie. She was everything Summer Avery was not.

****

Two hours later, Gil was regretting he'd ever thought Betty Flowers was motherly. She was a woman with one thought in her head—get him into her bed. The minute he'd invited her to dinner, she'd disappeared into the recesses of the preschool then reemerged from her living quarters a changed woman.

Prissy schoolteacher gone. Man-trap in her place.

Her staid white blouse and slacks had been replaced with a low-cut, sequined halter top revealing too much of her ample cleavage. Skintight leggings revealed every nook, cranny, and bulge. Strappy heels brought her close to his height. Her soft, round face sported ruby-red lipstick, fake eyelashes, and exotic purple eye shadow that made her look like an over-fed Mardi Gras queen. And to top it off, she'd plopped a black Cleopatra-style wig over her brown hair.

She looked garish, false, and determined. If he could have rescinded his invitation, he would have. But his mother had raised him a gentleman.

He held the door open. "Where shall we eat?"

She sashayed outside. "At the Tav, of course."

"The Tav?"

"The White Rock Tavern." She turned and pressed her breasts against him. "Don't you know it's the place *to see and be seen.*" She gave her wigged head a toss. "And I want to be seen with you, Gil Moses. But later"—her voice sank to a whisper—"maybe ... we might ... well, you know?"

Gil's stomach tightened. Underneath all the paint and bravado, Betty Flowers was a delicate blossom desperate for someone to love her and take care of her, and in Tide Harbor, her choices were limited. Unfortunately, as the newest unmarried man in town, she'd set her sights on him.

He gingerly helped her into the passenger seat, touching her as little as possible. She had no compunctions. Her hands brushed his chest and moved lower. He stepped back and closed the car door. She definitely planned to get him in her bed. Once there, he wouldn't put it past her to try to trap him into marriage.

And if she kept touching him, it just might happen. He'd been a long time without a woman. Dolores had kicked him out over a year ago. Summer Avery was off limits. Betty Flowers, on the other hand, was willing and able, and kind of cute when she wasn't dressed in her fantasy of a siren. And she was not someone from the States, but a Nova Scotian who knew who and what he was. He could do worse.

He climbed into the driver's seat, and Betty snugged up against him, wrapping her fingers in his ponytail. "I love a man with long hair." She sniffed along his collar. "You smell good, too. Like a forest or something." Draping herself over him, she slowly licked and kissed her way from his ear to his neck while one hand crept into his lap.

For a moment, he sat still. It would be so easy. He could whisk her back inside and replace the taste of Summer Avery with this woman's warm, willing mouth.

But no, it wouldn't be fair. Betty Flowers, the preschool teacher, deserved a man ready for commitment. He wasn't ready to marry again. He'd only cause her hurt. Better to keep it friendly until they were better acquainted.

Gil pulled his head out of reach and gently moved her hand back across the seat while avoiding looking lower where her ample cleavage was openly on display. "Betty, please. You're my daughter's teacher. I barely know you."

She sat back and pouted her lips. "Okay, I get it. You're not really interested"—she glanced at his crotch—"enough. But tonight, can you let a girl pretend? We can get to know each other a little more, and once that happens"—she patted his arm—"who knows what might come next?"

By the time they reached the White Rock, he knew more than he ever wanted to about preschool discipline, toileting accidents, and uncooperative parents—not including himself, of course. It was enough to dampen any sexual attraction he might have had for the woman and explained why she was still unwed despite her ample charms.

Praying the restaurant was empty, Gil parked the car and came around to help her out.

"Well, Gil, show's on." Betty settled her wig more firmly on her head, latched on to his arm, and snugged close. "Let's go. I can't wait to see everyone's faces when I walk in with Mr. Hot Guy."

"Hot Guy?"

Betty poked him in the chest. "You, silly."

He opened the door and a blast of beer-laden air escaped into the night. At the same moment, Betty clasped his head between her palms and kissed him hard.

Applause rose around him. Cat calls and cries of "Good catch!" drowned out the sound of plates and utensils. Someone on the karaoke stage broke into a rendition of Taylor Swift's "Mine."

He'd been had. His daughter's preschool teacher had declared them a couple. And in a small town like Tide Harbor, that could cause havoc.

Gil surveyed the crowd, hoping to see no one he knew. Halfway around the room, his eyes latched on to a pair of familiar blue-green ones. Summer, lips pressed tightly together, raised her hand then let it drop.

He should go to her, explain, but Betty had him by the hand. Before he knew it, he was sitting in the darkest corner, scanning a menu and staring into a well-satisfied woman's face.

Betty leaned in and made kissing sounds. "Okay, lover boy, I want the surf and turf. And order us a bottle of the *Jost* wines—a red, I think."

Gil glanced down at the prices, calculating the cost. It was enough to feed Lissie, Eagles, and him for a week. The exorbitant total fueled his anger.

"I'm not a wealthy man, Betty, and I don't like to be tricked."

She patted his hand. "Calm down, lover boy. It's only pretend"—she gave him a one-sided smile—"until it isn't."

"Mr. Moses."

Gil looked up.

Summer stood there, her eyes as dark as a forest at dusk, her lips pressed tight. "Are we still set to visit the Tidal Turbine Research Center on Sunday?"

Gil blinked. He'd totally forgotten about his invitation. He glanced at Betty, who was casting daggers at Summer while digging her nails into the back of his hand. He should say no, but how could he? She was trouble. She was untrustworthy. But she was still wearing his sweater.

He looked away. He had an out. He had equipment to repair, tests to run. He could refuse gracefully. Instead, he found himself agreeing.

"Uh, sure. Meet me there around noon." And in that moment, he knew he was a fool, just as his brother Aaron had always proclaimed.

Betty's nails dug in deeper. He turned to face her. She batted her overdone eyelids. "Can I come, too? School's closed on Sunday."

Gil let out a breath. Perfect, with Miss Preschool at his side, he could avoid being alone with Summer. "Sure, that's a great idea."

"So, that's settled." Summer rubbed her hands on her jeans and looked over her shoulder. "I hate to ask, but can you lend me a ten so I can get a bite? Cully Teed has my knapsack, and all my money is in it."

*Cully.* How could he have forgotten? Mr. Bearcat had a claim on her. Definitely off limits.

He stared at the overly made-up, bewigged woman sitting opposite him, suddenly grateful for Betty Flowers. He could afford to be magnanimous.

He took out his wallet and tossed Summer a ten. "Sunday, you can pay me back."

Summer frowned. "But I expected to see you tomorrow. It's Save the Sea Day. You must have heard?"

Gil grimaced. "Yes, I heard."

"Aren't you coming?"

"Not sure I'd be welcome."

She laughed. "Come. I'll protect you. Besides, you might learn something."

****

By the time he'd extracted himself from a very drunk, very amorous Betty Flowers and arrived home, Gil was ready to hit something.

He tiptoed through the living room and slipped into his bedroom, closing the door gently behind him. What he ought to do was go run or hike, but it was one in the morning, and he had to be at the boat early to finish setting up his equipment, install the webcam, and still have time to make an appearance at Save the Sea Day.

He fisted his hands. Why had he agreed? Being near her was like having his favorite chocolate fudge sundae sitting in front of him labeled, "*Do Not Touch.*"

He sat down on his bed, untied his shoes, and kicked them off. This was ridiculous. He had a job to do—catch the bomber, and instead of keeping his nose to the grindstone, he was knee-deep in woman troubles. Betty. Summer. Dolores.

Fish guts. He'd forgotten all about his ex-wife challenging the custody agreement. He needed a lawyer.

He chewed on his lip, worrying at a bit of skin. He knew only one lawyer he trusted.

Turning on the overhead light, he crossed over to his desk, powered up his laptop, and pulled up his email account. Barely breathing, he typed in the name then hesitated. He'd sworn never to contact Aaron again. Not after what he'd said about Dolores. But he had no choice. Only Aaron could straighten out the mess he was in.

He typed in the bare essentials and his cell number, hovered over the blue arrow icon for a second, and hit *send*.

Done.

He threw back his head and massaged his aching neck. He could hear Aaron laughing his head off when he opened the missive, chanting, "Told you so," like he had when they were kids. Aaron had always been the smart one, and he'd always been the fool left behind.

Gil sent an email to Seastroke Energy about the possible sighting of the bomber's boat and the dropping of another depth charge then went to close down his laptop, but stopped. He needed to take it on board tomorrow. He'd better back up all his data. Computers, small boats, and water were not always the best combination, and he hadn't done a backup since he'd contacted Seastroke about his equipment being destroyed and asking for more funds.

He shuffled through the papers littering the desk, searching for his portable hard drive. Where was it? It had been lying on the desk this morning. He gathered the papers in a pile, crawled under the desk, hitting his head in the process. The backup drive was nowhere to be seen.

He stormed out of the bedroom and threw open Mrs. Eagles' door. "Where is it?"

The old woman sat up, rubbing her eyes. "What?"

"My hard drive. Where'd you put it?"

She glanced down at his crotch and scooted back in the bed. "That's no way to talk to an old lady. You drunk?"

Gil slapped his hands over his face. The woman had no idea what he was talking about.

"No. No. It's a computer part. A black-box type thing about as big as my hand. It was on my desk."

"Don't know what you're going on about. I don't clean your desk. You made it quite clear your stuff was hands off."

"Get up. We've got to find it."

She struggled over to the side of the bed. "Fine, fine. Don't know why it can't wait till normal people waking time."

"Jiggers. It's vital to my work."

"You keep making a stir here, and your Lissie will wake up. Then we'll not be finding anything." She poked her crinkly feet into her kooky yellow slippers and stood. "Now calm down and tell me where you last saw it."

"On my desk, like I said." He stopped. "Could Lissie have taken it?"

She shook her head. "She's not been out of my sight all day."

*Bam.* He whacked the doorframe with his fist. "It's got to be here."

A screech rose from Lissie's room. The sound cut through him like a knife.

Mrs. Eagles turned on him. "Now you satisfied? No more sleep for any of us. What kind of father are you, anyway, thinking only of yourself?" She spun around and headed into Lissie's room. In the doorway, she stopped. "You have a precious child. She deserves your full attention and care, not you running around yelling and pounding on things." She stepped inside and closed the door firmly behind her.

Gil ran his hands through his hair. Mrs. Eagles was right. He was a terrible father. He'd let his anger spill over to his daughter. It was his fault Lissie had woken up frightened. He should have been the one rushing to comfort her. She'd made such progress.

He moved into the kitchen, pulled on his hiking boots and windbreaker, and went outside on the back deck.

It was a clear night. Millions of stars glittered overhead. Stars he hadn't seen in years. Even in the Boston suburbs, the sky was so light polluted only a few of the brightest were visible. He took a deep breath. After tomorrow, he would spend at least three hours every afternoon with Lissie. If it hindered his undercover work, so what? His heart wasn't in it.

If nothing else, the divorce had set him free to look for a professorship or a research project somewhere other than Boston. That was what he'd always dreamed of doing. All he needed to do was wrap it up here in Tide Harbor and quit Seastroke Energy.

*The hard drive.*

All of Seastroke's plans were on it—schedules, costs, competitor information, the data they had on the turbine terrorist. In the wrong hands, it could cause a major problem.

If he couldn't find it, Seastroke could sue him, ruin his chances at a new job. Not to mention tip off the bomber. He turned to go back in. Surely, it was in the house somewhere. They'd had no visitors, had they?

*Wait.* He wrapped his hands around the deck railing. Summer Avery had been here today for no good reason. Her mixed-up story about laundry had all the ear markings of a lie.

Heck. He'd been distracted by those kissable lips.

If EcoGreen Action's activist had stolen the hard drive, he was in big trouble, and so was she. He stamped down the steps and headed to his car. Summer Avery had some explaining to do.

# Chapter 19

## Summer

Summer opened her eyes to pitch darkness, her senses on high alert. Had she heard a noise? She lay still and listened. Wind whispered through the pines. Surf slapped the shore. Somewhere in the walls, a mouse, probably as hungry as she was, skittered.

Ignoring the growl of her near-empty stomach, she held her breath and listened harder. Nothing. Just her imagination.

She turned onto her side and yanked the comforter higher. She'd been having such a delicious dream about kissing a man who smelled like the forest.

*Crack.* A twig snapped. Footsteps crunched on the gravel drive. A man's shadow passed by her window. She shot up. Someone *was* outside the cabin.

Every muscle tensed. The flimsy door and cheap windows wouldn't keep a teen vandal out, and most certainly not a determined man.

Ingrid was right. This was *so* the wrong place to have rented.

Summer glanced around the barely furnished one-room living space. She needed something for defense, but the cabin was bare except for her sneakers, a heap of clothes, a few pots and pans, and a falling apart broom. Okay, the broom would have to do.

She grabbed the broom and hunched back on the bed, the end pointed at the doorway. She held her breath. Let the guy break in. She knew exactly where to aim.

*Thump.*

Summer tightened her grip.

*Thump.* More shuffling on the gravel.

"Anybody home? Summer. Summer Avery?"

At the sound of the voice, all the breath and tension she'd been holding in whooshed out. She lowered the broom.

Gil Moses? What was he doing here in the middle of the night? Shouldn't he be shacked up with Betty Flowers?

Heart pounding, she debated crawling under the covers and not answering. Would he leave?

She leaned the broom against the wall. Probably not. He had to know she was here with her car sitting in the drive.

*Thump.*

"Wake up. We need to talk, Summer."

She threw back the comforter. "Stop kicking the door. Coming." Shivering in the cold, she pushed upright.

"Hurry up."

Heaven's bells, he sounded angry.

She tiptoed to the door and stopped. Dare she let him in?

She looked down at the pink-flowered, thrift store flannel nightgown she was wearing. She looked like her demented granny Avery, who'd spent the last six years of her life shuffling around the farmhouse in her slippers. No way did she want Gil Moses to see her looking like a frump.

She whacked the door. "Okay. I'm awake. What are you doing here? Didn't work out with your date?"

"Date?"

"You know. Betty Boop. Our companion for Sunday."

On the other side of the door, Gil broke out in laughter. "Oh, right. She did look like a kewpie doll with that wig, didn't she?" The laughter stopped. "No. I'm here to get my hard drive."

"Your *what*?"

"My portable hard drive. The one you stole."

"*Stole?* How dare you come here, wake me in the middle of the night, and accuse me of stealing?" Summer stared at the door. She might be willing to lie for a good cause, but she toed the line at stealing outright.

"If you don't have it, prove it. Let me in."

Summer's toes curled on the cold floor. Her head screamed *no*. Her tingling skin and the heat swirling through her said *yes*.

She raised her voice. "No. Go away. Wake up the police. Let them come search."

"By the time the Mounties get here, you could have destroyed it."

There was a rub of cloth against the door, and Summer drew back. Captain Nemo must be leaning against it, that hot body, that kissable mouth, mere inches from hers. She pressed her palm flat on the thickly painted wood of the door then pulled her hand back. Dare she trust herself?

Summer pinched her lips together. She was a big girl. And a missing hard drive? She definitely had to know more about that. What did it have on it to send Mr. Moses rushing all the way out here in the middle of the night?

She clenched her fingers in the cloth of her nightgown. If it contained Seastroke Energy documents that revealed duplicity, pay offs to officials, or falsified data, it could be the key to bringing the whole tidal project to a standstill.

It might also reveal whether Gil had been truthful about being here to study lobsters. She clasped her hands together. Not that she was sure she wanted to know if he wasn't.

She leaned against the door. "Okay. If I let you in, you have to promise not to hurt me. Take a quick look around and leave."

The rubbing stopped. She imagined him moving away, his forehead creased in that little V that gave him the look of a small boy who'd lost a dime in a vending machine.

"Summer"—Gil's voice lowered—"I don't hurt women or children. I would never hurt you. Please, let me in."

Summer unlocked the door and opened it a crack. "Come in and look all you want. There is very little here. Nothing digital. Place has no wi-fi. I don't even have a computer." He didn't need to know it was riding around in Gary's truck. She hid behind the back of the door. "Do your worse before I change my mind."

Gil stepped inside, bringing with him the heady mix of sea-salted fog, woods, and the warm male scent that was his uniquely own.

Chilly bumps crept up her bare legs. She clasped the doorknob and pulled the door against her as if that battered wooden barrier could protect her from the desire churning up her insides. Letting him in had been a mistake.

She called out, "Make it quick."

His shadowed form lumbered deeper into the room. "Any lights in this shack?"

Summer ducked farther behind the door. "The switch is by the window."

*Click.*

Light from the bare bulb hanging from the ceiling flooded the room and illuminated the man. Why did he have to be so gorgeous? Long hair, straight-edge nose, sensuous mouth, broad shoulders. He wasn't a bruiser of a man, but he filled the room with his presence.

Gil peered around then set to searching every inch of the place. He looked under the chair cushions, beneath the sagging sofa, even along the windowsills.

"This place is the pits"—he wiped the dust from his hands—"and freezing cold. Doesn't the heater work?"

Summer bit her lip. "Not well. Seems to be mostly for show."

Doors banged as he opened and closed the metal cabinets on the wall over what passed as a cooking area. "Only a hot plate? No real food? Summer Avery, this won't do."

He stormed over to where she hid. "Okay. Come out from behind the door. We need to talk. I don't see my hard drive. Doesn't mean you don't have it. You were the only one at my house today, besides Mrs. Eagles and Lissie."

Summer's heartbeat sped up. Gary must have taken the hard drive while Cully argued with the housekeeper. No wonder Gil suspected her.

She'd been set up.

For a second, she was tempted to come clean, to tell Gil everything about Cully and Gary and that strange altercation with Mrs. Eagles. But if she got them in trouble, the whole anti-turbine group would think her a traitor—in cahoots with Seastroke Energy. They'd probably kick her out of town. Better she investigate what happened to the hard drive herself.

She huddled farther behind the door. "You promised to leave after you looked around."

He moved closer. "No. I promised not to hurt you. We need to talk and then"—he scanned the room a second time—"I'm moving you out of this dump. There's got to be a nice bed and breakfast in Parrsboro you can stay at."

Heaven save her from kind men with impossible intentions. Summer clenched the doorknob. "I can't afford it."

"You're broke? Is that why you stole the hard drive? To blackmail me?"

Summer pursed her lips. She really didn't like being thought of as a thief, but maybe if he had enough disgust of her, this attraction between them would die a nasty death.

"I didn't steal it. But you're right. Blackmailing you would be a great idea. Just might do that if I find it. What's on it that makes it so valuable?"

He stepped toward her and kicked the door shut. She cringed. Heavens. How could she forget? It didn't pay to antagonize a large male in small quarters.

"Enough." Gil closed in and stopped bare inches from her. His body warmth seeped through the thin flannel of her gown. "Let's start at the beginning. What are you really doing here?"

She wanted to fall into the heat of him, lay her head on his chest, join her mouth to his, and finish that kiss they'd started. Instead, she glared up at him. "I work for EcoGreen Action. You know that."

He shook his head, his breathing that of a man struggling for control. "No. That has to be a cover. You're too interested in me."

Summer narrowed her eyes and slowly looked him up and down. "Define interested?"

"You're here ... here to ... Oh, blazes." He crushed her against him. "You're here to drive me insane."

His lips met hers, his warmth and taste familiar and welcome. His hands clasped her body to his as if he were a drowning man.

He wanted her. She wanted him. The question was: could she succumb to his charms and still fight for what she believed in?

She put a hand on his powerful chest and pushed. "Wait."

Breathing heavily, he stepped back. "I am sorry. That was uncalled for. I meant only to talk, not—"

"Do you always apologize after kissing a girl?" Summer tilted her head. "I have to tell you, it's not the most romantic thing to do. Neither is this." She flicked his cheek with her finger. "Wearing someone else's lipstick while kissing me. Did you apologize to Betty Boop, too?"

"I didn't kiss her. There's nothing between us. It's all in her imagination."

"*Her imagination*? Really? So, how did her *imaginary* lipstick get all over your face?"

Gil rubbed his cheek with his palm. "Sor—"

Summer pressed her fingers over his mouth. "Don't you dare say it again." Against her fingertips, his lips were moist, his breath warm. Gil Moses was the wrong man, in the wrong place, and she was the wrong woman for him. But tonight, she was going to be selfish, ignore the consequences, and take what this man offered. And she wasn't going to be gentle about it.

After all, he had started it.

She wrapped her hands behind his neck and brought his stunned face down to hers. With a desperate need she had never felt before, she opened her mouth and raked her teeth over the inside of his lower lip, caught his tongue, drew it in, and sucked. Heat—welcomed heat—flamed through her.

For a moment, Gil let her explore. Then he joined the quest, their tongues meeting, their breaths mingling, his lips nipping and licking until she let him in.

Little by little, something inside her uncurled. She sank into his warmth. She'd been cold for so long.

She stepped closer so every part of their bodies touched. Gil Moses was all contrasts. Hard, sinewy muscle. Soft lips, hair, skin. His scent fresh, clean, and natural. And one thing was for sure—Captain Nemo was a world-class kisser.

She turned her head to get a better angle. A hum of satisfaction came from deep in her throat.

Gil yanked his mouth away. "Summer, slow down. I can't—"

"Oh yes, you can." He wasn't going to back out now. A few seconds longer, and he'd forget completely about that hard drive, and she'd get a taste of heaven.

She pulled the snaps of his nylon jacket apart.

"Oh, Summer." He shifted his weight but didn't stop her.

She glanced up. Gil peered down, his eyes dark with hunger. He was hers.

Fingers flying, she pushed the jacket down around his arms and off. The yellow nylon floated to the floor, landing with a soft *whoosh*. She barely heard it.

She shoved up his tee-shirt and ran her hands over the powerful muscles of his chest, brushing her fingers in the short, curly hair covering it. Her fingers reached the waistband of his jeans.

"No, Summer. Stop."

Suddenly, she was being lifted into his arms and carried over to the bed.

Panic set in. She flailed. Thumped his chest. She couldn't let him take control. Not now. Not when she'd had him where she'd wanted him.

She whacked him hard on the side of his head. He grunted and clasped on tighter. She renewed her efforts to twist free.

"Put me down. Let me—"

"Hush. I'm not going to do anything you don't want. I promised not to hurt you." He tripped and tumbled forward. She landed in the middle of the bed. He plopped down beside her with a thud that made the whole bed sag. Her breath caught. The old wooden bedframe creaked, shuddered, and—held.

Gil turned his head and peered at her. "Sorry?"

Summer released the breath she'd been holding and broke into gales of laughter. "You sure know how to destroy a romantic mood."

He gave a laugh and ran a finger down her cheek and over her lips. "I'm Canadian. According to the mimes, we say sorry a lot. However, I can be quite romantic, given the chance. But you need to give me that chance. Least you could do is keep the path to your bed clear of sneakers."

Tears—laughter tears, she lied to herself—gathered in the corners of her eyes. Gil Moses was a dangerous man. He knew how to make her laugh. He knew how to be kind.

"Hush. First of all, you deserve to be comfortable."

Summer opened her mouth to protest. He put his fingers on her lips.

He took the pillow and placed it under her head. "Next, you deserve to be warm." He sat on the side of the bed and fingered the neck of her nightie.

Summer's breath quickened. She gave a little shake. "Stylish, right?"

"Hmm." He undid the top buttons, leaned in, and kissed his way down her neck . "Soft, cozy flannel. Makes me think of winter nights curled up under the covers in my PJs, dreaming of a girl like you." He kissed her cheeks. First one. Then the other. "Dreaming of someone with silken skin that tastes like honeysuckle"—he slipped the nightgown off her shoulders and ran his tongue along her collarbone—"and nectarines, and I think"—he licked again—"ah, yes, and apricots." He blew on where he had licked. A chill rippled through her.

He lifted his head and peered into her eyes. "Do I hear your teeth chattering?" He stood and gently wriggled the coverlet from under her body and wafted it over her. It floated down, trapping her beneath its weight, trapping her heart.

Summer wrapped her fingers in the coverlet. She'd made a terrible mistake. Gil Moses didn't do one-night stands. He made forever love.

He ran a finger along her lower lip then pulled back. "Still too cold." He tugged the comforter up and over her head. "Ever huddle under the covers on a snowy winter night and pretend you were the only person in the world?"

She batted the polyester down and squinted at him. "Sometimes."

"I thought so." He tucked the cover around her.

Summer gazed up at him. The harsh light, streaming from the bare bulb overhead, caught the planes of his face, the high cheekbones, the broad forehead. He looked like a tribal warrior, a man who could drive away predators and keep her safe. She bit her tongue. But he couldn't.

She was set to unleash the biggest environmental protest in the Maritimes. By the time she left here, Seastroke's reputation would be in tatters, his research would be questioned, and his heart broken. If she got her hands on his hard drive, she'd use anything on it to bring him down.

No man had ever treated her so carefully, so gently. But no matter how much she wanted him, the right thing to do was to let him go untouched. Acting on this attraction between them was a mistake they'd both regret.

She pushed up on one elbow and, with what little moral righteousness she could muster, hardened her voice. "Okay, I got what I deserved. I'm comfortable and warm, all tucked in. Now go home to your little girl." She stuck out her arm and waved. "I'll ask around about the hard drive. I promise I won't blackmail you."

He caught hold of her hand. "First of all, you will not mention the theft to anyone *except me*. Second, there is one more thing you deserve."

"What?"

"To relax. You're wound up tighter than a tangled fishing reel."

He resumed his exploration of her skin. His fingers danced along her neck then wandered lower.

She flinched away

He stilled. "My fingers cold?"

Summer pressed her palm against his rock-hard chest. "No, you're a blasted furnace. I want to make it clear that I don't ... I don't do this—jump into bed with men I barely know."

He pulled back. "Trying to tell me there's nothing doing with you and Cully?"

She seized his hand and squeezed. Getting involved with the blowhard Cully after he abandoned her at Gil's place, even if he was on her side, was out of the question.

"Believe me. Definitely nothing. And there never will be."

Gil kissed her on the tip of her nose. "Good to know. I was feeling a bit like—what's his name?—Rhett Butler here." He pressed his lips against hers then stood.

She tried to untangle her hand from the sheets. Tried to catch hold, pull him back. "Wait—where are you going? We didn't ... finish."

He peered down at her. "I told you I'm a romantic. I don't do one-night stands, either."

Head spinning, she forced herself to sit up. He'd already donned his tee and jacket.

Gil exhaled and stepped back. "You're a beautiful woman, Summer Avery. And ... well, I promised not to hurt you."

Then he was gone. The door closing behind him with a snap. His car engine starting up. The tires rolling on the gravel. Then silence. Deep, lonely silence.

She wanted to chase after him. Insist he finish the deed. But she wouldn't. Gil thought he'd been kind. Instead, he'd pierced her through the heart.

Summer crawled under the comforter, drew her knees up tight to her chest, and tried not to think about the care and respect Gil Moses had shown her.

She tugged down the sleeves of the flannel nightgown. He'd even made the stupid granny nightie seem sexy.

Another shiver spread through her. She hadn't thought she'd miss anything when she eventually left Tide Harbor. Now she knew she would.

# Chapter 20

## Gil

Half an hour later, Gil stepped carefully over the trail of toothpicks leading from Lissie's room to the kitchen, glad he hadn't stomped on it in the dark. He slipped into his bedroom.

What a cad he'd been, fleeing like that. The woman probably thought him crazy. He shook himself. His sex-starved body definitely thought him crazy.

Still, Summer Avery had seemed so vulnerable lying there, wrapped in the soft flannel of her nightgown, her eyes full of something lonely and sad and frightened. He'd been afraid to go further. Bold and brassy Miss New York gave off sexy vibes, sure enough. But underneath, Summer Avery had secrets, and he didn't want to be the one who uncovered them. He had a feeling the man who did would fall so deeply in love he'd never come up to breathe.

Besides, getting entangled with a woman who most likely intended to bring the turbine project to a halt was not the brightest idea. Seastroke Energy would surely refuse to pay him. Then how would he pay Dolores her alimony?

He unlaced his hikers, kicked them off, and lay down. Then there was the hard drive. He was pretty sure Summer Avery didn't have it.

But if she didn't, who did?

Tomorrow, he'd check the webcam he'd set up at the wharf; see if it had caught any suspicious activity.

Maybe he'd get a break and uncover that bomber, at last.

*****

It was a perfect Nova Scotia morning. The kind Gil loved. Saphire blue sky. Virescent sea. Crisp air that cleared the lungs. And he had been happily enjoying it ... until Seastroke called.

Gil slipped his cell into his back pocket, a bad taste in his mouth.

His assignment had just gotten infinitely worse. His bosses at Seastroke didn't want to receive another petition or hear about another protest. Bad publicity was the last thing the company wanted. They'd moved finding the bomber down to second on his agenda and put a new item at the head of the list.

He was now tasked with shutting down the protest.

He glanced around at the milling Save the Sea Day crowds sporting the EcoGreen Action earth logo. A lot of luck he was going to have doing that.

He hadn't dared mention the missing drive. Nor Summer Avery.

Gil looked up and down the street. It was hard to believe one woman could stage something this huge in a few days. The outpouring of support from the community was overwhelming. Half the people walking up and down the sidewalk were wearing the bright aqua tee-shirts EcoGreen Action had provided. The other half were handing out brochures and collecting signatures on petitions. And every minute, more people poured in from Parrsboro, from Amherst, from Wolfsville, and even as far away as Halifax.

A whole contingent of grad students from Dalhousie's marine management program had arrived for an informational session at the town hall. He'd enjoyed talking with them. He'd not enjoyed the Halifax press who'd tried to interview him.

He waved to Ingrid, who was busy setting up a display of sea-themed, all-natural hair products outside her salon. Amazingly, all the small businesses along the main drag were participating in one way or the other. Some indicated they were donating a percentage of their sales to the anti-turbine cause. Others had set out tables featuring locally-produced crafts and foods, fishing gear, and posters about Tide Harbor's history.

Down the way, the school students stood behind a long row of tables, displaying their treasure troves of shells, rocks, and sea finds, along with reports they had written about the local marine life and why it needed to be saved.

He regretted not getting down to the dock earlier. Checking the webcam would have to wait. According to the information brochure, Cully and his buddies were taking out-of-towners for jaunts to the turbine site and demonstrating how lobsters and the various fish were caught.

He stopped at the baked goods display in front of the church and purchased a bag of sugar cookie starfish. Lissie and Mrs. Eagles would love them. He took one out and bit off one of the legs. Sugary sweetness filled his mouth.

Up ahead, Summer walked up and down the street, snapping photos. He really didn't want to see her after last night. He glanced back at the Dalhousie students. Or maybe he did.

He ambled down the street until he was behind Summer. He tapped her on the shoulder. "You know what you need?"

She spun around and blinked like a startled owl. She moved down the sidewalk. "I know what I don't need here. *You.*"

Gil trailed after her. "But you invited me, remember?"

"We saw enough of each other last night."

He raised his eyebrows. "You're lying, and we both know it." He waved his hand up and down the street. "You've done a great job pulling all this together. There's nothing wrong with wanting to save the sea. Even *I* want to save the sea, as hard as that is for you to understand. But the answer isn't fighting the attempt to produce green energy using the tides. Tidal turbines generate electricity naturally, eliminating the need for pumping oil out of the ocean floor and transporting it in tankers and pipelines, risking spills that do a lot more damage to your precious sea than carefully designed turbines ever will."

"The turbines aren't ready yet. They need more testing."

"Yes, they do. That's why Seastroke Energy is *testing* theirs." He tipped his head and gave her what he hoped was an irresistible smile. "See? Something else where we agree."

Two local teens passed them by. One of them spat at Gil's feet and hissed, "Turbine Toady."

Summer stepped away from the table and latched her arm in his. "You shouldn't be here." She tugged him toward the small cemetery next to the church.

He slipped out of her grasp. "I don't need your protection." He turned and watched the two boys sauntering away. "What I came to tell you is that I will be speaking tonight at the hall with the Dalhousie presenters."

She took a step back. "What? You can't."

"I am a graduate of Dalhousie's marine program. My old professor invited me to join them." He glared at her. "They're not stupid. There's a place for tidal turbines in the energy chain."

"You calling me stupid?"

"No. Just single-minded. Many of the grad students you've brought here to glorify fish and lobsters and clams, they're going to end up working in the tidal energy field. Turning this whole town against the turbines is counterproductive and dangerous. Turbines and fisheries can coexist. But it doesn't take much to bamboozle the public."

"Stupid? Single-minded? Bamboozle?" She rubbed her forehead. "I'm beginning to think you don't like me."

He made a low sound in his throat. "I think you know better."

She laid a hand on his wrist, setting his pulse thrumming. She lowered her voice. "Don't come tonight. Please. Some of the locals are a little riled up."

He stared down at her hand. "You're worried? I thought EcoGreen espoused nonviolent action?"

"Yes, but there are always rabble raisers, like those teens."

"I'm not afraid of some kids."

"For my sake, please, don't come."

He jerked his hand away. "Don't want your folks to hear good things about the turbines, do you?" He waved a hand at the action going on up and down the street. A photo crew had arrived and was taking pictures of the displays. A reporter held a microphone in Ingrid's face and was getting an earful.

He stiffened his shoulders. He shouldn't let his feelings for this woman make him doubt himself. "You like this— stirring people up, getting publicity. Acting like saving the environment is as easy as holding a party." He clenched his teeth. "Doesn't work that way. You're going to cause serious damage to these people's futures. The government is firmly in support of the turbine initiative." He shifted his weight from one foot to the other. "Plenty of environmentalists also favor the idea. No matter what you do, those turbines are coming, and there are going to be a lot of frustrated, angry people here." He stopped and drew in a breath. "They have to live here. While you ... you can waltz back to New York or to wherever." He turned to go, his hands fisted, his face hard. "Get ready. I am coming tonight."

****

Gil strode down the sidewalk to the parking lot where he'd left his car. Only Summer Avery could get his blood boiling so hot he lost control of what he was saying. Jiggers, he'd intimated she was only out for her own advancement.

Blasted woman. Either she was tantalizing him with her body or she was taunting him with her fool anti-turbine agenda.

She was too smart, too bold, too ... too ... *everything*. She rolled with the punches. Stood up to angry men accusing her of theft. With no whining. No running to others for help. The exact opposite of Dolores.

Not the kind of woman he'd ever thought he'd be attracted to. But he was falling for her, and he didn't know what to do about it. It had taken all his willpower to walk away last night. But if he'd feasted on what she so generously offered, he would never have been able to let her out of his reach again.

He swerved around a girl hawking plastic lobsters and crossed the street. The phone call he'd had from his boss at Seastroke rumbled in his head.

He searched out his car in the overcrowded parking lot and came to a dead halt. Someone had written *"Turbine Toady"* all over the doors, windows, and hood in yellow spray paint. He threw back his head and prayed for patience.

But a messed-up car was the least of his worries. He'd need a lot more than patience to get through this evening's protest meeting.

# Chapter 21

## Summer

Summer looked out at the mass of people in the assembly hall. It was standing room only. Normally, she'd have been thrilled to have garnered so much support so quickly for an environmental issue. She should be out there snapping photos, recording videos, and getting sound bites to send to EcoGreen's board to show them what a great job she was doing.

Instead, her stomach felt like it was full of lead, and her head throbbed with the start of a massive headache. She rubbed her temples. She never got headaches.

Any minute now, Gil was going to walk through the double doors at the back of the hall, and she had no idea how the audience would react. The Dalhousie representatives sat on the platform, waiting for his arrival. They assured her that his presentation would dovetail perfectly with theirs. She studied the bright, young faces of the grad students. She wasn't so sure.

Ingrid bounced up next to her. "Looky, looky at this crowd." She slapped her on the back. "We're going to be all over the news."

"I saw you bending that reporter's ear."

"Ya mean Dougal? Yummy guy. He and I have a hot date after the meeting. But don't worry—I'll make sure he gets the lowdown and writes it up for *The Chronicle*. He's staying for the protest, too."

Summer jerked her head around and frowned at her. "What protest?"

"The one we're having tomorrow at the Turbine Research Center."

"What?"

"It was a spur of the moment thing. Cully's idea. He thinks we should take advantage of all these people being here. It's not like Tide Harbor is a big draw for outsiders, even at the height of summer."

"But our group didn't discuss it or vote."

"Vote schmote." Ingrid wrapped an arm around her. "Sometimes, you have to seize the moment whether it's with a hunky guy or a demonstration. I got my hunky guy. You've got your demonstration." She let go. "As soon as we're done here, you need to contact all the government bigwigs and the national press. We've got a doozy of a protest planned for them."

Summer sucked air between her teeth. "When did you organize all this?"

"Gary, Cully, Betty, and I worked all last night, making the flyers and signs and stuff. The old ladies called everyone who signed our petitions. We would have asked you, too, but you were busy." She elbowed her in the ribs. "Heard you had a midnight visitor. Learn any secrets?"

Summer's headache pounded behind her eyes. "How do you know ...?"

"We got someone tailing Mr. Turbine Toady all the time."

Gil would not be thrilled to know that. "Whose idea was that?"

"Oh, Cully and some of the boys. So, spill. What's Moses like in bed? He a talker or one of those wham-bam kind of guys?"

There was a small uproar in the back of the hall. Was it Gil? Summer rose halfway out of her seat and scrutinized the new arrivals, but it was only Cully and a group of satisfied-looking fishermen trying to find seats. The noise settled down.

Ingrid glanced over at the presenters. "So, are we ready to start? Don't want our audience to get antsy, do we?"

"I thought another speaker might show up."

Ingrid frowned. "Looks like they're all here to me. There's the two crewcut guys and the three coeds in need of my hair styling skills. There's no one else from Dalhousie, is there?"

She shook her head. Ingrid would hate her if she found out she knew Gil was coming and hadn't told her.

Hands shaking, Summer grasped the microphone and, with an eye on the door, introduced the five presenters. The first student got up to speak, and she moved back to the folded chair near the side door emergency exit and focused her eyes on the enthusiastic young man talking about tidal flow. She rubbed her palms together in a vain attempt to warm them up. Where was he?

By the time the fourth speaker was finishing up a detailed overview of the ecology of clams, she'd chewed down one fingernail and started on the next. She clenched her fists. Enough with the waiting. As much as she might wish it, she couldn't imagine Gil wouldn't come. He'd been too adamant.

She looked over her shoulder and fingered her phone. Between presentations, she could slip out the exit and give him a quick ring to make sure.

The speaker droned to a close, and she jumped up as quickly as she could and snuck out the side door. Freezing cold air, thick with the scent of the sea, hit her the moment she was outside. After the overheated hall, the icy chill cut right through her unlined designer coat and set her teeth chattering.

She hadn't expected it to be so frigid or dark outside. She clasped the front of her too-thin designer coat together and slipped out her phone. She'd make this fast.

"You!"

Summer froze. The low, rough voice sent waves of panic through her. She backed against the brick wall and peered into the dark. "Who's there?"

A hunched form rose up from the rocks beyond the lee of the building. She flicked on the built-in flashlight on her cell and shone the light at the apparition. The glint from the cell caught the side of the man's face. Stubbly beard. Balding head. Opaque white eyes glaring at her.

Oh no. It was Owen Young, beer bottle in hand. She cringed. The man was rotten drunk.

He coughed and moved closer. "That you, city girl?" The reek of alcohol, old sweat, and dead fish washed over her. "Need to talk, you and me."

She wanted nothing to do with the old man. He was deranged. Unpredictable.

"Go away."

"Bad things coming down. Bad things."

Yeah, he was right about that. And he was one of those bad things.

She reached behind her and turned the doorknob. Locked. Stupid her. She was locked out.

She glanced over her shoulder. Only twenty feet or so to the front of the building and the well-lit parking lot.

Keeping flash app shining on the old man, she slid sideways, her coat catching on the rough bricks.

The man took a chug from the bottle, wiped his mouth with his sleeve, and moved closer. "That's right. You run. But that won't change things. The sea, she be angry. Not safe. You go back where you came from." He shook the bottle at her. "And take that Turbine guy with you. Let us locals handle it." He took another gulp, swayed, caught himself and, with a loud burp, stomped off into the dark.

Good riddance.

Summer turned and stumbled her way toward the front of the building, heading for light and safety. Halfway there, she tripped over a large lump and fell in a tangle of legs.

For a moment, she lay still, the air knocked out of her. Then the lump underneath her moved, and she jerked back.

"What the heck?" She scrambled away on all fours.

The lump slowly shifted. "That you, Summer?" Gil's normally brandy-smooth voice was hoarse and dry.

She clutched on to him. "Gil? What happened? Did Owen Young attack you?"

"Young? That old man? No. A bunch of fishermen happened. It was Young who chased them off." He pushed up and rubbed his head. "Good thing, too. I was way outnumbered." He scrabbled around in the dirt. "Bastards took my knife. Tried to take me."

Summer lifted her weight off him and ran her hands down his arms and legs and torso. "Are you okay?"

"Easy, girl." He caught her hands. "Nothing broken but got some tender spots. Punched me good in the jaw. Bit my tongue." He sat up and spat off to the side. "All the teeth are still there, though. That's a plus. My momma always said my teeth were my best feature."

She settled down next to him and leaned back against the wall. "I'm sorry."

He reached out an arm and pulled her against him. "What are you sorry about? You're not Canadian. It wasn't your fists that did this."

"I saw the men come into the hall. I had a feeling they'd been up to no good. Gil, I have to tell you something."

"Will you marry me?"

"No. Don't be ridiculous. The locals are following you around. That's how they knew you were coming here. They know you were at my place last night—wait." She turned and wished it wasn't so dark. Wished she see could his face. "Did you ask me to marry you?"

"Yes?"

"What in the world? Are you crazy?" She reached out and found the top of his skull. "You must be concussed."

Gil grunted and moved to stand up. "I'm definitely something."

"Where you going?"

"I'm going to get up and drive myself home in my newly decorated car. I assume speaking to the assembled multitudes tonight is a lost cause."

"But you're hurt."

"Not the first fists I ever ran into. I'll survive." He took a step, staggered slightly, and recovered. With a groan, he bent down and picked up her phone. "Kicked me in the shin. Probably some other spots I haven't noticed yet."

He exhaled sharply and helped her to her feet. "You'd better get back to give your rousing conclusion."

"Stop it."

"What?"

"Being so brave about it."

"Brave? I get knocked out by a bunch of idiots you riled up and that makes me brave? More like it makes me a fool. I should have been on the lookout for them."

"You're not a fool, Gil."

He wrapped her in his arms and kissed her on the forehead. "Oh, I'm a fool all right."

A car's headlights swept over them. He spun around.

"Got to go before the whole crowd comes pouring out." He turned and limped toward the lot.

Summer watched him get in his defaced car and start up the engine. At the last minute, she remembered the protest and called out, "Don't go to the research center tomorrow."

But he was already zooming out and turning onto the highway.

# Chapter 22

## Gil

Gil groaned as he hitched his way into the sunlit living room and sank down on the sofa. He knew there was no major damage from last night's fray, but his body thought otherwise. He slapped a bag of frozen peas on his shin and gazed at the thick, white envelope sitting on the coffee table. Dolores's custody documents had arrived.

His stomach tightened into a hard ball. He still hadn't heard from Aaron, and if his brother wouldn't defend him—and why would he after all these years?—then he stood to lose Lissie.

His cell phone rang, and he glanced at the display. Betty Flowers. The last person he felt like talking to.

He stuffed the phone back in his pocket then snatched it out again. Maybe she wanted to tell him something about Lissie, or better yet—cancel the outing to the Turbine Center.

He swiped it on. "Betty."

"Wondering if you could pick me up? My car's not been too reliable recently."

"You still want to go? Not much to see really." He thought about saying he was laid up then rejected the idea. He couldn't let the thugs think they could intimidate him.

"Of course I want to go. I can't wait to get your perspective on the turbines. Miss Avery still coming?"

"Don't know." Gil bit his lip. Summer probably never wanted to see him again. He had a vague memory of asking her to marry him. Surely, not one of his better moments.

Betty's tone softened. "That's too bad, isn't it? But I still want to go."

He looked at his watch. "That's ... great. See you shortly."

****

Thirty minutes later, he turned into the entrance road of the research center, a more normal-looking woman by his side. Thankfully, Flowers had dropped the wig and overdone makeup, lost the false eyelashes, and kewpie doll pout, too. Today, she looked like what she was—a preschool teacher, a little dumpy around the middle, her smile a bit awkward, but cute in a fresh-scrubbed way. The complete opposite of Summer Avery, flannel nightgown notwithstanding.

He'd be a lot safer cultivating a relationship with Miss Flowers.

He reached over and patted her hand. "I really appreciate you making the extra effort with Lissie. She's doing so much better since we came here. Mrs. Eagles is a wonder."

"Well, Victoria has her kindnesses. Good with the little ones. But ... well ... you should know"—she leaned in conspiratorially—"the old woman's considered a bit odd in the head. Lost a baby, she did." Betty peered out the window. "Oh, I say, what's happening?"

Gil brought the car to a dead stop, Mrs. Eagles' cheese omelet turning somersaults in his stomach.

Surrounding the research center was a mob of protestors waving anti-turbine signs and screaming into bullhorns. Reporters with cameras stood on the sidelines.

Seastroke Energy would definitely not want his face plastered across the local papers. He squinted at the three letters on the side of one of the vans. Correction—the national news.

He put the car in reverse and glanced in the rearview mirror.

Fish guts. A pickup truck had pulled up behind him, blocking the way.

Cully Teed leaned out the window. "Going somewhere, Mr. Seastroke Energy? Got some people here wanting answers to their questions. Surely, you can oblige." The lobsterman jumped out of the truck cab, stalked toward him, and yanked open the car door. "Get out, Mr. Moses. You, too, Betty."

"Fine." Gil slid out. "But Miss Flowers has nothing to do with this."

"Our Betty can take care of herself. She's one of us. It's you we want." Cully extended his hand toward the waiting mob. "This way."

Gil clamped his mouth shut and headed into the crowd. Jeers and catcalls rose around him. People pressed in, waving their signs, shouting curses in his ears.

One man in stained overalls grabbed his arm and dug his fingers in. "How dare you come tell us what to do with our Basin? Go stick the infernal machines in Boston Harbor. See how those city folk like it." He spat at Gil's feet. "Traitor!"

He shook himself free and pushed through the mob, aiming for the entrance to the building. Up ahead, he could see the visitor center's intern standing behind the glass door, twisting her hands and shaking her head from side to side. *Police coming*," she mouthed.

Gil sucked in a deep breath and readied his body. He could see the fear on the woman's face. No way was she going to let him inside. He was on his own out here with these people.

He turned around and faced the group. In his heart, he understood what motivated the angry scowls, shouted curses, and the stubborn set of their jaws. The technology was new and untried. Earlier versions of turbines had shredded whales and chopped up dolphins. The barrage design across the bay in Port Royal had changed the flow of the currents and affected fish populations.

He wiped his hands on his thighs. At the same time, the world desperately needed more sources of alternative energy. The tidal turbines planned for the Minas Basin would eventually provide all the energy needs for heating, cooking, and lighting to every home in Nova Scotia and beyond.

But people didn't like change, especially fishermen. Men who earned their livelihood at sea were probably some of the most superstitious and traditional of all Nova Scotians. You had to be when risking your life in a small boat on a wild sea, in the hope of making a haul.

And not everything made sense out there on the water. He'd been out in that world of sky and sea and seen incredible things. Water spouts. Green fog. Strange sea creatures not in any biology book.

Then there was the even more inexplicable. Whales keeping a drifting life raft heading in the right direction. Lines that mysteriously came untied or caught just in time to prevent disaster.

He looked out at the faces. Young college kids waved EcoGreen Action signs. Men with weathered skin and hard eyes held up *"Protect the Basin"* posters, stamped with the Fundy Fisherman's Organization logo. A group of First Nation men and women tapped drums. Mothers bounced babies on their hips, their eyes full of worry for their children. These were his people. He was one of them. He didn't want to hurt them.

A reporter stuck a microphone in his face. "Mr. Moses, tell us what you are doing here?"

That, he could answer. "Of course," he spoke into the mic. "I'm a marine biologist, here to study lobster populations around Seastroke Energy's test turbine installation and see if there are any impacts."

Another reporter pushed her way in. "But don't you work for Seastroke Energy?"

Gil pinched his lips together and prayed the Mounties arrived soon. "Yes. But—"

The crowd stirred. Boos rose all around him. Someone yelled, "Company shill!"

"I am a scientist, first and foremost. I will present the data as accurately and as objectively as is humanly possible."

Cully Teed shook his fist. "*Bah.* Fancy words that mean nothing. Go back to Boston and tell Seastroke Energy we want that turbine gone. Now!"

"Now! Now! Now!" the crowd echoed.

One of the student types waved an oar at him, the words *"Trash the Turbines"* emblazoned on the paddle in bright red letters.

Gil held up his hands. "Listen. Global warming is real, and it is acidifying the oceans. If we don't turn to alternative energy now, in a decade or two, there won't be any lobsters or shellfish or fish out there because the water will be unlivable for sea life. Already, we are seeing population drops across all species.

"Tidal turbines might affect the local ecology, but they will do far less damage to the environment than fracking for natural gas or drilling the seabed for more oil. In our grandparents' time, a kerosene cooker, a wood stove, and a few light bulbs sufficed. Not today. Are you willing to give up your televisions, your computers, your cell phones, and go back to the good old days?"

Gary MacDonald cupped his hands around his mouth. "No way will we let you destroy our fishery so Haligonians can stream videos."

Cully waved his fist in the air. "Get him, boys. Let's show Seastroke Energy what we think of them. Let's send Gil Moses back to his bosses with our message."

Several of the rougher-looking men surrounding him took up the cry. "Get him! Get him!"

At some pre-arranged signal, the group of toughs surged forward, a wave of fury trapping him against the building. Fear and anger turned their weathered faces into grotesque masks of hate.

In seconds, they were on him. Spit splattered in his face. A sign post whacked him on the side of the head. Another came within inches from his eye.

Saying anything had been a mistake. These men had their own agenda, and that was to bring him down. Gil tucked in his chin and kept his body tightly coiled. He didn't want to hurt anyone if he could help it.

Inch by inch, he slid sideways along the wall, but there was no escaping the angry-faced mob surrounding him.

Someone seized hold of his jacket. An elbow smashed into his shoulder. A knee caught him in the upper thigh, too close to his groin for comfort.

His mother had preached turning the other cheek. But as he'd always told her, nonviolence was a great concept until someone whacked you in the face. If he didn't defend himself, he was going to be incapacitated for weeks.

Tossing a prayer for forgiveness heavenward, he yanked himself free, threw a punch, and then another, aiming low, striking at the vulnerable spots—necks, ears, bellies— putting his attackers on the defensive while doing as little damage as he could. Fighting smart, the way his brother had taught him.

Men groaned and moved back. He wasn't a muscle man, but years hauling up lobster pots and working out in the university gym had given him a powerful punch. A small space opened around him, but the reprieve wouldn't last long. Cully Teed was pushing toward him, carrying the oar.

Someone grabbed his arm and tugged. He turned to shove the person away and came face-to-face with Summer. His heart skipped a beat. Beneath her hoodie, her face was contorted with fear, her eyes darting to the left.

"This way," she whispered, tugging again.

A fist flew at him. He pushed her behind him and ducked. Was the woman an idiot, barging into a melee? She was going to be injured, if not worse.

He elbowed one of the guys to the side, dodging more fists and kicking feet, no longer being careful, his only thought to get his would-be rescuer to safety.

Keeping her tucked behind him, he edged his way to the front of the building and what Gil hoped would be a way out of this mess.

Out of the corner of his eye, he caught a whipping movement as Cully Teed charged at him, swinging the oar and shouting, "Hands off the woman, bastard!"

All the attackers fell back, opening a path between him and Cully.

Cold sweat gathered under his collar. Adrenaline flooded through him. Had Summer Avery set him up?

The fisherman gave out a cry of victory and swung. The oar swooped through the air directly at his head.

Gil waited until the last second then dove sideways, knocking Summer to the ground in front of him. The oar hit the wall and splintered into a million pieces.

For a moment, Gil lay still, the *thunk* of the wood hitting the wall echoing through his brain. The man had meant to bash his head in. Meant to kill him.

He gave himself a shake. It made no sense. Why would a successful lobsterman risk a murder charge to do in one of Seastroke Energy's underlings?

In the distance, sirens heralded the arrival of the police. Finally.

Gil rolled over with a groan and assessed the damage. He had bruises on his bruises. His shin throbbed. Pain shot through his chest with every breath. One eye was already swelling—it would be black, for sure. He wiped his hand across the wetness on his cheek. It came up bloody. A cut from a ring.

A patrol car pulled into the lot and halted, lights flashing. The officer got out and spoke to a group of the protestors. Two women pointed toward him. The Mountie nodded and headed in his direction.

Gil pushed himself up and glanced around. The crowd had mysteriously thinned down to the stringy college kids sipping their coffees, the gray-haired elderly shuffling their feet, and the mommas minding their offspring. Cully Teed and his bruisers were nowhere to be seen.

The reporters hadn't left, though. Cameras at the ready, they trailed behind the Mountie like seagulls hovering behind a boat gutting its catch.

Gil rubbed the gravel from his palms and straightened up. How was he going to explain this to his bosses? He caught a glimpse of the Mountie's face. More importantly, how was he going to explain it to the police? Being arrested would only strengthen Dolores's custody demands.

Summer's fingers bit into his ankle. "Help me up, Mr. Turbine Man."

He twisted around. Summer lay sprawled beside him.

Ignoring the Queen's Cowboy advancing on him, Gil extended his hand and gently lifted her to her feet. He wanted to kiss her, hold her, make sure she was uninjured. But all the puzzle pieces were falling into place. The laundry lie. The stolen hard drive. Last night.

She had to have known about this protest last night at the assembly, and she hadn't said a word.

Anger flared, coursing red hot through his veins. He'd been had by another self-interested woman.

He scooped her camera off the ground and dangled it in front of her. "Was this your idea of a non-violent publicity event?"

She grabbed the camera and shoved the strap high on her shoulder. For a moment, her lips quivered then firmed. "Maybe. Do you want it to be?" She touched the slash on his cheek with her finger. "You're injured."

"You might say that."

The policeman halted in front of them. "Gil Moses?"

Gil broke away from Summer and her lies and nodded.

"Come with me. We have several complaints against you."

# Chapter 23

## Summer

Summer watched one of the officer's handcuff Gil and shove him into the back of the patrol car. One of the protestors was pushed in to join him. The other policeman took statements from several of the others. Then they were gone. All around her, cars slowly started up and disappeared down the drive. It was over.

"You did great. Distracting him like that was brilliant."

She whirled around and came face-to-face with Ingrid. Betty stood behind her, arms stretched out in the victory sign.

Ingrid wrinkled her nose at her. "Between you and Betty, the poor guy didn't suspect a thing." The hairdresser seized her hand. "Come. Cully can't wait to thank you."

Summer swiveled her head around. "Cully? Where'd he disappear to?"

"Into the woods. Has to protect his rep. He'll be back in a minute now the cops are gone."

Betty bounced up and down on her toes. "What a fight. I was sure Cully was going to get the bastard, but he missed."

She narrowed her eyes. "I thought you liked Gil?"

"Sure. Just the way you *like* him, eh? Between the two of us, we got him all confused, didn't we?" Betty elbowed her in the side. "Those recently divorced guys, always hungry for the gals. Bet he was two-timing his wife, too."

Summer stared at the woman. Had Gil lied to her? Had he been banging Betty Boop before he visited her? Was that why he hadn't—

Betty swung her arms out. "What a piece of shit. Those Seastroke people don't care a bit about us folks here. Sending us a lecherous Nova Scotian to shove their turbine down our throats. Well, we fixed him but good." She pointed to Summer's camera. "I hope you got some pics of him hitting the guys for the court case."

"Court case?" Summer swallowed hard.

"Already got us a lawyer. Gonna sue him and Seastroke Energy for medical bills and damages. Why, poor old Alan Hill's sporting two black eyes. One of the kids got his nose broken. We're lucky no one was killed. Turbine Traitor had a knife."

Summer shook her head. Gil'd said he lost it in last night's melee. "I didn't see—"

Ingrid patted her hand. "You were behind him. But don't you worry—everyone in Tide Harbor is ready to testify to his violent nature and unprovoked attack on innocent protestors."

"*Violent nature?*" She looked from one woman to the other. "*Unprovoked?*"

"You're not thinking straight, Summer. Think of all the bad publicity for Seastroke Energy. Corporate bastards will be happy to take their turbine and run by the time we drag them and their sorry employee through court."

Betty leaned over Ingrid's shoulder. "A big, scandalous trial will be covered in all the major newspapers. Be on TV. Gonna put Tide Harbor on the map. Show the world we won't stand for a huge corporation sending thugs to attack us. Wait till you see what we plan to do next."

Ingrid yanked on Betty's sleeve. "Enough. Let's go congratulate our hero. This was all his idea." She waved toward a truck parked near the main road. "Cully's back."

Summer curled her lip. *Some hero.* Hiding in the bushes while everyone else took the blame.

She rushed across the gravel lot, not sure if she should give Cully Teed a dressing down for attacking Gil or play nice and find out what was going on.

She pictured the blood running down Gil's face, the oar coming down toward his head. He might be on Seastroke's payroll, but he didn't deserve what the mob had done to him.

Somehow, she'd lost control of the protest group she'd started, and if things kept going the way they were, she was sure to get the blame. If someone was severely injured or worse—killed—in a protest under the auspices of EcoGreen Action, she'd be kicked out of environmental work forever. Heaven's bells, if someone died, she'd never be able to live with herself.

Cully lounged against the side of Gary's truck, looking no worse for his altercation with Gil.

Ingrid gave Summer a push forward. "Here she is, Cully. Worked out great. We had a front row seat, so to speak. And Summer couldn't have done better if she tried."

With a wink in their direction, Cully stood up and approached her. "Now you see what we're fighting. Did you hear the garbage Turbine Guy was spouting?" He took her by the shoulders and shifted her around so she faced the sea. He waved his hand toward the Minas Passage. "Destroy all this so the rest of the province can power all their fancy electric stuff. That's just plain fish-brained. You can't eat cell phones or computers or televisions." He nodded at Betty and Ingrid. "We're never going to let that happen."

He snugged Summer against him. "And here's our secret weapon. We have one more thing planned. After that, there will be no more need for you to pretend you're hot for that toady anymore. Gonna be just you and me, city girl." He gave her a smacking kiss on the cheek. "You and me and a turbine-free sea." He turned to her two companions. "Right, ladies?"

"Yay!" Ingrid pumped her fist in the air.

Betty grinned. "You got it, Cully."

"Let's go, Bets." Ingrid tugged her sleeve. "Give the lovebirds a little *privacy*." They took off across the lot.

Summer gazed after them. The last thing she wanted was to be left alone with Cully. Mr. Bearcat might act all jovial and easygoing on the surface, but minutes ago, he'd shown his true nature. He'd been a furious bull, intent on doing deadly damage to a man who was only trying to do his job—measure lobster populations.

Sure, he was probably jealous after Gil's midnight visit, but bashing the man's head in was beyond extreme and certainly not the way to win over government officials.

If she hadn't needed the anti-turbine group's support to stop the tidal energy project, she'd have stomped off after the two women. Instead, she swallowed down the bile gathered in her throat and steeled herself.

She wiggled out of Cully's hold. "I'm nobody's weapon. I don't know what you've planned, but all this is getting out of control. EcoGreen Action supports *nonviolent* protests, not what happened here today. You nearly killed the man."

Cully's hand came down, cupped her bottom, and gave her a pat. "Nearly doesn't count."

Summer arched away from him.

He drew her back against him. The rigidity in his arm held a warning. "There's going to be a big story breaking any day now involving our Mr. Moses. He's not who you think he is. You wait and see." He reached behind the passenger seat of the truck, whipped out her backpack, and handed it to her. "Here you go. You're going to need your goodies to do the job."

Finally, she had her stuff back, after all the runaround he'd given her.

She snatched the bag from his hand. "What job?"

"You're going to put some information on Mr. Moses' computer for us."

"Huh? What information?"

"It's on the hard drive in your bag."

Summer gave her pack a shake. It felt bulkier and heavier. She peeked inside then glanced up. "That's Gil's missing hard drive. I thought so. You and Gary stole it."

"Of course." Cully laughed. "And you were so kind not to mention that little tidbit to him. Now all you have to do is give it back."

"What's on it?"

"Nothing to worry your pretty head over. Let's just say it will get Mr. Moses all fired up."

"I don't think—"

Cully pressed his finger to her lips. "No thinking necessary. Plug in the drive and download the file labeled *Tide Harbor Turbine* onto his desktop."

"No. It's wrong. You should never have taken it in the first place."

A dark look flashed across Cully's face, sending shivers down her spine. Then it was gone, hidden behind that free-and-easy smile and those weather-crinkled eyes, blue as the Minas Basin on a sunny day. He shook his head. "You haven't gone all sweet on him, have you? 'Cause he's the enemy, remember?"

Summer swallowed. She *was* sweet on Gil—more than sweet. But that was irrelevant. Gil Moses definitely wasn't sweet on her, especially after today. But she didn't really want to hurt him any more than she already had.

"I'll never get to his computer without him knowing."

"Mr. Moses is going to find himself charged with assault. That should keep him hemmed in and out of your hair for a while. If you hurry, it'll just be the old lady and the kid."

"Assault? But—"

"Didn't you see how he broke that boy's nose?"

"But he was under attack, defending himself."

Cully shrugged. "No difference to the law. The Mounties will let him out on a peace bond, but he'll have to pay a fine and avoid anything to do with the turbine protests. Not get into any more fights." He winked. "Of course, that might just be a little hard to avoid. Tempers are quite riled around here."

He scuffed his feet in the gravel. "You know what, Summer? Go ahead. Take a good look at what's on that hard drive. You'll see. Gil Moses is a lowdown, lying bastard who'll do anything to get those turbines installed, even shack up with you."

Was it true? Summer swallowed, remembering how desperate Gil had been to find the drive. She slung the pack over her shoulder. "Okay. I'll check it out. Then I'll decide what to do."

A smile slowly spread across Cully's face. He opened the truck door and put one foot inside. "I'll be at the Tav if you need a shoulder to cry on."

Summer headed toward her car as fast as she could. She couldn't wait to see what was on that hard drive. Because as much as she tried, she couldn't imagine the man she was coming to love was the villain Cully thought he was.

****

An hour later, Summer pulled her Hyundai into Gil Moses' driveway and turned off the engine. She was so angry every part of her body was shaking. Hands clutching the steering wheel, she glanced at the drive lying atop her backpack.

It was all there in the files. Gil Moses wasn't in Tide Harbor to do a valid research study. Studying lobsters was his cover. He reported to Seastroke Energy regularly. His assignment was to catch the turbine bomber. Number two was to stop her protest movement. The man even thought she might be in league with the crazy bomber.

All those kind words, those soft kisses, that almost love scene, the ridiculous marriage proposal, had been designed to distract her, while he undermined her. And Seastroke Energy worked behind the scenes, wooing the government officials and big-name businessmen. The list of the pro-turbine supporters, she'd found, was impressive and depressing.

She slammed her hand on the dashboard. Gil Moses deserved every blow and kick he'd gotten. He deserved whatever surprise Cully had put on the hard drive. She'd love to know what it was Cully wanted her to download, but the file required some special program to open it.

Didn't matter.

She scooped up an EcoGreen Action flyer with the picture on the front of the Minas Basin she'd taken that day on Gil's boat. She brushed her finger over the photo. He'd seemed so honest, so concerned for the environment, while he was helping Seastroke stick that turbine in the Minas Passage. She crumbled the flyer and tossed it to the floor.

Enough railing. Time to take action.

She stuffed the drive in her backpack, slammed open the car door, and stomped up onto the deck. She'd tell the old lady Gil had sent her to check something on his computer, do the dirty deed, and get out of the place. Who knew when the police would let Gil out?

Before she could knock, Mrs. Eagles opened the door wide and gave her a cheery smile she didn't deserve. "Miss Avery, a pleasure to see you again. Come in. Come in."

Summer put on her most innocent expression. "Gil asked me to hook this up to his computer." She held out the drive.

Mrs. Eagles wrinkled her nose. "What is that?"

"A hard drive."

The old woman raised an eyebrow.

"A part for his computer."

The woman threw out her hands. "Oh, that's what he was looking for. Come in. You can put it on his desk."

Summer stepped fully inside, tossed her coat and backpack over the arm of the chair nearest the door, and inhaled the aroma of roasted chicken wafting from the kitchen. Her stomach growled. She'd been running on one granola bar since dawn.

"Smells delicious, Mrs. Eagles."

"My gran's recipe—maple chicken. Come snitch a taste." The old woman peeked around her. "Where's Mr. Moses?"

She eyed the hallway that led to the bedrooms. She needed to do the dirty deed fast. Last thing she wanted was to have a long-winded talk with Mrs. Eagles. Still, the woman deserved to know what had happened.

"He's been arrested for assault, but I'm sure it will be fine. He was only defending himself."

The old woman twisted her hands in her apron. Her lips trembled. "*Assault*?"

Summer couldn't help feeling sorry for the woman. If Gil left, she'd be out on the street again. "He'll be home soon."

"Daddddddddy." Lissie bounced into the living room and stopped dead. She rocked back and forth on her bare feet, her mouth flapping open and closed. "Daddddy?" She bobbed her head and, with a hop, disappeared back into her room.

Mrs. Eagles sank down on the sofa. "She's a little clockwork, Lissie is. She knows it's time for him to take her to Miss Betty's."

"You want me to take her?" The little girl didn't need to suffer because her father was a louse.

The old woman raised her hand. "Don't bother. Lissie's happier here, to tell the truth. Miss Betty does her best, but she doesn't understand her the way I do."

"Kermiiiii!" Lissie charged out of her room, Summer's garish green sweater swaddled around her neck. "Kermiiii!" She halted in front of Summer and jumped up and down, yelling at the top of her lungs, "Kermii! Kermiii!"

Summer peered at the housekeeper. "She remembers me."

Mrs. Eagles grinned. "Of course she does. She's smart, my little princess. Really smart."

Lissie stopped inches away from Summer and jerked her head back and forth, curls bouncing with each jerk. Smart? Summer had plenty of experience with children. She'd raised two younger brothers.

She knew how to look the other way when her brothers ate all the cookies she'd baked to sell at the farmer's market. She knew how to patch a pair of jeans torn on a barbwire fence so that they could be worn to school the next day. But she had no idea what to do with this jerking, hopping sprite. Watching the little head spin back and forth was making her dizzy. Her normal reaction would be to grab the child and hug her tight. But that hadn't worked so well the last time she'd tried it.

She looked at Mrs. Eagles. "Make her stop. She's gonna give herself brain damage or something."

The old woman pursed her lips. "Seems to me Lissie wants to play with you. Try doing what Mr. Moses did. I'm off to rescue the chicken before it burns up."

"Huh? Act like a frog? How's that going to help?" She glanced up. Mrs. Eagles was gone. She looked back at Lissie, who had edged closer. She could hear the child's teeth snap with every jerk of the head. "Okay, okay. Gribbet? Gribbet."

Lissie swung her head faster.

She slipped the hard drive into her pocket and looked longingly at the hallway. So much for a quick in and out. She could never ignore a child.

Summer sat down on the sofa and rubbed her hands on her thighs. "Sorry, Lissie, I'm not real good at frog sounds.

But I tell you what, I do know a frog song." It was probably not the most appropriate song, and really wasn't about a frog, but it had been her brothers' favorite, sending them into gales of laughter even when they had little to laugh about. She hummed the melody, searching for the words.

Lissie's head stopped its frantic spinning. Her tongue poked out. She tipped her head sideways and, in a tiny voice so at odds with her usual screams, said, "*Sing.*"

"Here goes, girl." Summer took a deep breath and sung the first words she remembered adding a special twist. "*Five little Kermies jumping on the bed, one fell off—*"

The front door opened. Gil, a vicious red cut marring his cheek and a dark bruise beneath his eye, stepped into the living room and stopped dead. He blinked hard, as if that could make her disappear.

"*You.*"

Summer glimpsed the weariness in his posture, the pain in his eyes, and the song died in her throat. Yes, they were on opposite sides, but all she wanted to do was wrap her arms around him and take the hurt away.

She would have fled if she could, but she was trapped. Her coat and daypack rested on the chair behind Gil and, more importantly, Lissie stood in front of her, inches from her knees.

Lissie looked at her then at her father. Her brow furrowed, as if making a major decision. Then, with the quickness only a young child was capable of, she clapped her hands in Summer's face. "*Sing.*" She turned to her father and clapped again like some primo conductor at the Met. "*Sing.*"

Gil's mouth dropped open. He glanced at Summer, lifted a shoulder, and joined her in belting out the song, complete with hand gestures and wiggling shoulders and hips.

Summer eyed those gyrating hips, and her face grew hot. For a moment, her voice faltered. She hated that she was attracted to the man. It made what she had agreed to do to his computer so much harder. Though at least he'd have the hard drive back.

She forced herself to refocus her attention on the bouncing child and kept singing.

Lissie glanced back and forth between them, wiggling along with them as they sang a mishmash version of verses.

The song ended. Laughing, Gil flopped down on the sofa next to Summer. The seat cushion sank under his weight, tipping them together. Summer fisted her hands and held her spine rigid, but it was no use. He was so close the heat of his body soaked into her. His scent filled her nose. And all her anger fizzled into cold, hard guilt.

Gil Moses could never be a villain.

She'd known he was for the turbines from the beginning. He worked for Seastroke Energy. Of course he would want to silence the protest group and stop the bomber. Heck, she wanted to stop the crazy guy, too.

Those things didn't make him a bad man. It made him hard-working, loyal, and good at what he did.

He turned to her, his battered face alive with joy. "Lissie talked." Their eyes caught and held. His irises, dark brown like the depths of a cedar pond, had a softness in them that spoke of gentle touches and long-lasting passion.

For a second, all her resolve twisted. She could forget the hard drive. She could forget the promotion at EcoGreen Action. She could turn her back on Cully and all the anti-turbine supporters, and she could have this man.

He was a good man. He would forgive her. He would keep her warm and fed and comfortable. He would give her children and grow old with her. He would give her his heart.

And she would break it.

They'd always be on opposite sides. He was a company man, and she would never break her promise to her father and stop fighting to save the environment.

She gave Gil a weak smile. "That chicken sure smells delicious. I'll go see if I can help Mrs. Eagles with it."

# Chapter 24

## Gil

Gil watched Summer slip into the kitchen. He'd been wrong about her. She'd be a wonderful mother. Lissie had attacked her. Twice. Still, she hadn't pulled away or ignored Lissie the way Dolores would have. She'd sung to her. He couldn't remember Dolores ever singing—not a lullaby, not a nursery rhyme, not a pop hit.

And they'd laughed. It had been a long time since he'd had any reason for laughter. A long time since he'd seen Lissie so animated. The "Five Little Monkeys" song earwormed through his head. He rubbed his ear. And to choose that ridiculous song. Somewhere in Summer's past, there'd been a fun-loving child.

"Daddy. Boo-boo." Lissie extended her finger toward him.

Gil stilled. From infancy, Lissie had avoided making direct eye contact on her own. Head down, she looked at her feet or the rug or something only she could see.

He'd done everything to get her to look up—waving a toy in front of her, cupping her face between his palms, pushing up her chin. And she'd fought back, keeping her neck so rigid he feared he'd injure her with his efforts. It hadn't helped that Dolores had considered his attempts useless and mocked him at every turn. The child was an idiot; what did it matter if she grew up crooked?

He'd given up, content to get a glimpse of a perfect pink mouth, a turned-up nose, and a flash of eyes when she was awake.

But now he could see what he'd missed while he'd been slaving to provide Dolores with her dream, followed by a year living alone in an apartment downtown, fighting for custody. Lissie had grown and left babyhood behind.

Her fingers were less chubby. Her cheeks no longer baby round. Her nose straighter. There was a hint of cheekbones and heavy-lashed eyes. She looked so much like his sister that goosebumps ran up and down his arms.

Lissie edged closer, her finger outstretched, totally focused on *him*.

He held his breath. When she made contact with the cut on his cheek, the touch was no more than that of a butterfly settling. But it felt like she touched him all the way to his heart.

She tipped her head. "Ouchy, Daddy."

Not only was she touching him, she was showing empathy. Something they'd been told she'd never be capable of.

Gil wanted to pull her into his arms, tell her he was all right, that they were going to be all right. But he knew better. He settled for a smile, a smile so big, so wide, she had to see it.

Lissie stared at him for a second, her mouth opening and closing like a landed fish. Then, slowly, her lips pulled up into a small matching smile. And in that moment, everything was perfect.

Then all bedlam broke loose. Something fell and smashed in the kitchen. Mrs. Eagles said a word he thought outside her vocabulary, and Lissie, screaming, slapped her hands over her ears and curled up on the floor in tight little ball.

"I agree. Too loud. Too angry. I'll fix it, sweetheart." Gil gave a groan and forced himself to get up. He had bruises all over his body, the worst on his shins and ribs. Nothing earthshaking. But it hurt. And he was definitely going to be stiff for several days.

He headed for the kitchen and cautiously popped his head in. Summer was standing with two potholders in her hands and a broken casserole of chicken at her feet. She peeked at him from under her curls, her mouth twitching.

"Sorry?"

He would have laughed if Mrs. Eagles hadn't looked so furious. The old woman put her hands on her hips. "Sorry doesn't do it, lady. That's our dinner decorating your feet."

Gil moved past the housekeeper and bent down to gather up what was left of the meal.

"Wait." Mrs. Eagles laid a hand on his shoulder. "You're hurt, Mr. Moses. Just look at that eye." She scowled at Summer. "You didn't say Mr. Moses was injured, or I'd have taken care of it right quick. Treated many a black eye on my old man." She turned back to Gil. "Now, you sit right down here. Let her clean up the mess she made. Need potato juice on that swelling, or you'll not be seeing straight for days."

Gil frowned. "Potato juice?"

Mrs. Eagles opened the refrigerator door. "Works wonders. Luckily for you, I still have a few spuds left."

He looked across at Summer, who was bending over, giving him a good view of her rear end, and grinned. "That's me—lucky."

****

Two hours and a pizza delivery later, Gil wasn't so sure about his luck. Mrs. Eagles was driving him crazy, pressing cotton balls dripping with some gross liquid against his sore eye, leaving the front of his tee-shirt sticky with the starchy drips. Lissie had crawled under the twin bed in her room

186

and wouldn't come out. And Summer refused to listen to him.

He pushed Mrs. Eagles' hand away, stood, and tried again. "You can't go back to that pit you're staying in. It isn't fit for human habitation. Stay here tonight. Tomorrow, I'll help you find something better. Should have done it yesterday."

Summer twisted her hands together. "Don't need your help, Gil Moses. Don't need anyone's help. I can take care of myself."

Gil took a step toward her. Having the woman here, so close—he inhaled the sweet, honeyed scent of her with every breath—would drive him mad. But a gentleman did not let a woman put herself in danger. And the dump she was in *was* a danger, if not to her health, to his. He'd not sleep a wink thinking of her there all alone.

He worked at softening his voice. "Be reasonable. It's late. It's dark. Anyone can break into that place. I'd worry about you."

Her mouth scrunched up. "Don't need your worry, either."

"Let her go. There's nowhere here for her to sleep," Mrs. Eagles huffed behind him.

He was not going to be dissuaded. He had a bad feeling about letting the woman out of his sight. She'd lied to him and ratted on him, and she'd let her protesters run amuck, but he didn't think it was personal. In fact, after her response to him the night before last, he knew it wasn't.

Gil turned and glared at Mrs. Eagles. "Have you seen that dump Keddy's rented her? It's unlivable. It would be criminal to let her stay there another day. She can sleep on the sofa, for heaven's sake. Even the floor here would be better. Now stay out of this."

The old woman backed up a step, her mouth pinched tight. "Whatever you say, Mr. Moses. You're the boss."

Summer circled the table and pressed her hand against his chest. "Go ahead. Browbeat your *employee* all you want. Can't boss me around. Sorry, Mr. Good-Deed Moses, but I'm leaving." Her voice lowered. "You'll thank me in the end."

Gil held his breath, all his senses focused on the heat of that small palm pressing his wet shirt to his skin. "Thank you?"

Her hand slipped a little lower. She bit her lip and nodded. "Thank me." She gave him a little push then stomped into the living room, hips swinging as she maneuvered through the doorway.

Gil trailed behind. He wanted to wrap his arms around her and never let go, but if she insisted on leaving, he couldn't physically stop her, as much as he wanted to. That left begging, and he hated to beg. Oh jiggers, he'd beg.

"Stay. Please. You can help with Lissie."

Summer picked up her coat and slipped it on. "Mrs. Eagles is better with her than I am."

"She likes your singing."

"Shows she has no taste. Better expose her to some Aretha Franklin quick like." Summer peered around the room. "Where's my backpack?"

"That red thing?"

"Yeah. I put it down on the chair with my coat." She cast a glance around the room again. "My car keys are in it."

"Uh-oh,"—Gil couldn't help grinning—"you might be staying after all."

"Wipe that look off your face. Perhaps I left it in the car." She opened the front door and went to step out.

Gil slipped past her. "Hold on. I'll look." He dashed down the steps and tried the driver's side door. "Locked!" he yelled back as he circled the car, testing every door. "Definitely locked. And not a glimpse of a backpack." He bounded back up the steps. "Sorry. Looks like you're staying."

Summer stuck her tongue out at him. "And you're not sorry one bit."

Gil put his hands on her shoulders and turned her around. "It has to be in the house somewhere. We can look for it in the morning."

She arched away from him. "We can look for it right now."

They stepped back inside.

Mrs. Eagles stood, hands on hips, her mouth twisted. "You looking for a red bag, Miss Avery?"

"You found it?"

The woman wrinkled her forehead. "Could say so. Lissie has it under the bed with her."

Gil's stomach sank. He was going to have to let Summer go. "I'll get it."

Mrs. Eagles moved in front of him. "No. She's curled up around it, asleep. You'll have to wait till she wakes up in the morning."

Summer pushed her hand through her hair. "The couch, it is."

Gil shook his head. "You won't be comfortable there. Take my bed." He lowered his head and studied the carpet. The word bed gave him all sorts of ideas he shouldn't be having, especially about a woman whose followers had attacked him only hours ago.

She rolled her shoulders. "Concerned about my comfort again?"

He gave her a hard look. She was avoiding his eyes and looking down at her hands. Her snappy retort lacked its usual zing. He wasn't the best at figuring out women's feelings—just ask Dolores—but the way she was behaving looked a lot like guilt to him.

He should want her to feel guilty. His face throbbed. Every breath hurt. He was going to have tell Seastroke Energy he'd been arrested, and Dolores—blasted—the arrest gave her a basis to demand custody back.

But first, he needed to straighten things out here. And for some reason he didn't want to examine too closely, he didn't want Summer feeling guilty, not about him.

He stepped toward her and put a hand on her cheek. She flinched but didn't pull away. "Look, some bad things happened today. But I don't blame you for what your followers did."

She raised her head. "That's magnanimous of you."

Her eyes were so big and her mouth so enticing, he couldn't resist the invitation. He dropped a quick kiss on her lips.

Summer jerked back, a hand over her mouth. "What was that for?"

He licked his bottom lip. "For thinking I'm magnanimous."

Mrs. Eagles glanced from Summer to Gil. "So, that's the way of it. Well, I'm telling you, Mr. Moses, better not be planning on shacking up, the two of you. Not under the same roof with me and that darling child. Don't know how she'd react, but I do know how I will."

Gil wanted to strangle the woman.

He spoke through gritted teeth. "I would never do anything to harm my daughter."

"Good. You're injured. You sleep in the bed"—she pointed a finger at Summer—"and she sleeps on the chesterfield. And that's exactly what I want to see when I wake up in the morning. No hanky-panky." With that, the woman stomped into her bedroom and shut the door.

"Bossy employees you have here, Gil." She gave him a Cheshire cat smile.

It took all his willpower to answer. He kept his voice low. "She's right. Except about where you're sleeping. You get the bedroom."

"Do you always have to be a gentleman?"

"Always. My momma taught us boys right." He winked. "Ladies come first."

She walked over and put a finger on his lips. "I would have liked your momma."

All he had to do was open his mouth and suck that finger in. Pull her against him and taste her again. But one taste would never be enough.

He pinched his lips closed and stepped back. "Scoot. My room has its own bath. Take a shower. Relax. And lock the door."

Summer tipped her head. "Can't quite figure you out."

"Yeah?"

"You've got too much control for a man. Sooner or later, something's going to give."

Gil turned his back to her and rummaged in the coat closet, pulling out the extra blanket and pillow. Control? Miss New York might be a liar and a trickster, but one part of his anatomy didn't care.

And if she didn't get out of his sight soon, she'd learn exactly how uncontrollable he could be.

Holding the pillow strategically, he turned to face her. "Go get some sleep, Summer. There are circles under your eyes."

She snapped her head around and pursed her lips at him. "Very romantic, Mr. Moses, very romantic."

"You heard my bossy housekeeper. Not trying to be romantic. Go to bed. Lock the door."

"*Fine.*"

From the corner of his eye, he watched her disappear through his bedroom door. The woman moved like a siren— shoulders back, hips swaying. He fought the urge to get up and follow her.

The door shut. The water came on. Good. She was in his shower, using his soap.

Gil sank down on the sofa, whipped off the sticky tee, slipped out of his jeans. Then he plumped the pillow under his head and drew the cover over him.

He hadn't seen her body in the dim light of her cabin, but he'd touched enough of it. Right now, water was running over that silky skin, running down her curves. Touching her in all those places he wanted to touch. Darn it all, he wanted her.

He threw off the blanket. Temptation was a few feet away. All he had to do was sneak in and—

He clamped his teeth together and rolled over to face the sofa back. Mrs. Eagles was right. He had no business thinking about making love to Summer Avery. She was a temptation all right. One that was set on making trouble for him.

The only way the protestors could have known he would be at the research center at noon was if she had told them. Then pretending to help him so the crowd would be incited to more violence? Miss EcoGreen Action was in cahoots with the crazier elements of the anti-turbine group. It was her fault he'd gotten arrested.

He rubbed a sore spot on his ribs. The charges against him would be taken care of. Seastroke Energy would probably fire him after all this, but as long as he was on their payroll, they'd defend him. But he didn't like fighting, and he didn't like being tricked. He just wished Summer Avery wasn't so attractive and smart and good with Lissie.

He'd had more fun with Summer in the few days he'd known her than he ever had with Dolores. Dolores had been his dream woman—perfect, fragile, too good for a boy who'd grown up a lobsterman's son. A princess to put on a pedestal and worship. Summer was bold and stubborn and tart-mouthed and didn't put up with his nonsense.

And she wanted him.

The way her face looked when he'd left her that night, lying swaddled in that flannel nightie, had nearly broken his resolve.

Enough tormenting himself. He closed his eyes and concentrated on mentally organizing all the equipment he would use for his data collection foray scheduled for tomorrow. Luckily, everything he needed was in his car. He'd get up at dawn and head down to the wharf. Along the way, he'd check out the boats out on the water and the webcam.

He'd only had a glimpse over a distance, but the boat that had dropped the depth charge during daylight had appeared to be deep blue below and white on top. It wasn't a Tide Harbor working vessel. He'd checked. Most of the locals considered dark blue an unlucky color for a boat. But there were plenty of coves and inlets along the coast where a non-commercial boat could be moored out of sight.

The shower stopped, and all thought of boats and nets fled, replaced by the image of a naked Summer. She'd be getting out. Drying herself with his towels. Climbing into his bed. Snuggling under his sheets.

Gil shifted again on the sofa and groaned. It was too small and too narrow, and he was too aroused to sleep. Making love to that woman was inevitable. But not now. Not with Lissie sleeping a wall away.

He should maintain some decorum in the house. He had no idea how Lissie would react if she found him in bed with Summer. And it certainly wouldn't help his custody case to be sleeping around within a few months of the divorce. Aaron would kill him. Lissie had to come first.

Gil jerked up, heart thumping. *The custody suit.* Paperwork had to be filed by the end of the week, and he still hadn't heard a thing from his brother.

He pressed his fingers to his temples. Maybe Aaron had emailed. He hadn't checked his cell phone or the computer today, what with the arrest and the distraction of Summer. That woman sure messed with his head.

He reached down to the floor and searched through his jeans pocket. No cell. That's right, he'd left it in the car, along with all his other belongings the police had packed neatly into a plastic bag. Battery was probably dead, anyway.

He peeked at his bedroom door. Dare he sneak in and take a peek at his laptop?

Swallowing down a groan, Gil rolled off the sofa. He'd never sleep worrying. Besides, Summer had to be asleep by now. He'd make it quick.

Holding his breath, Gil slipped silently toward the door, his footfalls muffled by the carpet. He held out his hand and grasped the doorknob. He'd told Summer to lock the door.

Part of him prayed she had. The other part—

The cold metal knob turned. *Yes.* Unlocked. His heart beating so loudly he feared it would wake everyone in the house, he slipped inside and glanced at the bed. Faintly illuminated by the clock radio, a hump of bedding lay in the center of the mattress. Good, Miss Temptation was buried under the covers, not a hair showing.

He tiptoed to his laptop and flipped it open. The screen saver disappeared, and a blinking icon appeared on the desktop, probably one of those annoying pop-up ads. He'd take care of that in the morning. Right now, he needed to hurry.

He clicked on his account, opening his email and quickly scanning the inbox. Most were from Seastroke Energy, but there, finally, what he been waiting for—Aaron's reply. He held his breath and opened it. The message didn't say much, but he hadn't expected much. Not from Aaron.

He read the words: *Coming. Bringing papers.* And below, almost as an afterthought, *Stay out of trouble, Gilly Boy.*

A chill ran down Gil's spine and settled like a stone in his stomach. Aaron was coming. He'd sworn to never see him again. If bigwig Halifax lawyers, like his brother, needed papers signed, they overnighted them or sent them with a lackey. They didn't deliver them personally to clients in back-of-nowhere places like Tide Harbor.

Gil gave himself a shake in a futile attempt to chase away the chills crawling up and down his spine. Why was

Aaron coming? Their whole relationship was based on them never meeting in person ever again in this lifetime.

He slumped in the chair, unable to summon the energy to move. All he could see was Aaron's furious face the day he and Momma had left. The day they'd buried their sister.

He leaned forward to turn the computer off then stopped. He clicked the flashing icon and groaned.

"Bad news?"

The whisper cut through him. He snapped the laptop closed and spun around.

Summer stood behind him, wearing one of his old tee-shirts. It hung to her knees but clung in all the right places. The radio's neon blue light illuminated her like a museum spotlight on the statute of some exotic sea goddess.

Gil threw back his head and drank the vision in with a hunger he could not control. His gaze traced the curve of her neck, the convexity of her breasts, the small indentation where her waist flowed into her hips, then followed the line of her legs down from her thighs to her calves to her curled-up toes.

She batted her eyes at him like some *femme fatale* in a bad French movie. "Couldn't stay away, could you?"

"Sorry I woke you. Had to check my email. Now back into bed with you before Eagles hears us." He scooped her up and laid her back on the bed. Big mistake. She smelled of sleep and warmth, his shampoo and her own natural sweet scent that drove him wild. It was a heady mix that washed away all his control, all his reservations. He lowered his mouth and kissed her.

# Chapter 25

## Summer

Heavens, the man could kiss. She'd been imagining him kissing her since he'd arrived home, looking like a battered knight errant.

Gil lifted his head, breaking contact. He put his finger to his lips and whispered, *"Quiet."*

She bit her lip and nodded. She'd be as silent as the ocean depths as long as he didn't stop.

He returned to kissing her. Thoroughly. Everywhere.

"You"—he peered into her eyes then placed a gentle kiss on her forehead—"are"—he kissed each cheek—"so"—he kissed her chin—"very beautiful."

Summer closed her eyes. Those magical lips were saying words every woman longed to hear. But they were untrue. He saw only the outside of the woman she was, not the dark, sneaky, grubby creature underneath—the ambitious woman who was going to use him and betray him. She remembered the hard drive—already had.

Summer tangled her hands in his hair and pressed her lips to Gil's wonderfully warm ones. He tasted like a minty sea, sweet and salty at the same time, and she couldn't get enough. She wanted all of him, no matter the consequences.

She couldn't forget how he'd put his body between her and Cully's oar. No man had ever protected her like that before. Her brothers had been too young. Her father too broken.

But *this man*—his tongue pressed against the seam of her lips—this glorious man—she opened her mouth and let him sweep in and claim her—this heartbreaking, gentle man was going to be hers. Tonight. She would let herself pretend that she wasn't going to see betrayal in his eyes come morning.

She reached behind his neck and undid his ponytail, filling her hands with his hair. Heavens, she'd wanted to touch his hair and set it free ever since she's seen him on the ferry and mistook him for a backwater fisherman. There was something incredibly sexy and brave about a man wearing long hair.

She gathered the dark strands up, amazed at the length and the unexpected softness of it. She ran her hands down his chest. His muscles bulged. For a man with a desk job, Gil Moses was one hard body.

He let out a low moan. She pushed him flat onto the mattress and gingerly climbed on top of him, avoiding the worst of his bruises. This time, he was not going to get away from her.

He stared up at her. "Be gentle with me, warrior maiden," he whispered. "I have a lot of tender places."

She gazed down at that poor, battered face. What she was doing was wrong, so very wrong. His child slept a wall away. Prudish Mrs. Eagles would think her a tramp. Worse—tomorrow, Cully's surprise would be waiting for him on his computer, and she would be out on the street, calling the wrath of the protestors down on him and his company all over again.

But none of that mattered in this moment. In the still of the night, in the dark of this room, they were one man and one woman, finding pleasure in each other.

A door opened, and slipper-clad feet shuffled in the hall.

Gil flopped onto his back. "I swear Eagles has ESP."

There was a tap on the door, and Mrs. Eagles' voice, groggy with sleep, echoed through the wood. "I'll be leaving in the morning, I will." The slippered feet moved away. They could hear her mumbling, "... to expose a child ..."

Gil folded his hands behind his head. "I think she's a bit of a prude." His voice was barely above a whisper.

"But you need her."

He yawned. "I'll sweet-talk her in the morning. She has nowhere else to go."

"She can't take Lissie, can she?"

"No." He turned and kissed her on the nose. "She's a bit prone to dire pronouncements. No wonder her husband took off."

"You know the story?"

"Yeah, Betty filled me in on all the local scuttlebutt. Eagles shares an apartment with another old bitty. Seems they had a disagreement over Victoria's junk collection, which now resides here." Gil ran a finger down her cheek. "If she does leave, I'll hold her stuff hostage till she comes back."

"Speaking of Betty, I can understand what she sees in you, but what do you see in her?"

"Too syrupy-sweet for my taste. And that wig ..."

She nudged him with her elbow. "So, why are you sleeping with her? I thought you kinder than that."

He rolled to his side and ran a hand through her hair. Little ripples of pleasure followed. "If she said that, she lied. But it's good to know you don't mind sharing."

"You ... you ..." She sat up and slapped him across the cheek. "I do mind. Stay away from Betty Boop." She drew her hand back, trembling. She had no right to claim him. Soon, she'd be gone. Betty would stay. She stuck her stinging hand under her armpit. "Sorry."

He unburied her hand and kissed the palm. "Reminds me it never pays to tease a lady." He gently placed her hand on the sheets, scooped up the coverlet, gave it a shake, and floated it over her. "Stay warm. I'll be right back, and I'll show you a little more kindness."

"But Mrs. Eagles?"

He leaned in and kissed her. "Damage done. We might as well enjoy ourselves." He pushed up from the bed and headed to the bathroom.

Summer licked her lips. The night wasn't over. If she were going to have regrets come morning, she might as well make them huge ones.

Gil came out of the bathroom and stopped dead. "What the heck?" He snatched a pair of binoculars off the nightstand and moved to the bedroom window.

Summer sat up. "What's the matter?"

Gil grabbed a pair of jeans from the wash basket, slid them up one leg then the other, did up the zipper, buckled on his belt. "There's a boat out there. On the turbine site." He tugged out a tee-shirt and pulled it over his head. "I can see the lights."

A ball of knots formed in her stomach. "It's unusual to fish at night?"

"Yes and no. On a clear night and with the fish running, an inshore fisherman might head out, but not on a night like this with no moon and with the wind picking up, looking to rain."

He turned and gave her a half-smile. "I've got to go check it out. It could mean nothing, but ... well ... it's part of my job." He hesitated. "That's why I'm really here, you know—to catch the idiot dropping depth charges on the turbine."

She chewed her lip and stopped her protests. "Can't the Coast Guard check it out?"

"Take too long. And it may be some yahoos having a party or something." He bent over and kissed her. "Don't worry. If it proves to be the bomber, I'll call in help."

Summer threw back the covers. "Let me come with you."

He shook his head. "With a storm coming on? You're prone to seasickness, remember? You'd slow me down, Summer. You curl up in bed and stay there until I get back. Mrs. Eagles won't bother you if you play possum. Wait for me to come rescue you."

*Click.* He opened the door to the hall. For a brief second, light flooded the room. Then the door shut, and dark settled over her like a blindfold. She rolled over and buried her head under the covers still redolent with his scent.

She didn't envy him heading out into the cold and sloshing around on a boat in the middle of the night. Just the thought of it made her stomach turn over. And he was probably right. He'd turn up kids having a beer blast or two old men fishing.

She shot upright. And he could be wrong.

She tossed off the covers and searched for her clothes. That crazy guy might be there right now, doing his worst.

He couldn't go alone. Somehow, she'd get her knapsack from Lissie, find her car keys, and follow Gil.

Five minutes later, Summer wasn't so sure she'd be going anywhere ever again. In front of her, Mrs. Eagles stood wide-legged, the old woman's bushy white eyebrows forming a menacing V across her forehead, a broomstick in one hand, Summer's pack in the other. Behind her, Lissie lay on the floor, flailing her arms and emitting piercing screams. Extracting the backpack had been notably unsuccessful. The child was more alert than a sleeping cat.

"I told you not to disturb her." The woman kicked at Summer with her fluffy yellow slipper. It was like getting hit with a feather boa, but the intention was clear. Mrs. Eagles hated her.

"I'm sorry. The last thing I wanted to do is to hurt Lissie. Look, this is an emergency. Gil could be in trouble. I need my car keys. Give me the pack, and I'll be out of here."

"Mr. Moses can take care of himself. Don't need no bad luck woman." The housekeeper lowered the broomstick. "I want you to promise to stay away from him and my Lissie. I know what you and Cully are up to. We don't need your type here."

Her and Cully? The old woman had to be crazy to pair the two of them together. But none of that mattered. She'd had her few moments of selfish pleasure. After tonight, Gil would hate her anyway.

"Sure. I promise. Anything. Give me my bag, and I'll disappear."

Mrs. Eagles tossed the pack at her and pointed the broom handle toward the door. "Go."

Summer worked her way to her feet and dashed out the house. If she drove at tornado speed, she just might make it to the dock before he cast off.

# Chapter 26

## Gil

Gil slammed his car door, slung the duffle with his equipment over his shoulder, and then headed down the pier. The slap of the tide against the hulls of the boats and the chilly sea air transported him back to his childhood. How many times had he followed his father to the wharf before dawn, lugging the heavy metal lunchbox his mom had packed? How many times had he stood on the dock, waving goodbye, always trusting his dad would come back? Until he didn't.

Goosebumps crawled up his neck. No use thinking about that. It was the way his father would have wished to go.

He pulled up his jacket collar, missing his wool sweater. He pictured Summer standing in his kitchen with the sleeves rolled up, and he wasn't cold any longer.

He peered out at the water. Hopefully, it'd be a group of crazy teens having a party, and he'd be back in bed with his feisty activist in less than an hour.

He tossed in his duffle and jumped aboard *Hell'za Poppin'*. The deck shifted beneath his feet, the boards slippery wet with sea mist. He flexed his knees from old habit, rolled with the boat, and ducked into the wheelhouse.

The engine started right up, humming smoothly. He took the portable VHF marine radio and GPS out of his duffle and hooked them up, undid the lines, and checked the position of the boat moored behind. The last thing he wanted to do was damage someone else's boat. He threw the engine in reverse and turned the wheel to pull away.

"Wait!"

"Summer?" Gil squinted over his shoulder. The last person he needed at the moment. Didn't that woman listen to anything? He put the boat in neutral.

"I'm in time." Summer leaned over the side of the pier. "I am going with you."

He pointed his chin at the camera slung around her neck. "Got your pack, I see."

"You angry?"

Gil shook his shoulders. "No. Just frustrated. My reward for going out in the middle of the night without my wool sweater was that I would come home to a nice warm bed *with you in it*. Instead, here you are. I'm freezing my butt off, the bed's getting cold, and you're wearing *my* sweater."

Summer looked down. "Sorry. If you take me with you, I'll stand nice and close to you to keep you warm."

"What freezin' cold man could refuse that invitation? Come on down." He offered up his hand. "Put your foot on the combing, and I'll catch you."

In minutes, she was in the boat, her arms wrapped around his waist, her lips on his neck, and he was trying to remember why it was so important to check out the turbine site.

"So, are we going?"

"Yah, sure." He reversed the boat, maneuvered away from the pier, and headed out.

Summer squeezed him tighter. "I love your accent."

He put his arm over her shoulders, suddenly glad she had come. "Well, I agree there's a lot about me to love. Let's see ... I'm smart. I'm a hard worker." He wiggled his eyebrows at her. "I know how to kiss you senseless."

Summer batted at him.

"But my accent ... what's to love about that?"

"Well, you don't have one as heavy as the Tide Harbor folks, but you definitely don't sound American what with the *yah sure's* and the dropped *n's* creeping in."

"You know, technically, Canadians are Americans. Last I looked, Canada was in North America."

"I meant from the States."

"The States, right. Well, I've been living in the Boston area for over ten years. I would think my accent pretty washed out."

She nuzzled her face against his chest. "It's coming back. How'd you end up in Boston?"

"After Dalhousie, I did post-doc research at Woods Hole. Taught some courses at Boston U. as an adjunct. Met Dolores, was hired by MIT, and settled in." He stared off at the blinking light of the first buoy out of the harbor. "Whole family bit."

"How could any woman toss over such an incredible man? You're a rarity, you know."

He patted her on the back. "Like my kisses?"

She nuzzled against him. "I've kissed a lot of frogs who turned out to be snakes. Your Dolores is a fool."

Gil swallowed. "She was happy enough with me. I gave her everything she wanted. It was Lizzie she wanted rid of."

"You're bitter."

"No. Not anymore." He tangled his fingers in her hair. "I was the fool—fell in love with the wrong woman. She was beautiful, accomplished. A pianist. Always dressed to perfection. Always knowing the right thing to do at the right time. She was Boston Brahmin to the core—a Cushing descendant. Way out of my league."

"And she married you?"

He snugged his arms around her and trailed kisses down her neck. "I can be extremely persuasive. And I landed a tenure track position at MIT. That, plus the *Doctor* in front of my name, made me acceptable to her nose-in-the-air parents."

Summer slipped out of his hold and put some space between them. "I'm no different. I probably remind you of her."

"You did. At the beginning." He laughed. "Those boots. But you are not Dolores. Dolores would never be out here on the water in the middle of the night"—he ran a finger down her cheek—"wearing that sweater. She called it my ratty sweater."

"Ratty?" Summer looked down. "It's a beautiful sweater, not worn or anything."

"My mother knitted it from natural gray wool she got from a neighbor in the Cove who kept sheep. Dolores said the color reminded her of a rat."

"What a horrible person."

Gil pressed his lips together. "I loved her."

"Oh, I didn't mean ..."

"It's okay. She is horrible. She means to take Lissie away from me."

"Can she do that?"

"Probably. It was a fluke to get full custody in the first place. Thing is ... she wants to put her in an institution." He gripped the wheel and held the boat steady as the bow met the swells running across the harbor entrance.

"I thought institutionalization was frowned upon even for the severely handicapped. Lissie's not so out-of-control she needs to be locked up. She's a little girl who's overly sensitive. I get that."

He rubbed the top of her head. "So says the woman Lissie literally tore the skin off of." Gil leaned forward and peered through the mist-spotted glass. "Idiots are still out there. I was hoping they'd hear my motor and take off."

"What do you plan to do when you get there?"

"Don't need to get too close. If you bend down and open my duffle, there's a pair of binoculars. It's dark, but if I can make out the name or number of the boat, I'll report them to the Coast Guard, and they can do the face-to-face stuff."

Summer rummaged in the bag and came up with the binoculars. She pressed a hand on her stomach. "Oh, I don't think I should have done that. I was fine until I moved."

"Come here." Gil pulled her close. "See? Here's something else to love about me—I make a good antidote to seasickness. Hold on and stare straight out the front. Better?"

She blinked up at him, her eyes almost black in the dark. "You're an antidote for a lot of things."

Gil glanced away. He was in love with this woman. Not the New York fashion-plate with her brassy nose in the air. Not the sneaky activist he was beginning to think was in league with the bomber. No, he was falling for the girl in his rat-gray fishing sweater, with drops of mist in her hair and the look of a well-loved woman on her face.

He took the binoculars from her and focused in. The boat was little more than a dark, shadowy shape on the water, the color impossible to discern. Even so, he could tell it was not much bigger than *Hell'za Poppin'* and had an old-style wheelhouse. Nothing like any boat out of Tide Harbor.

"Can you make it out?" Summer asked.

"Nope. Too far. Too dark. Sitting awfully quiet in the water, though. Not a party. Unless they are lying low, waiting to see what we're going to do." Gil throttled down the engine. "Don't like it. Seems to be anchored to the spot."

He peered out again. Could someone be in trouble? He didn't think so. The mystery boat was bobbing directly over the turbine site. That kind of accuracy didn't happen by accident.

Summer shifted in his arms. "My camera has a night vision setting. Let me have a look." She jerked against him as she struggled with the strap. Then she was swaying beside him, peering into the dark.

Gil snugged her tighter. "See anything?"

"No …" She turned sideways, leaned out, and peered across the port side of the boat. "Wait a minute. Looks like something moving around. Could be a man. Hard to tell." Summer lowered the camera. "Can you get closer?"

"Not sure I want to. By now, whoever's on that boat knows we're here. If we close in, they may panic and take off. If I keep heading off a ways, they will think us some fishing boat setting out real early, giving them an eyeful."

*Splash.*

Summer's hand squeezed into his. "Did you hear that?"

The hairs on the back of his neck rose. He'd heard lots of things fall into the sea. That was the sound of something large and heavy being dumped overboard. He held on to Summer and waited for an explosive reaction. None came.

He squinted through the dark. Fog was forming along the surface of the water, making visibility even more difficult. If there was a name on the boat, it was hidden or covered over. His breath came a little faster. Something was definitely wrong.

He clasped Summer tighter. He shouldn't have let her come and put her at risk. He looked over his shoulder. They could still turn back.

But no. He'd lose the chance at identifying the bomber, save his job, and stop the threats.

*Splash.*

He jerked around. What was that?

He listened again. A faint, rhythmic lapping, like oars dipping in and out, traveled over the water. Someone could have launched a dingy or kayak from the opposite side. But that made no sense out here in the night. Only a fool or a desperate man would be in a small boat over a mile from shore with a storm threatening.

Still, it was possible.

Heck, anything was possible.

He glanced at Summer. The message on his computer had been clear. The blasted bomber wanted Seastroke Energy to pay five hundred thousand dollars in return for ceasing his bombing activities. And if he didn't get it, he would do something dire to him—Seastroke's shill—and to Lissie.

No one threatened his daughter. That bastard had to be found and stopped.

He tapped the console. It would be easy to overtake a man rowing. First, he'd check out the silent boat. To do that he'd have to leave Summer alone on *Poppin'*. The idea made his stomach clench. He'd only be a few minutes, but it never hurt to be prepared for the worst.

He lowered his voice. "Reach in my jeans pocket and take out the card I have there."

"Card?" Summer's fingers crept inside his pocket and gave a little wiggle. "I'd rather be reaching for something else, Gil Moses."

He kissed her on the top of her head. "Soon. That bed's calling." He ran his fingers down the side of her face, hoping his suspicions were wrong. She looked so beautiful, felt so right in his arms, but he was having a hard time trusting her.

Gil peered out at the anchored boat. "I'm going to circle around and come in closer. But I want you to know how to call in reinforcements, if needed. The directions are on the card." He turned on the marine radio and showed her the red distress button. "If you have to, push that button and shout *mayday* three times."

Lit only by the instrument panel, Summer's face was barely visible. "Are we in danger?"

A bone-chilling prickle crawled across his shoulders. He hated to make her nervous just when she was getting comfortable being out on the water.

He kept his voice calm. "No. But it's good practice to know what to do in an emergency." He turned the card over and jotted a series of numbers. "That's our current longitude and latitude. You say that three times after you give the mayday signal. Then say the problem three times."

Summer flipped the card over. "I always thought good things came in threes."

"Being rescued *is* a good thing. Now take the wheel; you're going to drive." He showed her how to hold the course and turned on his flashlight. Then he ducked into the cuddy to fetch the survival suit.

He tugged the coverall out from under the bench. Where it had been, something shiny glinted in the beam of light. He bent over. It was a sharp filleting knife. He worked it free from between the decking and hefted it in his hand. It was old, the wooden handle scratched and worn. He bet this was Mr. Eagles' long-lost knife.

Holding it in one hand, he grabbed up the suit with the other, and popped back up on deck.

Summer's eyes widened. "What's the knife for?"

"Found it in the cuddy." He placed it on the console and set the suit down. He sure hoped he didn't have to get Summer to put it on. But the sea *was* getting rougher.

Gil took back the helm, turned the wheel, and *Hell'za Poppin'* came around.

"In a minute, we should be able to see the name of the boat. Be near enough to halloo."

The shadowy boat grew closer. Gil clamped his lip in his teeth and prayed he was doing the right thing. He really didn't want to find out who was on that boat. If it was the bomber, and he set off a depth charge, it would kick up some mighty big swells or even damage *Poppin*'s hull, and they wouldn't last long in the water at this temperature if the boat capsized.

Still, if someone was on that boat, they had to know they were here. Sounds magnified over water, after all. And it might not be the bomber, but an old fisherman in trouble.

When they were within shouting distance, he cupped his hands and shouted, "Hey yah. Needing help?"

The other boat sloshed in the wake they were kicking up, but there was no answering cry.

Gil clenched his teeth. If there were people on that boat, they were either drunk or injured or dead.

Summer looked through her camera lens again. "It's weird how no one is calling to us. And it looks like the name is wiped out or something." She lowered the camera. "There has to be someone on board, doesn't there? Or were those splashes someone going over the side. Going for a swim."

Gil turned to look at her. "You *are* a landlubber. Us fisher folks avoid falling in the water at all costs. The sea here is too cold for swimming. Most lobstermen don't even learn how. Better that way." He shook his head. "You get dumped in the sea without an immersion suit, like this one, and you'll stay conscious about ten minutes at most in dead winter. Even now in October, the temperature hovers at or just below fifty degrees. It would be touch and go. You could lose dexterity in less than ten minutes and succumb to hypothermia in an hour or two, if'n you didn't just die from the shock."

He bit his lip and tasted salt and blood. "My dad died that way. Went over with a pot. Leg caught in the line. My brother hauled him up in less than five minutes—dead. They said the cold shock killed him, not drowning."

The rain was picking up. He picked up the suit. It was time. He hoped it didn't panic her more.

"Here, I want you to put this on."

"What is it?"

"An immersion suit. If you fall in the water, it will keep you warm for several hours. Long enough to be rescued. The color helps rescuers see you."

"You're scaring me." Summer looked around. "We're not going to sink, are we?"

"Nah. But rain's starting to pound down. I would feel better if you were in it. It'll keep you dry."

"Yeah. You just want to see what I look like as an orange frog."

"Well, there is that." He held up the suit. "Step in."

It took a bit of doing to get her bundled up and she did look like an orange frog. He zipped up tight.

Summer looked down. "I do feel warmer. Maybe looking like frog is a good idea." She glanced up. "Wait—where's your suit?"

"Only bought the one. Took a good part of the grant money. They're pricy."

Summer's gloved fingers crept into his. "Will your lifejacket help?"

He hesitated. "A lifejacket will keep your head out of the water if you manage to flip yourself up and back." It just didn't help with hypothermia. But he wasn't going to tell her that.

She pressed against him. "Can you swim?"

"Yah, sure." Not that it would do much good in the coming storm.

Gil slid his hand out of hers and turned the wheel. "We should probably check and make sure no one is injured. That's the only explanation I can think of. Let's hope whoever's on that boat is dead drunk and not worse. I'm no doctor."

Gil throttled down as they approached the silent boat. There was a sucking rattle, and then the engine sputtered.

He slapped the helm hard. Fool. Summer's anti-turbine fanatics had destroyed his equipment. He should have figured they'd mess with *Poppin'*, too. He glanced out at the boat bobbing next to them. This was starting to look like a setup. But how could anyone have known he'd come investigate in the middle of the night?

Summer looked around her. "What was that?"

"I think someone messed with the engine."

Her head jerked up. "Messed with this boat?"

"Some anti-turbine mischief, most likely. Poked a small hole in the fuel line. Damaged the fuel pump. Mean-spirited, but at least not as dangerous as the attack at the research center. Thought I was a goner there between Cully and that oar. We're safe for the moment." He hoped.

"I'm sorry about that."

"I thought you said you'd do anything to stop the turbines being installed?"

"Anything non-violent."

Gil listened to the engine cough and catch. Blazes. The last thing he wanted was to be stranded out here with a storm coming. He'd circle the mystery boat and head in.

Summer grasped the sleeve of his jacket. "Someone caused a leak on purpose? Spilled diesel into the ocean?" She tipped up her chin. "Wasn't my people. The anti-turbine people care about the environment."

Gil couldn't keep the anger from his voice. "Don't be a fool. No one truly cares about the environment. It's all about money. That's what motivates people, pure and simple. Think about it. If tidal energy was going to bring tons of money to Tide Harbor so no fisherman ever had to go out in the freezing cold and haul traps until crippled by arthritis, do you think they'd be fighting it? No, they'd lie back in their lounge chairs, sip beer, watch hockey, and give not a whit about the fish."

Summer pulled away. "I didn't realize you were such a cynic. Is that what motivates you? Money?"

"Yah, sure. I might be a great kisser"—he wiggled his eyebrows at her—"but I'm no saint. Your friends are right. I'm getting paid by Seastroke Energy. I needed a job in

Canada, and I needed one fast. I'm in debt up to my neck what with alimony and lawyer's bills. Probably be a pile more of those from the riot. And I have to support Lissie.

"Someday, I'd like to move on, do real research again. Be someone whose work makes a difference. So yes, I'm doing it for the money right now." He let out a breath of air. Time to put Miss Save-the-World on the spot. "Come on. Aren't you doing the same thing?"

"What?"

"Farmer's daughter wearing over-the-top leather boots and designer clothes. Flaunting hard-nosed big city ways. You might be slumming here for a few days, pretending you're happy in that pit of a cabin, wearing thrift shop clothes and being all outdoorsy, but appears to me environmental activism pays you well enough. Ain't been no manure on your high-heeled boots in a long while, and spending time out here in nature doesn't make your blood thrum. Don't tell me you aren't money-grubbing like the rest of us. If your protest succeeds and shuts Seastroke Energy down, what will you get out of it?"

Her body went rigid against him. "You don't want to know."

"But I do. Because whatever it is, it's making you feel guilty. And I don't want you feeling guilty." He kissed the tip of her nose. "I'm getting quite fond of you. Even if you are a thief."

Summer jerked away. "Back to that accusation, are we?"

"Tell me then, why are you here?"

"Okay, okay. You've got a right to know. I do care about the environment. A lot. I'm aiming for the head director's job at EcoGreen Action's headquarters in Atlanta. I want to shape the agenda. Forget pretty-sounding slogans and make-the-earth-green sing-ins. We should be using our platform to help the little guys take on the sleazy corporations, like the one that poisoned the water on my family's farm."

He steered nearer to the blue boat. "Who poisoned your farm?"

"Some corporation fracking for natural gas."

Gil shook his head. "Tell me." Keeping her talking would distract her from the fact that the wind was picking up, and ole *Hell'za Poppin'* was tipping and rocking more.

He cast an eye on the glowering sky. The storm was moving in faster than he'd expected.

Summer wrapped her arms across her chest and leaned back against him. "They swore that they had nothing to do with the pollutants in our water. And the local court, run by people hoping to make a killing, believed them. Not us, who watched our fruit trees die, and our dog, and my mother. But we didn't have the money to fight the decision. So, I got a degree in environmental science and swore I would fight these callous corporations with my last breath." She pressed her hands to her face. "But you're right. I got sidetracked by money. Got into marketing, intending to represent the environmentally aware businesses. But they can't afford top-quality PR people. And I found myself representing companies like the one that destroyed my parents' farm." Her voice became a whisper. "My father has never forgiven me, and he's getting old. I want to earn his respect before it's too late."

She stepped away, swayed as a wave slapped the side of the boat, and came back into his arms. "So, I am not going to give up. Not going to follow the rules. I'm going to hurt you, Gil. I won't stop the fight until those turbines are gone from here."

Gil pressed her against him and breathed in her scent that drove him crazy. Why did he always fall for the wrong women? He hugged her tighter. "Thing is, you think your cause is so righteous you don't mind trampling on people who disagree with you. I think you lie most of the time. Steal when you have to. Maybe even sleep with a guy to get what you want. So ... Miss Fancy Feet"—he kissed her on the nape of her neck—"am I a frog or a snake?"

She twisted around and faced him. "How dare you?" Another wave rocked the boat. She bobbed against him then pulled back. "It wasn't like that ... I didn't ..."

Gil put his fingers against her lips. "No lies. That why you took my hard drive?"

Her chin went up, and she gave him a push. "I didn't touch your blasted hard drive. Other parts of you, but not that one."

He peered through the windshield. They were nearing the bow of the boat. He glanced back at her. "So, you have no idea how it got back on my desk tonight?"

Her mouth twisted, and so did his heart.

She rubbed her neck. "Okay, I put it there. But I didn't steal it."

"But you know who did?"

The boat rocked again.

"And I'm not telling." She looked up. "We all have things to hide."

He studied the boat bouncing alongside *Poppin'* then peered down at the woman in his arms. Was she working with the blackmailer? Only she could have put that message on his computer. Was she so desperate to win this fight she'd threaten Lissie? He couldn't believe that. Something just didn't add up.

At that moment, the engine hitched and went silent. He turned the key in the ignition and listened to the engine suck air. He dropped his hands. Silence wrapped around them and settled into his gut.

Summer gripped his arm. "What just happened?"

"Engine stalled."

Summer Avery's treachery no longer mattered. He had bigger problems. The next few minutes were going to be rough unless he could get the engine started up again or caught a tow. He looked at the other boat. "Hold onto the wheel."

"What?"

"The wheel. We're drifting up on the other boat. When we hit, I'm going to make fast, go aboard. Investigate. See if we've found us a terrorist or a drunk. Or better yet—see if I can get it started. Then we'll tow ole *Poppin'* in."

She tightened her hold on his arm. "Don't go. It's too risky."

Gil extracted his flashlight from his pocket and gave her a hard look. Everything they were doing was a risk. A storm was moving in. The swells were getting rougher.

He pulled away and shone the light on the deck of the other boat. "Looks abandoned. I'll take a quick look in the cuddy. See if the engine starts."

He set out the sea anchor, undid the bowline and, ignoring the way her hands shuddered, handed it to her. "Toss it across when I'm over."

A wave rolled in, and the boats hit with a soft *thunk*, bobbed up and down, the sides grinding against each other. He uncoiled the stern line and, timing his jump, leaped between the shifting boats, landing with a *thud* and a near slip on the wet decking.

He belayed the lines and worked his way forward. Boxes and pieces of cardboard littered the deck like someone had been unpacking equipment. The open-back wheelhouse stood empty. He shone the flashlight in front of him and headed for the cuddy.

Sliding the door open, a combination of noxious smells assaulted his nose—long dead fish, tar, old sweat, decay, and on top of it all, the metallic odor of blood.

Holding his breath, he aimed the flashlight into the dark and gasped. No, it couldn't be. He moved forward, tripped, and landed hard on his knees. His flashlight went flying and winked out.

In the blackness, he reached down and found the trip wire. The boat had been booby trapped. He had no wish to see what else awaited him. He turned, fumbling in the black toward the hatch.

Gil clenched his hands. He shouldn't have left Summer alone.

Not without telling her he loved her.

He bent over to pass through. Something brushed his shoulder.

*Snap.*

A heavy object fell from above and smashed the back of his head so hard his brain rattled in his skull. Everything went brilliant white, then blue, then deep, deep black.

# Chapter 27

## Summer

Summer gripped the wheel and prayed that Gil would return soon. The wind had changed. Gusts whipped around her, carrying needles of sleet that stung her face each time she peered out looking for him. Rough waves battered the boats, knocking them together and pulling them apart.

With every bump, the boats shifted, the lines stretched and tautened. She didn't know much about boats, but there was no question those two ropes would not hold much longer.

She squinted through the dank gloom. How long could it take to search a small boat? He'd said he'd be only a few minutes.

She shoved the wet strands of hair from her eyes with the side of her glove and yelled at the top of her lungs, "Gil!"

Nothing. Just the roll and crash of the waves.

She shouted over and over, but her words were sucked away into the wind. She might as well be whispering. He'd never hear her.

A huge wave rose up next to the boat. Beneath her feet, *Hell'za Poppin'* shuddered and dipped then jerked toward the other boat. Summer drew in a breath of water-laden air and latched onto the wheel as tightly as she could.

*Smack.* The two boats hit. The blow slammed through her body. *Poppin'* dropped down, gave a shake, and rose up again.

With a snap heard above the wind, the lines joining the boats gave way.

Waves surged over the sides and sloshed across the deck. Cold sea water splashed her face. With a shudder, *Poppin'* twisted around and swirled into the black.

Summer clung onto the steering wheel and risked a glance over her shoulder, fear curling up tighter and tighter inside her chest. Searching. Hoping. Praying.

But she could see nothing. No blue boat. No Gil. Only black sea and black sky and sheets of rain pouring down.

But he had to be out there. He couldn't be gone.

*Poppin'* dipped, and she clamped her hands tighter to the wheel. Her heart numb. Her thoughts jumbled. Tremors ran up and down her body. She needed help. She needed to be rescued. Gil was right. She wasn't the outdoorsy type.

Wait. She shook her head to clear it. Gil had shown her how to call in a mayday.

With awkward gloved fingers, she fished out the card he'd given her. Fumbling in the dark, she flipped up the cover of the radio and pressed the distress button.

First the mayday. Next the numbers. Then her cry for help. Three times. She had to say everything three times. Her voice cracked as she struggled to be heard above the wind and rain.

For the longest time, there was no answer. Suddenly, the radio crackled to life. The faint voice of the Search and Rescue team dispatcher came on. A woman. Cool. Calm. Controlled.

They were coming. Sending out a helicopter. All she had to do was hold on.

She peered out into the darkness, her fingers clenched to the wheel. How would they ever find her?

*Crash.* A huge wave hit the boat. Water thundered up into the air and over the decking.

Closing her eyes, Summer concentrated on holding on as the boat pitched and yawed in the wild sea.

Suddenly, the boat bucked beneath her, ripping her hands from the wheel. She flew across the deck and landed in a sodden heap in the corner of the wheelhouse, her left ankle twisted under her. Pain shot through her. Saltwater filled her nose and burned down her throat.

Another wave breached the boat. The *Hell'za Poppin'* tipped, and she slid backward toward the stern, closer to the roar and crash of the waves.

She threw her arms out desperately, grasping for something—for anything—to slow her slide. There. Her gloved hand caught hold of the end of one of the flapping ropes. Heart lodged in her throat, she wrapped it around her waist and prayed for strength as the sea washed over her again and again.

Minutes. Hours. A lifetime later. As if through a tunnel, she heard something.

The drone of an engine.

Was that another boat?

Lights appeared out of the black. The whirring noise came closer. The ear-splitting roar grew louder. A beam of light moved along the surface of the water.

A wave sloshed over her. Summer came up gasping.

Help had arrived. She licked her salt-encrusted lips and used the last of her strength to flail her arms.

In seconds, the beam of light shown down on her. Moments later, there was a clank. The deck beneath her tipped. A man, in a matching orange suit, scuffled aboard, his boots clumping toward her.

Another wave hit, and she came up spitting out seawater. Then he was unpeeling her benumbed fingers, strapping her against his chest and lifting her above a wild, reckless sea. They swung out into space, the helicopter blades whooping overhead, and were hauled up into the belly of the copter.

She grabbed the suit of the man holding her and tried to get her frozen lips to move. Gil. She had to tell them about Gil. But her voice had turned to nothing. She tried again. The words broke forth, shallow, barely a whisper. "Gil. Gil Moses. On the other boat."

Her rescuer leaned in and spoke in her ear, "Yah, sure. Boats looking for him."

The Nova Scotia expression created a hollow in her heart.

Would she ever hear Gil say that again?

# Chapter 28

## Summer

By the time the helicopter landed, Summer was no longer numb, but she wished she was. The cuts and bruises on her face stung like a thousand needle pokes. Every part of her body ached from being tossed around on the boat. Her ankle most of all. Broken, the EMTs had said. It hurt. But not as much as not knowing if Gil was safe.

She squeezed her eyes closed as the stretcher was unloaded on the helipad at the hospital. She couldn't have lost him, not when she'd found the one man who could make her body sing. The one man who knew exactly who she was, but still cherished her.

She opened her eyes and peered skyward at the dissipating clouds. Sweet heavens, she'd gone and fallen in love with the turbine man.

The stretcher bounced over some unevenness in the pavement. She turned and upchucked into the vomit bag they'd given her. She hadn't thrown up once on the rolling boat or in the helicopter swinging about in the sky as it searched for Gil. Now on dry land, she couldn't stop.

She heaved again. Came up for air. There was nothing left in her stomach, but she kept retching. It was like her body wanted to turn inside out, shed all the harsh words, all the lies she'd thrown at Gil until all that was left was her love for him.

She shifted on the stretcher. Nothing could relieve the stone-hard lump in her chest. Gil couldn't be gone. Not with that little girl relying on him to keep her safe. Gil's ex-wife would put Lissie in an institution.

She gagged and spit again. The only good thing about her upset tummy was that it kept the policeman standing at the side of her stretcher at bay, while the search and rescue team fussed with adjusting the straps and IV that was supposed to be helping with the nausea.

There was a commotion to her left, and the blare of an ambulance siren. Beside her, the police officer's radio crackled, something about the other boat rescue, and he took off toward the ambulance. The orderlies on either side of her turned to watch. Could it be had they had found Gil?

Summer turned her head in the direction they were looking and blinked to clear her vision. Two police cars, lights flashing, zoomed across the hospital parking lot as the ambulance crew unloaded a stretcher.

"Gil?" Summer lifted her head as far upright as possible, the blanket slipping from her shoulders, the wind whipping through her hair. She had to see.

The other stretcher turned. The same wind ruffled the blanket, revealing a face.

*Oh no.* She snapped her head back, wishing she hadn't looked. The man on the stretcher wasn't Gil. It was Owen Young, the collar of his tawdry plaid shirt covered in blood, his toothless mouth gaping open.

Owen Young. Dead. Murdered.

Summer twisted around. Where was Gil? A rubber-gloved hand caught her, and a young fresh-faced nurse in a winter ski jacket blocked her view.

"Stay still, Miss," the girl said as she pulled the blanket over her. "Time to get you inside."

Summer pushed against her. "Where's the other man? Gil Moses?"

"They're already treating him, Miss."

"He's alive?"

"Yah, sure. Ambulance brought him in fifteen minutes ago. Coast Guard boat picked him up."

She twisted out of the girl's grasp. "I've got to see him."

The girl caught her with more strength than seemed possible and wrestled her shoulders back down on the stretcher. She fastened the straps more firmly over her. "Later, Miss. Your man'll be okay. They got to him in time."

"How bad?" she whispered.

The girl shook her head. "He was in the water for a while." She took a position at the head of the stretcher, the other orderly held on to the side, and they rolled her away toward the emergency room doors. "First, let's get you feeling more yourself. The police want to ask you questions."

Summer's stomach twisted. "Questions?" She tipped her head and glanced back. A knot of men in uniforms stood around the ambulance. Two were walking her way.

She swallowed down the bad taste in her mouth and tried to put the pieces together. Had Owen Young been the bomber? He was creepy enough.

It had to be him. Sneaky bastard.

The stretcher bounced over the doorsill. Summer gasped. Heaven help her. Had Gil murdered that old man to protect the turbine? Was that what Seastroke Energy had sent him to do?

Could the man who touched her so gently, who cherished his poor struggling daughter so intently—the man she loved—be capable of killing? A shiver crept up her spine. Perhaps, it had been an accident?

Then she remembered the blood. That was no accident. And the knife? Had Gil taken that wicked-looking knife he'd found with him when he had boarded the other boat?

Beside her, the nurse undid the strapping, rolled the top of the throw-up bag closed, and threw it away. If only her poisonous thoughts could be tossed away as easily.

She shook her head. In a few minutes, she'd have to answer questions, and she had no idea what she would say.

# Chapter 29

## Gil

Gil groaned. Where the heck was he? His head throbbed. Every breath sent waves of fiery hot pain through his ribs. His hands were dead weights on either side. Beeps, hums, and gabbled voices assaulted his ears. And the smell—a mix of plastics and chemicals with a hint of bleach—burned his nose and throat. He coughed, and the pain tore through his gut.

"Gil? Can you hear me?"

He opened his eyes a slit. A blurry shape surrounded by white light stood over him. It came closer bringing with it the honeysuckle scent he loved. He formed her name with his lips. "Summer."

"Look. I'm not supposed to be here." Something brushed his cheek. "Snuck in. I have to know. What happened? Did you kill him?"

*He killed someone?* He remembered the weight smashing into his head. Yes, someone had tried to kill him. And the blood. There'd been blood everywhere. And there'd been the lines breaking and him jumping into the cold, freezing water, trying to reach her as *Poppin'* swirled away into the storm. But none of that mattered. Summer was here. He had to warn her.

He opened his mouth, sucked for air, but no sound came out, only a low moan from deep inside him.

He choked in another breath and huffed out his fear. "Lissie. Go. Stay with her."

A cool hand brushed his brow. "I can't, Gil. I'd lose all my cred. I'm sorry, so sorry." The shadow that was Summer pulled away. A door clicked shut. Only emptiness remained, and the shouting in his head.

He could deny it no longer.

The woman he loved had no heart. He could understand her turning her back on him—he worked for Seastroke Energy—but refusing to help an innocent child? That he could never forgive. All she cared about was her cause.

The next time he woke up, Gil knew where he was—a hospital. There was no mistaking the drawn green curtains, the IV drip hanging above him, nor the bustling woman wearing a pale blue uniform with a stethoscope around her neck.

"Good. You're awake finally." The nurse pushed the drapery back. Sunlight streamed across the foot of the bed from a window on the wall to his left side. "Doctor's coming. See how that head of yours is doing."

He lifted his hand, dragging the IV line with it, and touched his brow. "Feels like I was hit with a brick."

"Something hard, for sure." The nurse leaned over and inserted a plastic-covered probe in his mouth. "They did an MRI. Nothing broken upstairs. Concussion, for sure. Few cracked ribs. Lots of scratches and bruises. Going to be achy for quite a while. Poor guy must have fought like the dickens."

Gil slid his head sideways to get a better look at her. "What poor guy?"

"The one you murdered."

"But I didn't—"

She jerked the probe out of his mouth and wrote something on her chart. "No fever. I'll send the officers in now. You can tell *them* what you didn't do."

# Chapter 30

## Summer

Summer pulled into Gil's driveway, her heart thumping triple time. She was a fool. She should be staying far away from here. The headlines were blasting the news everywhere: *Seastroke Energy employee viciously kills a poor fisherman trying to save his livelihood by dropping some homemade depth charges that the police called laughable.*

A huge demonstration was forming outside the Royal Canadian police station. Owen Young might have been a drunk and curmudgeon and turbine bomber, but he was one of them. Sympathy protests were being organized in Halifax and St. John.

She should be out on the street, leading the protestors. Screaming for Gil's blood. Demanding that underhanded Seastroke Energy pull out of the Basin for once and for all. And if not doing that, she should at least be contacting the national press, alerting EcoGreen Action. This was the kind of newsworthy breakthrough every activist longed for, one big enough to put anti-turbine slogans into everyone's head.

Instead, she was here.

She glanced up at the white cottage, looking homey in the morning mist, rolled her shoulders, and got out of the car. The fog settled around her, cold and damp. She should definitely turn around and head back to town.

But while the police were having no problem pinning Owen Young's murder on Gil, she didn't buy it. She would check his laptop again, look through his papers, be absolutely sure he was guilty before she and her followers went wild.

Summer peered down the road. And she had to do it before the police arrived to confiscate his computer. They had to be close behi.

Awkward on her hospital-issued crutches, Summer grabbed her pack, hoisted her way up the steps. She thumped on the door. No answer.

She caught her lip between her teeth and glanced around. Red, yellow, and orange leaves flitted to the ground from the ornamental maples in the front yard. Dew drops glistened on the blades of grass. From down below the cliff, the sea lapped at the shore. So normal. So quiet. She gave herself a shake. Too quiet.

She rubbed her hand on her coat and knocked again as hard as she could. With all this banging, Lissie should be screaming or making some kind of noise.

She crossed over and peered through the window into the living room. What she could see of the house looked dark and empty.

A shiver crawled up her spine. Maybe the police had already come and taken Lissie and the housekeeper somewhere.

She went back and tried the door handle. It turned. Her gut tightened. Mrs. Eagles would never leave the house unlocked.

Shifting her weight on the crutches, Summer took a deep breath and used her hip to push the door open.

The house held that stale cooking smell that houses had when their owners had gone out for a few hours. The living room sat empty, bathed in the pale gray light filtering through the window. She peeked into the kitchen. No sign of a recent meal—the counter tops squeaky clean, no dishes in the sink.

Okay, no one home. They must have stepped out or gotten a lift to Betty's. Lucky her.

She smacked her lips together and headed to Gil's bedroom. If the computer was still there, she'd do a quick search then go.

She crossed the hallway, peering into Mrs. Eagles' room as she passed. Through the partially open doorway, she spied a half-packed suitcase lying sprawled open on the floor. Two plastic bags of Lissie's clothes sat next to it. A bad feeling tiptoed up her spine.

Summer pushed open the bedroom door and stopped dead.

Cully Teed stood with a knife pointed at Mrs. Eagles' throat. Gary Campbell sat at the desk in front of Gil's laptop.

Cully grinned at her. "Welcome to the party. Been wondering if you'd show up. Digging up some nice dirt on your lover boy or"—he raised an eyebrow—"heaping some more dirt on him. Depends on your point of view. Either way, we'll bring those Seastroke Energy bastards to their knees." He gave her his extra-wide grin. "Shame Seastroke Energy's shill will end up in prison. But we all have to make sacrifices to save the fishies, don't we?"

She glanced at Mrs. Eagles. The old woman's lips were white, her face ashen.

Summer kept her eyes on the knife. "How do you know about the murder?"

"Came in on the police scanner," Gary yelled over his shoulder.

Mrs. Eagles pressed back harder against the wall. "Murder? You never said anything about murder, Cully."

"Don't be getting all wishy-washy now, Auntie." Cully pressed the tip of the knife into her fleshy neck. A trickle of blood ran down. He grinned at Summer. "Victoria here has been so helpful. Letting us know all about Gil's movements and such. Got cold feet at the last minute, though. Didn't want us to kidnap the little girl. Caught her packing. She was planning on high-tailing it out of here with the brat."

Gil's words flashed through her mind. Half-dead, accused of murder, and his only thought had been of his daughter. He'd wanted her to watch over Lissie. And she'd refused.

She had been so focused on the protest she hadn't considered the little girl to be in danger. A pressure built in her chest.

"Where *is* Lissie?"

"That's what I'm trying to find out," Cully said. "Victoria hid her somewhere."

Mrs. Eagles peered down at the knife blade. The skin beneath her eye twitched. "Don't know. Took off when you guys barged in."

Her shoulders tensed. So far, Cully thought she was on his side. It was vital she maintain that illusion. She had to keep him from getting his hands on that dear little girl.

Keeping a close watch on Cully's knife hand, she worked her way to the desk and peered over Gary's shoulder. The man might act like a gape-mouthed fisherman, but he was a whiz on the computer. Somehow, he had gotten into Gil's Seastroke Energy directives. His gloved fingers flew over the keyboard.

She leaned in closer. "You're doctoring his orders. I don't understand."

Cully gave her a twisted-mouth smile. "It's the perfect plan. By the time Gary's fixed Mr. Turbine Man's papers, not only will Gil Moses be going to jail for a long time, but Seastroke Energy will be accused of setting up a brutal murder of a poor old fisherman. *Voila*! No more turbines."

His knife hand twitched. "Gonna pay me and Gary a lot of money, too, or we'll go to the press with the charge."

"You're framing Gil Moses as a hitman for Seastroke Energy? That seems farfetched."

Cully shrugged. "Why not? You took us for simple-headed fisher guys." He twisted up one side of his mouth and winked at her. "In a little while, you're going to find out there's a lot more to me than a sweet-faced guy who takes no for an answer. We're going to have that party I've been promising. How's the song go—'Just You and Me, Baby?' You and me and the half-million Seastroke Energy's gonna deposit in my off-shore account for keeping all this quiet. Not to mention the other million their competitor is going to pay out to us for bankrupting Seastroke."

Summer shivered. Going anywhere with Cully Teed was definitely not on her agenda.

Gary pushed away from the desk. "Done. Let's go."

"We got Victoria here to deal with," Cully said.

Gary shrugged. "She'll not say anything. Else we'll spill the beans on what really happened to her husband." He looked the old woman in the eyes. "Everyone in Tide Harbor knows old Billy boy got his just desserts, but the Royal Cowboys won't agree. Even sweet little old ladies can go to jail for murder."

Mrs. Eagles? A murderer?

Summer stared at the terrified woman. "Come on. No way could she have killed anyone."

Cully looked over at her. "Thought you were smart. Poor old Auntie Victoria's rather handy with rat poison." He flicked the knife in her face. "According to Owen, that's what you used, right? Way I hear tell, you fed your husband some doctored chili. And Owen helped you dump his body at sea."

Mrs. Eagles spat in his face. "Owen was on to you. He knew you were responsible for those bombings. He'll tell the truth. He won't let you get away with this."

Cully wiped his cheek. "Your brother, Owen, is dead. Your boss murdered him."

"*No ...*" Mrs. Eagles pressed her hands against her heart and slowly sank to the floor. "Owen? My Owen? Dead. It can't be? And Mr. Moses killed him?"

Cully turned to Summer. "Tell her."

Summer twisted her hands together. "The police have arrested him."

Cully laughed. "We're holding a big demonstration today in Owen's memory. Old drunk's going to be famous. They'll put that murdering Seastroke guy in prison for a long time. I promise you that, Auntie. But right now, we got to run." He slapped Gary on the back. "We need to get that kid. She's our insurance that we'll get our money."

Gary flipped his hand and strode out the door. "Forget her. She's an idiot. We can pretend Summer is our hostage, if we're cornered."

"But the kid's a witness."

"*Bah.* No one will believe anything she says about us being here. If'n she even has enough upstairs to remember."

Cully hesitated, pocketed his knife, and latched his hand around Summer's upper arm. "Come along. You and me got a big protest to stage. Betty and Ingrid have been calling everybody since the news came over the police band."

No way was she helping these two rats carry out their plan. The police were on their way to the house. All she needed to do was detain them here a while longer. She slowed down and pretended to struggle with her crutches.

"Come on." Cully tugged her forward.

She loosened her grip on the far crutch and lurched to the side.

"Whoa." Cully caught her around the shoulders and scooped her up in his arms. "Forget the crutches. Won't need those where we're going. Been waiting for that Gil guy to be out of the picture for days now." He kissed her on the neck. "You did a terrific job bamboozling him. Time to christen that new bed on my boat. We've got plenty of time. Got my eye on a nice little island in the Caribbean."

She flailed against him. "Wait. Put me down. I have to get my bag."

"Got it." Gary stood in the doorway, swinging her knapsack in his hand. "Our star organizer is gonna need her computer and stuff."

Time to play it cool.

Summer pasted on a smile. "Thanks, Gary." She placed her palm on Cully's chest and pushed. "Let me down. I really do need those crutches. Broke my ankle."

He snugged her tighter. "Don't think you do. I like having you at my mercy. Don't want you taking off now we're in the driver's seat."

She pounded on his chest. "Idiot. It doesn't work that way. I got to call in the big media. Contact EcoGreen Action. Have them send support."

"You're sounding a bit ungrateful to me. It was Gary and me who got the turbines in the news with those bombs we dropped. You're not thinking your Gil guy is innocent, are you? 'Cause he isn't, and you know it. Way we heard it, you and he were the only ones out there with poor old Owen, right?"

Summer looked from one man to the other. "But Owen could have been murdered before we got there."

"You sure? Owen's throat was slit with Moses' fancy knife."

A chill slithered down her back. How did Cully know that? These two men knew way too much about the murder of Owen Young. None of those details were public yet.

Round-faced, red-cheeked, overly friendly Cully Teed didn't look like a killer, but neither did Gil.

She remembered the splashes they'd heard. Could Cully have murdered Owen Young then slipped off the boat and rowed away? She ran her gaze over the broad shoulders, the weathered skin, and calloused hands. Then she remembered. He was a sea kayak enthusiast. A champion, Mrs. Eagles had said.

Of course, he could be the murderer. She couldn't prove it, but deep inside, she knew it to be true. Cully Teed was responsible for the gruesome knifing Gil was accused of. Cully Teed and Gary were not only the bombers, but murderers, too.

Gary pushed past them. "Come on. Time's flying. We can use Summer's car." He opened the front door.

Police sirens filled the air.

"Uh-oh." He pulled the door closed. "Trouble coming our way. Good thing we came by kayak. Move it, guys. Out the back." He called over his shoulder. "Aunt Victoria, answer the door. Play cool with the policemen." He dodged into the kitchen.

Tears glistening on her cheeks, Mrs. Eagles tottered out of the bedroom, pushing past them. She gave Summer the evil eye. "You really are a whore, aren't you? Shack up with anyone."

Cully hefted Summer higher and dashed after Gary. "Be nice to the lady. She sacrificed her honor for our cause."

Mrs. Eagles *hmphed.* "Not my cause. Wasn't Owen's, either. He wanted you to stop bombing that tidal thing. Stirring up the sea wraiths."

"Sea wraiths? A drunken man's hallucinations." Cully shrugged. "Old guy was crazy. He was gonna turn me in for dropping those depth charges, that's what. That's why he's lying dead."

Summer broke out in a cold sweat. Cully Teed *was* the bomber and a murderer. She had to get free. Go to the police. Get them to release Gil.

She thought fast. "Wait, Cully. You have to leave me. My car's out front. The cops will want to know where I am."

"Don't think so." Cully carried her through the living room and turned sideways to pass by the kitchen cabinets.

There was an ear-curdling screech, the under-sink cupboard flew open, and a wild-haired demon in a green sweater whipped out and sank her teeth into Cully's calf.

"What the devil?" Shaking his leg violently, Cully let Summer slip to the floor. The child clung on. Cully reached down and took hold of the child. "Gotcha."

Lissie screamed. Mrs. Eagles walloped him over the head with a frying pan and the child tumbled free.

Cully groaned, hung still for a moment, and then he gave himself a shake and rose up to his full height. He yanked out his knife and spun to face the old woman. "Should have poked you before. You and Owen are like two loony seagulls. Don't know what's good for you. Owen refused to blow up the turbine, and you defend that bastard Moses' kid." He gave a low roar, lunged forward and stabbed the knife into her belly. "Go join your rotten brother."

Eagles slapped her hands over her stomach and slowly sank down against the refrigerator door.

Summer gasped.

Lissie screamed again.

He whirled around, eyes wide. "Blast it all!" He grabbed her by the arm and gave her a shake. "Shut up, kid."

Summer focused on the knife clenched in his hand. Her pulse pounded in her ears. Would he harm an innocent child? She had to do something.

She crept closer so she was between the knife and Gil's daughter and peered into Lissie's eyes. "Run. Hide." Then she threw herself into Cully.

Lisie broke free and disappeared into the living room.

Cully rose up, roaring, "Look what you have done!"

She forced a teasing lilt into her voice. "Calm down, Cully. Remember, we got to get to the demonstration. Look, Eagles isn't dead. She'll be all right." Summer looked at the old woman from the corner of her eye.

Eagles lay on the floor, her hands covering the growing red stain on her belly. She hoped she was right.

Car tires rolled into the driveway. A car door slammed. Footsteps ran up the steps. The front door banged open.

"Lissie."

Summer turned at the sound of the voice. *Gil.* If he was here, did that mean he hadn't been charged? Hope blossomed.

"Come on." Cully grabbed her by the arm.

She yanked back. "You're murderers. The police will be here in a minute."

"Changing sides, city girl? Fine, then you can be our human shield." Knife in one hand, Cully dragged her out the screen door. Before she could draw breath, he picked her up, threw her over his shoulder, and ran.

# Chapter 31

## Gil

Summer? He couldn't believe she'd gone with them. He'd thought her smarter than that.

Gil ran across the lawn, down the rise, and stopped at the fence. He could see nothing through the thick fog except the incoming tide lapping at the foot of the cliff. The small beach was already under water.

He squinted, but there was no sign of Cully or his partner-in-crime. His heart skipped. No sign of Summer coming back to him.

He fisted his hands, wishing there was something he could hit. He really was a fool. Here he'd been worried to death about Summer because he'd abandoned her to face the storm alone. Worried because she had broken her ankle. Relieved that despite her gut-wrenching no at the hospital, she had come to his house to care for Lissie as he'd asked, instead of ramping up the crowd at the police station. He'd seen her car and been ready to throw his arms around her and pledge to love her forever.

But that wasn't going to happen. Not now.

She'd betrayed him.

He gazed out into the fog. She'd come to join up with Cully and his sidekick and help them kidnap his daughter.

He glanced back at the house where the kind EMT lady was standing guard duty beside the bed Lissie hid under, clutching that horrible green sweater.

Luckily, they'd failed.

Anguish shot through him, trapping his breath, pulling his muscles tight. What was the matter with him? He'd been tricked again by a woman. Was he so love-starved that he could be made a fool by a brassy New Yorker?

He rolled his shoulders and inhaled. Forget the sad stories and luscious kisses. Summer had said she'd do anything to stop the tidal energy project, and apparently, that included kidnapping his innocent daughter and holding her for blackmail.

All that kindness she'd shown Lissie? It must have been to make his daughter easier to handle when they abducted her. How could he have been attracted to such a heartless person?

Dolores was right. He was a failure as a father.

He gripped the fence rail tighter.

A failure as a man.

Thank heavens, Mrs. Eagles had been there to protect Lissie. The poor woman. If she survived, he vowed he'd take care of her for the rest of her life.

He should go back, comfort his daughter, and forget Summer Avery

With one last look at nothingness, he let go of the railing and turned to go.

*Splash.*

*Swish.*

*Splash.*

*Swish.*

Gil jerked around. Sound did strange things in the fog. But he recognized that one—the steady dip and pull of a kayak paddle. It was the perfect way to escape—silent, easy to land on an uninhabited shore, and quickly hidden.

With the fog as cover, those bastards would be gone before the police could find them. Once they rounded the point, they could slip in anywhere along the coast and be out of the province in hours.

He took a step toward the house. He had to inform the police.

Someone screamed, followed by a giant splash like a person being thrown into the water. More splashes. A woman's screech for help. Cully swearing. He spun around.

*Summer.*

She was in trouble.

He peered into the fog. He should go back to the house. Fetch the police. Let the EMTs rescue her. He shouldn't care what happened to her.

But he did.

If she was in the water, the cold would sap her strength, and with the tide coming in, she'd never reach the steps in time. He had to save her.

Gil leaped the fence and dashed down the cliff path, his only thought to save the woman who, despite all reason, he still loved.

At the water's edge, a kayak paddle floated in and out on the incoming rollers. He reached down and grasped it.

Suddenly, Cully loomed up in front of him, a wet, gray mass rising from the sea mist, wading toward him through the hip-high waves.

He shook his fist at him. *"Give me that paddle."*

"I don't think so." Gil gripped the paddle tighter and let the man come closer. "Where's Summer?"

"Drowned, for all I care. We could have been out of here, on our way south. Crazy woman flipped the kayak and lost us the paddle. But she'll not get far. The water's cold, and the tide's rising. She'll be pounded to death against the cliffs."

Gil's blood roiled. He'd been wanting to hit something. Now was his chance.

As Cully climbed up out of the water, Gil drew back the paddle and walloped the slimebag in the face. His nose broke. Blood spurted. But he didn't fall.

Instead, Cully's hands clamped around the paddle and pulled him down under the water. The sudden cold stole his breath, but he didn't let go. He found his footing and fought to hold on.

He rose to his feet and struck out again. But Cully hadn't spent the night lost at sea. Hadn't just left a hospital bed so he could plead his case and prove he hadn't killed Owen Young. Hadn't been beaten and concussed in a riot the day before. It was all too much.

Gil's fingers slipped, and Cully jerked the paddle away. Then it came down.

*Crack.* Pain radiated down his shoulder.

*Whack.* The paddle slashed across his jaw.

He fell back into the water.

Freezing cold seawater sent shocks through his already battered body. His teeth chattered. Hypothermia was setting in, making him move slow, think slow. He pictured Mrs. Eagles, her blood pouring out. Heard Summer scream again.

Cully Teed might be bigger and less exhausted, but he was not going to get away.

Gil had lifted a ton of lobster pots in his life. Heavy objects had a lot of pull, all downward. He might be wearing down, be he had gravity on his side.

Gil rose up and grabbed for the paddle, latched on to one end, and yanked it toward him. He rose out of the water and slowly moved back up the steep path, climbing the cliff. One step. Then another. They tussled like two boys playing tug-a-war. But they weren't boys. They were dead serious.

"Got you, you fool." Cully pulled with all his might.

Gil turned slightly and let go. Cully flew backward, landing on the rocks below.

*Crack.*

The murdering bastard's leg bent back at an impossible angle. His head bounced.

Gil held his breath.

Cully groaned then passed out.

He climbed down and dragged the man up the path as far as he could then stopped. Someone would find Teed eventually.

Right now, he had to save his strength to rescue Summer. But where was she?

Gil peered through the mist. The fog was brightening but was still so thick he couldn't make out anything farther than twenty feet away.

He climbed back up the path a few steps. Summer had to be in the cove and, with the tide coming in, washed up close to the cliffs.

He shouted her name. Then he stilled, closed his fog-blind eyes, and listened for the slightest change in sounds. It was a game he and his brother had played as children on foggy days, each taking turns hiding and calling out until the other found him.

He held his breath. If she were alive, he would hear her.

Water slapped against the rocks. In the distance, a foghorn blew. A gull cawed. And there—a squawk or was it a woman's gasp?

He shouted again. The squawk answered. So not a seabird. That was Summer pleading for help, her voice fading.

She was close. Somewhere to his left.

Gil shouted again then scrambled across the cliff face. Stones loosened beneath his feet and splashed into the water below. The waves inched higher. The wind cut through his wet clothes. His injured shoulder burned as he wedged his fingers between the boulders and cantilevered himself across the escarpment. The cries grew louder.

Then he saw her, a gray speck, clinging to a jutting rock. Her face stark white. Her body rocking in the surf as the waves washed over her, threatening to tear her loose. And with each roller, the water rose. The high-tide mark stained the rocks well above her head. She'd be underwater in minutes. She didn't have long. He had to hurry.

He pushed himself to go faster, found one foothold, and swung wildly across. Then another and another, his feet sliding. The rocks stripped the skin from his palms and tore his jeans. He would get there no matter what.

Then he heard another voice coming from above.

*"Daaaaddy."*

He pushed out from the cliff as far as he could. Lissie hugged the fence. Her dear face pressed against the wire. Her arms tangled in the green sweater.

*"Daaaaddy."*

Her cry cut through him. Where was the Mountie who should have been watching her? Where were the Mounties who should be looking for him and for the culprits?

He glanced back to where Summer clung for her life just in time to see her slip into the sea. He took one long look at Lissie. Would this be the last time he'd hear his little girl call him daddy?

But he couldn't abandon Summer, not when he was so close.

"Stay there, Lissie. I'll be right back."

Then, as much as his body rebelled at the thought, he dove into the water and breast-stroked toward the last place he'd seen her.

It was hard going. Already chilled, weighed down by his wet clothes, buffeted by the surf, his shoulder a dull, constant ache, he was more than exhausted. But he refused to give up. She was here somewhere, and he would find her.

He looked for the rock she'd clung to, called her name, then listened.

"Help."

The cry was as soft as a baby bird's, but it was hers.

A spurt of adrenaline shot through him. He wasn't too late.

He kicked toward the sound. Then he saw her. Summer had wedged herself into an indentation in the rock face where the waves were calmer. Her white-knuckled fingers gripped an exposed root.

He bobbed up above the water. "Stay there. I'm coming."

She made a weak nod.

In seconds, he was there, holding her. Her head lolled against his shoulder. Her arms and legs were limp. There was no warmth left in her body. Not much left in his own.

"Gil, I'm so sorry," she whispered.

"Nothing to be sorry about."

"You have to know. They used me—Gary and Cully. They killed Owen. They were going to kidnap Lissie and blackmail you."

"I know. If anything, I love you even more for standing up to those two men."

"But ..."

"Hush. Save your breath. We'll have plenty of time to talk later."

He grabbed on to the root, wedged a foot on a protrusion, and clasped his other arm around her, feeding her the last of his remaining body heat. She had to survive. He couldn't bear the thought of losing her.

She breathed in his ear, "Is Lissie safe?"

"Yes, she is. And waiting for us."

A wave swept up and splashed their faces. Summer choked.

"No, waiting for you."

Gil clutched her tighter. "For us. She needs us both."

Water swirled in around their legs. He could barely feel his toes. Soon, it would cover them. They had to move.

"Come. We have to get farther up the cliff. Above that gray line up there."

Summer trembled in his arms. Her voice came out a rough croak. "Let me go. Save yourself. Your little girl needs her daddy."

"Where's my feisty New Yorker who stole that paddle from two murdering bastards?"

"I saw you. Fighting Cully. Did you kill him?"

"Broke his leg. Last seen, he was out cold. I don't think he will be bothering anyone for a while."

"Good."

He scanned the escarpment. Here, the waves had undercut the cliff below the pines, leaving no way to reach the top. He studied the cliff face.

"There. There's a crevice far enough above the tideline to keep our heads above the waves, and there are branches and roots exposed by the sea to help us get there."

"I have no strength left, Gil. Everything's gone numb." Her lips were blue.

Gil pressed his face into her hair. Hyperthermia was setting in. She would die if she wasn't warmed up soon. He had to get her above the water.

He glanced down. The last thing he wanted to do was get back into the water, but he had no choice. He took off his yellow nylon windbreaker and tied it around her head and torso.

Summer batted at it. "I can't ..."

"Leave it. I know it's wet, but it should keep the scrapes to a minimum and help me find you again. Now I'm going to lift you up. Be ready. Grab for a root or rock." With frozen fingers, he inched his way down into the water until he was below her and could grasp her legs.

An icy wave splashed over him. He shook the saltwater from his eyes and called up, "Ready?"

He felt an answering shake.

He took a breath and heaved with every bit of strength he had left. For a moment, her weight was too much, and then it was gone. He peered up. She'd made it.

"Bravo." He waved. "I'm going for help. Don't go anywhere." He pulled himself out of the water. He wanted to crawl into that crevice with Summer. He wanted to hug her and tell her how much he loved her. Propose again. But she needed help fast. They could talk later.

Calling on some hidden inner strength, Gil began the long, dangerous climb back to the path.

# Chapter 32

## Summer

Summer pushed her hair out of her eyes and peered after him. In a scene that would have looked amazing in a *Tarzan* remake, Gil swung from rock to rock then scrambled up the cliff and disappeared.

She bit her lip. He'd come for her. Saved her. He truly was a good man. Too good for a manipulating, lying woman who had betrayed him at every step. Gil Moses was not for her. He needed to take care of his daughter.

She glanced at the rising tide. How long would it take for the water to creep up her legs, over her torso, until it reached her mouth and nose. Would help get here in time?

She shivered and gazed out at the water. The fog was lifting. She could see the white ball of sunlight trying to break through. The ocean was less gray and more green, but the tide was still coming in. Still rising.

The thought struck her. If she died here, her death would be a headline story. Famous eco-activist killed trying to stop the turbines.

But no. No one would know her story. At best, she'd be called an idiot tourist who went out on the beach and got trapped by the tide. At worst, a coconspirator working with the murderous turbine bombers.

She peered out at the ocean. Yep, that's what happened to farm girls with big dreams who thought they could bring down the bad guys.

She gave herself a shake. Heavens, that was not the last thing she wanted to be thinking about when she sank beneath the water.

She closed her eyes and pictured Gil smiling at her, laughing, teasing. Treating her like someone who mattered. Kissing her until her toes curled. Touching her like she was precious. Yes, that was the image she would cling on to as she sank into her watery grave.

"Ma'am, stay back. Emergency Rescue here." An orange cable skittered down the rocks above her and landed in front of her. Gravel and stones rained by.

Summer peered up. A woman in a yellow jacket swung out over the cliff edge and belayed herself down.

"We'll have you safe in nothing flat."

Summer gave a shake and let the woman slip a harness around her. She'd been ready to die. She wasn't sure she was ready to live.

*****

Done. Summer pushed her laptop to the side of the hospital bed and leaned back against the antiseptic-smelling pillow. She gazed down at her body. No missing toes or fingers. No more broken bones, beside her ankle. A few bruises. A minor concussion. A press release sent. EcoGreen's board of directors notified.

She should be filled with joy. Cully and Gary had been caught. Seastroke Energy, in light of the bad publicity and the huge protests erupting everywhere, had put the tidal energy project on hold.

The EcoGreen Action board had submitted her name for the directorship. They couldn't wait for her to get down to Atlanta. Some oil company was trying to cover up a billion-gallon oil leak, and the environment needed her passion to save it.

She covered her face with her hands. It didn't matter that she had stopped the turbine project and gotten her promotion. She'd lost something precious in the process. Something she hadn't known she'd wanted—love.

Gil and his imp of a child had weaseled their way into her heart—she fingered the note he'd sent—and she was going to leave them.

She maneuvered to the edge of the bed, stuffed the rest of her belongings in her pack, and worked at putting on her sneaker and air boot.

And if she loved him, loved his child, she would have to leave. It didn't matter that he'd said he loved her or wanted to marry her. It didn't matter her heart was crying. She was the wrong woman for him.

He deserved a soft, gentle mother for his daughter. He deserved someone who loved boats and water and Nova Scotia. Someone who didn't find Tide Harbor too small, too isolated, and too full of memories.

Leaving Gil Moses was going to be the hardest thing she ever did, but she was tough. She'd been doing the hard stuff since the day her mom had died and when her father had lost his case against the fracking company.

She slung her pack over her shoulder. Gil was somewhere in the hospital, sitting by Lissie's side while they made sure she was all right after her concussion. Poor child had fallen trying to climb the fence and reach her daddy, who'd been busy rescuing her. If nothing proved she was the wrong woman for him, that did. She didn't need to see the recriminations in his eyes or feel the guilt compress her chest.

She was going to Atlanta. Her plane ticket was bought. Her Hyundai waiting in the hospital lot, brought over by a helpful Mountie.

Gil would not know she'd left or where she'd gone. It was better that way.

A nurse stuck her head in the door. "Ready to go, Miss Avery?"

Summer nodded over her shoulder.

"Great. I'll get the wheelchair."

Minutes later, an orderly was rolling Summer through the shimmering green hospital lobby, crutches across her lap, a new gray walking boot on her left foot. Through the glass entry doors, the sun shone, and people hurried in and out. She would be gone in moments.

A tall woman with straight black hair gathered severely back from her brow by a ski band cut in front of the wheelchair. She bumped into the end of Summer's crutches, knocking one down. The metal hit the floor with a loud *smack*, the sound echoing in the two-story high atrium. The woman's lips pinched into a pout as she swerved around it.

"You'd think people would have a care for the actual patients here," the orderly said. He pulled the wheelchair to the side then bent down to pick up the crutch. He placed it back in Summer's lap. "Probably worried about a loved one."

Behind her, the red-aproned receptionist's voice rose. "Wait a minute, miss. I need to see your identification."

The woman slapped the countertop. "This is an emergency. I demand to see my daughter at once." The thick Boston accent sounded out of place. "Lissie Moses. Pediatrics. The people back in that Tide-Something hamlet told me she's here. I've been driving all over this godforsaken wilderness trying to find her. If he's hurt her—"

*Lissie Moses?* Summer brushed her hair away from her eyes to get a better look and studied the woman in her expensive ski jacket more suited to a Vermont ski resort than maritime Nova Scotia.

*That* was Gil's ex? His Dolores? The woman who wanted to put Lissie in an institution?

She grabbed the wheel of the chair. She had to stop her from finding Lissie. It was the least she could do for Gil.

She signaled the orderly. "Wait. Hold up. I think I know that woman."

The orderly spun his head around. "Got a fire under her, that one. She's already heading toward the elevator."

Summer held up her hand. "Can you follow her, please?"

"No can do. My job is to take you to your car."

"Stop. I'm getting out." She gripped the arms of the wheelchair, kicked up the footrests, and pushed herself up.

"Wait." The orderly blocked her way. "You have to be careful with that ankle."

Summer gave him her patented don't-mess-with-me stare. "I've been adrift in a runaway boat, nearly drowned, and been yanked up the side of a cliff. Haven't made it worse yet. Now get out of my way. I can definitely reach that elevator."

Summer slipped her arms into the cuffs of the crutches, shoved past him and, with the fluid ease she'd perfected over the last two days, swung her way down the hall toward the elevator. Just as she pulled up behind Dolores, the door slid open, and a man wearing a suit and tie stepped out.

Dolores fell back. "Aaron Moses. What are you doing here? You said—"

Summer stared at the man. This was Gil's brother? He might have the same dark eyes and same full lips, but his hair was close cropped and his suit top of the line. This man was no fisherman.

Gil's brother wrapped his hand around Dolores's upper arm. "We have to talk." He spun the woman toward the exit doors.

"How dare you?" The woman jerked against his hold. "My daughter's up there. Your brother broke the custody agreement. The child is mine."

"She is not your daughter, and you know it."

Dolores's eyes widened. "What are you talking about? Of course, she is. I have papers—"

"I knew Gil made a mistake marrying you. Not only are you a money sucker. You're a liar." Ignoring her sputtered protests, he hurried her through the lobby and out the door.

Summer trailed after them, her heart pounding in her chest. Gil had abducted Lissie? She didn't believe it.

Outside, the woman turned and grabbed Aaron's lapel. "I've filed international abduction charges against Gil. My lawyers had no trouble with her papers. Now get out of my way." She whirled around to go back inside and plowed straight into Summer.

*Whoosh.* Her crutches flew out, and she tumbled to the pavement, dragging the woman with her.

Summer groaned. "Should watch where you're going, lady." She moved as if to get up, making sure to poke Gil's ex with the end of the crutch.

"Sorry, miss." Aaron Moses gave her his hand and helped her to her feet. He peered hard into her face. "You okay?"

Summer readjusted her crutches. "Yeah, sure. Just a broken ankle. Been falling all over the place." She shifted to the side and leaned against a column. "Got an appointment to get to."

Gil's ex was still sitting in a tangle of leather-booted feet and cashmere scarf. As Summer watched, Aaron yanked her upright.

"Hands off me." She spun around and took off for the hospital entrance.

"No, you don't!" Gil's brother yelled and caught hold of her by the shoulder.

"That's it." Dolores extracted her cell phone from her pocket. "I'm calling the police."

"Go ahead. I'm sure the Mounties would love to hear the truth. Lissie was never properly adopted here in Canada.

She's still in my custody. Drop the legal challenge unless you want to be charged with kidnapping."

The woman's mouth dropped open. "You gave her to us. You said you took care of the paperwork."

His jaw tightened. "I knew the minute I handed the baby to you, you didn't want her. You held her like you did Gil. No expression, no warmth. Not even a kiss. Like another possession added to your collection of things for your perfect life. You're a cold woman. Colder than any fish I ever pulled from the sea."

Dolores drew back. Her lips squeezed against her teeth. "Nothing wrong with wanting a nice life with nice things, like my parents provided. You may not believe it, but I loved Gil. I thought he wanted the same things I did." She shifted her weight from one foot to the other. "I loved Lissie, too. I still love her. I want the best for her."

"*Love*? How dare you talk of love and want to put her in an institution?"

"A home. A lovely place for children like her where she can get therapy, be with others like her." Her fingers twisted her purse strap. "I couldn't handle her, Aaron. She frightened me. And Gil was never around to help."

"Then it's just as well she will not be traveling back to the States with you. Go home, Dolores. Go home to that empty house and enjoy all the possessions my brother showered on you, trying to please you." He took a step back. "And stay out of their lives. You have no claim on either of them."

The woman ran her hand over her perfectly smooth hair. "Can I see her? Say goodbye? I did come all this way to this"—she glanced around—"this *place*."

"No." He whipped a folded paper from his inner suit pocket. "Turn around and move your butt right out of here before I call the Royal Canadian Police and show them this restraining order."

Dolores tilted her shoulders and studied his face. "So prepared. You're the cold one, Aaron Moses." She ran a finger down his lapel. "I may be a cold fish, but you're Ice Man. You have no right to lecture me about love. You turned your back on your brother. Broke his heart *and* your mother's." With that, she spun on her heel, stomped down the pavement, and out to the parking lot, her perfect hair swinging, her tight jeans revealing her perfect butt.

Gil's brother let out a curse and whirled around, crashing into Summer.

"Oh dear." He grabbed her arms and kept her from falling again. "I'm so sorry." He made sure she was stable on her crutches then let go.

Summer peered at the face that was Gil's, but with sadder eyes and a mouth set in a bitter twist. This was a man living with guilt. She might not be able to give Gil the love he deserved, but she could at least give him back his brother's.

She tipped her head toward the fleeing Dolores. "I couldn't help overhearing what she said. She's wrong, you know."

"Huh?" Gil's brother straightened and gave her a wary look.

"You did what you did out of love. Your brother will understand. He's a kind man, your brother."

"You know Gil?"

"Our paths crossed." She hiked up her crutches and wended her way down the sidewalk in the wake of Gil's ex.

# Chapter 33

## Gil

Gil leaned on the hospital room windowsill and let out the breath he'd been holding. Down below, Dolores, her ponytail flapping in the breeze, stalked across the pavement and crossed over to the parking lot.

When Aaron had told him Lissie's adoption had never been legal, he hadn't known whether to smack his brother in the jaw or hug him. But at the moment, he'd been too preoccupied with Lissie's recovery to pay Aaron much attention.

Gil rubbed the stubble on his chin. He'd spent a sleepless night at Lissie' bedside, calming her every time she woke and became petrified by the strange lights and sounds of the hospital. When the desk called up to say Dolores was here and coming up to the room, his brother had taken off to intercept her.

He glanced out the window again then turned away. Aaron had been successful, it seemed. But Aaron had always been successful.

The door opened, and his brother peeked in. "Can I come in?" he whispered.

Gil nodded. "She's asleep."

Aaron stepped in and stood over the bed, peering down at the sleeping child. "She's beautiful."

Gil moved over to the other side of the bed. "Spitting image of Gracie at that age, isn't she?"

Aaron fingered a lock of Lissie's hair. "I'm sorry for what I did. I should have told you I never filed the papers. I was so angry. Gracie dead in that drug house. Mom insisting you and Dolores should have the baby. You and Mom taking off in the middle of the night. Leaving me alone to deal with the legal aftermath of Gracie's death."

"It wasn't your fault Gracie died. She made the wrong choices."

"Yes. But I didn't stop her that night. I knew where she was. I could have picked her up and forced her into my car."

"Gracie? She was more stubborn than any of us. Remember Dad liked to call her his rock head because nobody could drill any sense into her? Thinking about it, I wonder if she didn't have a bit of autism like Lissie. When we were little, she was so afraid of sounds and strangers. I used to cover for her. Make excuses when she'd disappear at a party or acted up in school."

"You were a good brother."

"She was my twin. When she died, it was like a limb had been cut off. I wasn't thinking about you at all. And when you cursed me, I should have known you were grieving. Grief makes us do strange things. Even tell the truth. You were right about Dolores not wanting the baby, but I was grieving, too, and didn't see it. All I saw was the last piece of Gracie on Earth, and I had to have her."

Lissie stirred under the covers. Her eyes opened. Her hand came up and brushed his face. "Dadddyyyyy."

"I'm here, Lissie. I will always be here."

Aaron pushed away from the bed. "I should go."

Lissie's head turned in Aaron's direction, her eyes opened wide. "Daddddyyy?" Her head spun from him to his brother and back.

Gil laughed. "That's Uncle Aaron. He's my brother. We do look a lot alike. Can you say hello to him?"

"El-oh."

"That's my good girl." He glanced up at Aaron. "She's made tremendous progress living here. I turned my resignation into Seastroke Energy. I'm staying in Tide Harbor. Don't know what work I'll do. Can always go back to lobstering, I guess. Find a nice Nova Scotian girl to marry."

His heart tore. It wasn't a local girl he wanted. He wanted his wild, passionate EcoGreen Action activist. He wanted Summer Avery.

But he couldn't have her. He understood that. Where would she wear her designer jeans? What work could she do here? An ambitious environmentalist would go crazy in isolated Tide Harbor. And she'd hate being tied to Lissie. It would be like marrying another Dolores.

He gazed down at his daughter. But Dolores would never have sung to Lissie the way Summer had nor, as Mrs. Eagles avowed, put her body between Lissie and a killer's knife.

Aaron gave him a smile. "You don't need to shack up with anyone yet, Gil. Give your heart time to heal."

Lissie rocked rhythmically, moaning over and over. "Kermmmiee."

Aaron glanced across at him. "She keeps saying that. What does it mean?"

"Remember Kermit the Frog? She adores the green puppet. I left hers behind in Boston."

Lissie shook her head violently from side to side. Her body twitched. "Kerrrrmmmie."

Aaron drew back in alarm. "She having a fit? Should I get a nurse?"

Gil took a deep breath. "No, she's trying to communicate. The old housekeeper might have been a spy and murderess, but she taught me a lot about my own child.

In fact, I'm hoping you'll defend Mrs. Eagles so I can hire her back. I owe the woman."

Aaron grinned. "A murderess? Not asking a lot, are you?"

"I think she had cause. From what I hear, her husband was a nasty man."

Lissie wiggled some more. "Kermiee."

He softened his voice. "You want Summer, don't you?"

Lissie's motions slowed. "Kerrmmie. Sing."

"Summer—that's the woman you mentioned who saved Lissie?"

"Yeah. Some amazing woman. Survived a storm at sea. Suffered a terrible battering trying to stop those bastards from getting away. She's somewhere in the hospital. I don't think they would have released her yet."

Not that he'd checked. He didn't know what he was going to do about Summer Avery. She'd never said she loved him. As far as he knew, he'd just been another frog she had to kiss to get her way.

"Golden-brown hair, incredible sea-green eyes, New York accent?"

"You've seen her?"

"Ran into a woman on crutches at the hospital entrance. Gave me a message about you."

Gil's head snapped up. "What did she say?"

"You're a kind man."

Kind. He sank down on the bed. That was all he was to her. Someone who'd been kind to her.

He fisted his hands. He certainly didn't feel kind.

When he saw her ... "Wait—you saw her in the lobby? Where'd she go?"

"She left. Right after Dolores."

"She's gone then." Off to save the Earth.

He ran his fingers through his hair. He wasn't fool enough to go after her. He had Lissie to worry about and a new job to find. Now that he and Aaron had made up, he could even go home to Seal Cove and see the rest of the family—his younger brother, Jordan, and his two older sisters. It was better this way.

He inhaled sharply. Now, if only he could convince his heart to believe that.

# Chapter 34

## Summer

All passengers proceed to their vehicles."

Summer Avery peered out the window as Yarmouth harbor came into view. She couldn't believe that EcoGreen Action had let her come back to Nova Scotia again. Not after the fiasco in Tide Harbor. Yes, she'd stopped the turbine project for now, but Seastroke Energy was suing EcoGreen Action for libel.

But they wouldn't win, not with the brand-new study showing their turbine design did affect lobster populations, at least according to a research project carried out by a marine biology team from Dalhousie, led by a researcher named Dr. G. Moses.

She picked up her pack and headed down the stairs to the car deck. No more turbines for her, though. She was here with her father's blessing to investigate salmon farming. Somewhere buried in her knapsack were the names and addresses of anti-fish farm groups and prosperous fish farmers. And if the salmon farms in a fishing village named Tide Harbor were at the top, that was only because she had a longing to see the place again.

She trotted down the stairs, wove in and out of the parked vehicles, and climbed into her Hyundai. She was a little better funded this time around, and reflecting her new status with EcoGreen Action as a director, she was going to have an assistant this time—Cat Silva. The girl was scheduled to fly into Halifax in three days.

She drove down the ramp toward the customs' booth. Deep green water rippled against the pilings. The scent of salt air filled her lungs and made her eyes water. She wiped the wet away—Summer Avery didn't cry—and set her GPS to her destination. Tide Harbor.

****

Aaron nudged his brother in the ribcage. "You sure about this lobstering business?"

"Positive. Wait till you see her." Gil pulled the truck to a stop and sucked in a breath of tangy sea air. Nothing was more beautiful than Nova Scotia on a warm June day, especially when you had a brand-new boat to call your own.

He climbed out of the pickup and grabbed Aaron by the arm. "Come on. I can't wait to take you for a spin."

Aaron shook Gil's hand off and grinned at him. "I have been on boats before, you know, bro. It's one reason I'm a lawyer. You do remember that lobstering season is in the winter, right?"

Gil hip-bumped him like he'd done when they were kids. "You haven't been on *my* boat before. And besides, in the Minas Basin, lobster season is now and the water is glass. Tell me you don't want to be out there with a fishing line in your hand."

"Oh, come on with you." Aaron laughed. "Mom always said you were the one with the highest dose of sea salt in your blood."

Gil pointed. "There she is."

His brother stopped, pushed his black Halifax Moosehead cap farther back on his head, and made a show of running his gaze from stem to stern. "A beauty. A real

262

beauty. Don't know about the name though. *Summer Girl?* Think there might be a story there."

Gil whacked him on the back. "My boat. My loan. I get to name it. That's the rule." He knew the name would catch Aaron's attention, but he didn't care. Let his brother wonder.

He hustled his brother forward. "Wait till you see the equipment." Gil couldn't keep the jaunt out of his step as they approached the gleaming white and turquoise boat tied up on the end of the pier. He felt like a kid again, excitement swirling through him like that day long ago when his father had lifted him into the new boat he'd bought.

Gil glanced up at the blue sky. He couldn't wait to get her on the water. Run her through her paces.

Out in the harbor, sailboats swooped. The day tripper with its load of tourists putted out toward Southwind Island. In minutes, he'd be out there, too, engine thrumming under his feet, bow cutting through the waves. Everything perfect.

A twinge ran across his shoulders. Almost perfect. If he couldn't have a curvy woman with sea-glass eyes nestled against his side as he zipped around the harbor, then he'd be satisfied with this lovely lady beneath his feet and his brother standing next to him.

On the pier, Aaron stood, ready to untie the bow line. Gil jumped down into the boat and started up the engine. He unlocked the door to the wheelhouse, slid it open, and retrieved the champagne he'd stowed there. Before they took it out, he would christen this boat but good. He bent down to close the hatch.

"I'm looking for a fisherman to take me out to view the salmon farm pens. I've tried every wharf up and down the coast. Either nobody's around, or they're not interested. Then I remembered Tide Harbor. Someone once told me it was a friendly place."

Gil froze, every muscle pulled tight, his heart rate soaring. He'd know that twangy voice anywhere. *Summer.*

Had she come to tell him she loved him, or was this one of those horrible coincidences that Fate threw at people to test their inner strength?

"Hey, yah," Aaron said in answer, putting on the heaviest Nova Scotia accent Gil had ever heard. "Yah, sure, but yah'll have to ask the captin', eh? He's in the boat."

Gil put down the bottle and stood. Summer Avery peered up at him, loose-limbed in short shorts that revealed long, tanned legs and a tight navy tee-shirt that displayed those perfect breasts that haunted his dreams.

Her signature red knapsack, a bit more worn, dangled from one hand. The other hand clutched a straw hat, threatening to blow off in the breeze. Beneath the brim of the hat, her hair was a mess of wild curls. Around her neck, an unpolished lump of sea-worn amethyst hung on a silver chain. The amethyst rose and fell with her breath and gave him hope.

He saw the moment when she caught sight of him. She glanced sideways, her mouth dropping. She looked over at Aaron, who was now grinning at them both like a crazy fisherman who'd landed a record halibut, then back at him.

He waited. If she turned and walked away, he'd still have Lissie. He'd still have the boat. But this time, she'd take what was left of his heart. But it had to be her choice.

Summer took a step forward, her eyes squinting in the glare sparkling off the water. "Would you be interested in taking me for a ride, Captain?"

"Only if you don't mind if it is a long one."

She edged closer to the edge of the pier. "How long?"

"A lifetime wouldn't be long enough." He jumped off the boat and put his hands around her waist, breathing in the sweet scent of her. "Marry me, Summer Avery, and we can save the ocean together."

She pressed her palm against his chest. The heat warmed his heart and sent blood pummeling through his veins. She tilted her head. "Warning: I might get seasick."

"Don't care. Got lots of ginger candy in the cuddy."

"I ... I might not know how to cook fish and lobster, or whatever fisher folk eat."

He tossed her hat onto the wharf and ran his fingers through her hair. "Not to worry. We have Mrs. Eagles to do the cooking. My brilliant brother got her off." He nuzzled her ear. "I'm a pretty hot cook, too."

"I still want to save the Earth."

"Of course, you do. We can do it together."

She slid her hand a little lower. "I might not know how to be a good mother."

"You'll do fine. You have good instincts. Every day, Lissie asks for the Jumping Kermies song."

"She's doing well?"

"Lissie's still sensitive to noise and commotion, but she's talking more now. Terrific with numbers. I think she might be mathematically gifted."

"That's amazing."

He drew her closer. "No. It's what happens when you love someone so much you accept them as they are and give them the space they need to grow. Have I given you enough space?"

"Too much. I tried to deny it but my heart's in Tide Harbor. I've missed you and Lissie so much. This is where I belong." She threw her arms around his neck. "With the man I love."

"Then marry me, Summer girl."

She raised herself up on tiptoes and planted a kiss on his mouth then gave him the answer he'd thought he'd never hear.

"Yes."

COMING NEXT

# SNEAK PEEK

## *Lost Beneath the Tide*

Book 2 in the Tide Harbor Suspense Series

## Chapter 1

Alex Harris steered his pickup onto the bumpy road leading to the abandoned dock. He looked over at his daughter. "This will just take a minute, Ellie."

Wearing a pout worthy of the starring role in a kid's TV drama, the six-year-old crossed her arms in front of her and shook her head. "But you promised we'd go. There's gonna be popcorn and ice cream and everything."

"Soon as I check out what's going on at the fish pens, we'll head right over to the town hall. We still have time." He glanced at the clock on the dashboard and grimaced. Between working overtime and doing extra leg work for the boss, he would have to step on it to make it to the annual Southwind Harbor ice cream social.

Not that he had any desire to sit around chatting with the local moms while the kids got wound up and sticky, and the divorcees eyed him like he was tastier than the ice cream they were doling out. But he hated to disappoint his daughter. Ellie was everything to him.

She was why he got up in the morning. Why he worked at a job he despised. Why he was driving down this dead-end sand-buggy track to check out what was probably a great big nothing for a paranoid boss who saw eco-terrorists around every corner.

He jerked the wheel to avoid a pothole. The ancient pickup he'd inherited from his father needed to be coddled, not gunned down washed-out dirt roads. But the spit at the head of the harbor had the best view of the fish pens from land. If some eco-freak was messing with the fish pens, he'd see them.

If anyone was going to get the lucrative head of security position at the Halifax offices of Cowling Fish Farms, it would be him. So, if his boss wanted him to check the pens after hours, then check the pens, he would.

Once he landed the job, he'd buy a new truck, and leave Southwind Harbor and its memories behind. His daughter would have so many more advantages in the city. She'd go to a big fancy school. Make new friends who weren't going to grow up to be fishermen. Best of all with an office job, he'd be home every night. No more dragging his little girl with him on wild goose chases. He could get her the puppy she wanted so much.

The truck thudded over a rock in the road and came down hard.

Ellie latched onto his arm. "Daddy, why we driving down this bumpy road? Dorchester doesn't like it."

"Huh? Who's Dorchester?"

"My puppy."

Alex made a quick scan of the cab and then raised an eyebrow. "Where're you hiding a puppy?"

Ellie laughed. "Dorchester's not real, Daddy. He's a pretend puppy." She moved her hand as if she were petting a dog. "I'm practicing so I'll be ready for a real puppy someday. And don't you worry. Dorchester is very good. He won't cause any trouble, I promise."

Alex slowed the truck to a crawl and put a hand on Ellie's shoulder. He didn't have many bright spots in his life, but his daughter was one of them—the most important one. "I promise we'll get a puppy as soon as I get that promotion. Say, why don't you be my lookout and tell me if you see any more rocks in the road."

Ellie sat up straighter on her booster seat and gave him a salute. "Aye, aye, Daddy. I'll pretend I'm Uncle Matt in the crow's nest looking for swordfishes." She made a tiny barking sound. "Dorchester can help look too."

With Ellie and her imaginary pet guiding them, and by inching forward at the speed of a sea slug, Alex managed to avoid several more rocks and a pothole the size of a dory. Finally, they arrived at the edge of the old dock.

Alex stepped on the brakes, and the old pickup rattled to a halt, all four tires thankfully still intact. He peered out the windshield. A postcard-perfect sunset loomed on the horizon, the kind his mother used to call a soda pop sky, because the oranges, purples, and golds illuminating the clouds mirrored the artificially colored sodas she refused to buy for him and his brothers.

He glanced over at Ellie who was talking in a tiny voice to her imaginary pet. He sure missed having his mama around. He had no idea how to handle pretend pets or little girls who missed their mothers. But one thing he did know was he needed to do better at being father.

Letting out a puff of air, Alex pulled out his binoculars from between the seats and rolled down the window. From here, the circular pens were only several hundred feet away, as close as one could get without using a boat. Which was fine by him. He hadn't been in a boat in a long time.

Alex scanned the water around the nearest pen. Nothing. Then the next. Nothing. He focused on the third ring. There. A black object bobbed up and down in the water. Seemed his boss had been right. Something was out by the pens. Now, was it a seal or a runaway beach ball? He adjusted the binoculars' focus.

Behind him, the passenger side door squealed open and then slammed shut.

He spun around only to see his daughter dash toward the water. "Ellie, come back. The dock's not safe." Heart in his throat, Alex jumped from the truck and charged after her. "Ellie, sweetheart. Stop." He grabbed her shoulder just as she stepped on the rickety wood of the old dock.

"Let go, Daddy." She shook off his hand. "I'm just going to get that shell. It can be Dorchester's water dish." She pointed to a small clamshell wedged between the planks just a few feet from the shore.

"You've got plenty of shells like that one at home. Now stay right next to me."

Ellie looked up at him, her hazel eyes so like her long-gone mother's. "Can you get it for me?"

He looked at the gleaming white shell, and the water slapping against the piers. A cold shiver ran down his back. It might as well be on the outer islands. He put the binoculars up to his eyes. "No. It's just an old shell. I'm here to make sure the salmon are safe."

She scuffed her sneaker in the gravel. "Stupid fish. All you ever do is worry about the salmon."

"The salmon pay our bills, Ellie." He watched the bobbing object disappear under the water. "Might be a big bad seal out there trying to eat them. We can't let that happen, can we?"

For a few moments, she stood quietly next to him, then she pulled on his sleeve. "We aren't going to make it to the ice cream social, are we?

He shook his head. "Tell you what. We can stop at the supermarket and buy popcorn and ice cream and have our own party at home. I'll read you your favorite book."

Her little mouth puckered and then she nodded. "Okay." She reached up. "Can I look too?"

How could he refuse after letting her down? Alex lowered the binoculars and placed the cord around her neck. Then he stood behind her and held the glasses to her eyes as he adjusted the focus. Narrowing his gaze against the glow of the setting sun, he guided her to the spot he'd last seen the object. "There. That black blob—can you see it?"

She gave a little jump and pointed. "Yeah, there it is. Oh, it's coming towards us." She waved. "Here, Mr. Seal. Here. Don't eat my daddy's fishies."

Alex peered out over his daughter's head. The seal or whatever it was, dipped and splashed toward the shore. Now that was rare. Sea mammals usually moved sleekly through the water. A bad feeling washed over him. "Can I use the binoculars for a minute, sweetheart? Not sure that's a seal."

Ellie held them up, and he peered at the creature as it neared the far end of the crumbling pier. For a moment, it dipped below the surface, then popped up again. With a twist, a black-suited scuba diver hitched up onto the dock and sat with his feet hanging over the edge.

Silhouetted by the setting sun, the diver removed his facemask, tore off his hood, and shook out his hair. The long, wavy strands of hair glowed pink in the sunset.

Alex focused in closer. Silhouetted against the dying light, the swimmer was all feminine curves. Not a he. A she.

For a second, he was stunned. Then he gave himself a shake. What was a strange scuba diver doing nosing around the Cowling fish pens? It didn't matter it was a woman, a gorgeous one, at that. Whoever the diver was, she'd better have a good explanation, or she would be in deep trouble. Nobody messed with Cowling's fish pens.

Ellie slipped her fingers into his and tugged. He glanced down. His daughter's face was round in wonderment. She pointed toward the diver. "Look, Daddy. It's a mermaid. Maybe she's seen mommy?"

He glanced again at the woman, who'd slipped off her oxygen tanks and was now busy checking the gauges. In a minute, she'd turn and see them.

Alex scooped up his daughter and hurried back to the truck.

Scuba Diver Lady would be trouble all right. Trouble he didn't want to have.


Visit www.TideHarborSuspense.com to find out more.

# YOUR FREE BOOK AWAITS ...

Thanks for taking the time to read *Concealed by the Tide*. If you enjoyed it, please take a minute to give me a review on Amazon. I really appreciate your feedback, as I depend largely on word of mouth to promote my books. To receive updates when more of my books are coming out and a chance to win a new romance every month, sign up for my newsletter at www.ZaraWestRomance.com and receive one of my books, *Inside the Skin:* a multi-holiday, sweet contemporary romance, for FREE.

If you would like to know more about the Nova Scotia setting, and how I went about writing the Tide Harbor series, check out www.TideHarborSuspense.com.

Want to be an early reader of the next book in the series? Join Zara's Z Squad on Facebook.

# ABOUT ZARA WEST

Zara West loves all things mysterious, adventurous, and heart-stopping as long as they lead to true love. Born in Williamsburg, Brooklyn, Zara West spends winters in New York where the streets hum with life, summers in the Maritimes where the sea meets the shore, and the rest of the year anywhere inspiration for tales of adventure and love are plentiful.

In a life full of misadventures, she has had sunstroke on the top of a Greek mountain, been partially trampled by a herd of four hundred sheep, and while she has never been kidnapped, she has been marooned on an uninhabited island in the middle of the Canadian wilderness for longer than she wants to remember.

A member of Romance Writers of American, and Women's Fiction Writers of America, Zara is an award-winning author of both fiction and non-fiction in the fields of ethnography, education, and the arts. She has published the award-winning romantic thriller series The Skin Quartet. Writing as Joan Koster, she is the author of the Write for Success series and the Forgotten Women biographical novel series

Zara teaches numerous online writing courses and blogs about:

Romance at www.ZaraWest Romance.com
Writing Tips at www.ZaraWest.me,
Forgotten Women at www.JoanKoster.com

# OTHER BOOKS BY ZARA WEST

**The Skin Quartet: A Dark, Sexy Romantic Thriller Series**
*Beneath the Skin*
*Close to the Skin*
*Under the Skin*
*Within the Skin*

**Historical Fiction under the Name Joan Koster**
*Beneath the Mask* in *The Eve of Love Anthology*
*Solstice Promise* in *The Light of Love Anthology*
*That Dickinson Girl: A Novel of the Civil War*
*Censored Angel: Anthony Comstock's Nemesis*

**Write for Success Series**
*Fast Draft Your Manuscript and Get It Done*
*Revise Your Draft and Make It Shine*
*Research Your Subject and Validate Your Writing*
*Power Up Your Language and Make It Sing*

Tidal Waters Press